GEM

Opal

FREYA BARKER

OPAL

ISBN: 9781988733838

Cover Design: Freya Barker
Editing: Karen Hrdlicka
Proofing: Joanne Thompson

GEM: a privately-funded organization operating independently in the search for—and the rescue and recovery of—missing and exploited children. Although, at times working in conjunction with law enforcement, GEM aims to ensure the victims receive justice... by whatever means necessary.

GEM Operator Opal; multifaceted, versatile, a chameleon.

She hides in plain sight, adapts, and infiltrates.

When Opal goes undercover in a youth center several teenagers have disappeared from, she's shocked to find a ghost of her own traumatic past at the helm. However, her worry for the missing kids is greater than her concern being recognized and she risks her own safety to discover the truth.

To complicate matters, a familiar FBI agent shows up conducting his own investigation and almost blows the whistle on her. It takes some doing to convince him to join forces with her but as it turns out, they work well together.

In the course of uncovering an organized group of child molesters, they find themselves falling—for each other.

PROLOGUE

JANEY AND I GET DRESSED FOR BED QUIETLY.

Mostly because we know we're being watched.

Compliance comes easy when even at only seventeen you've been made to believe you have no rights, no importance, no voice.

Yesterday we were told it was time for more 'personal development.' Like Pavlov's dogs, we immediately fell silent as we climbed into the van taking us from the group home to our destination, our minds automatically detaching from our bodies. It's how we protect ourselves, knowing the next however many hours our bodies are no longer ours to command.

"Kate?"

I barely get into my bottom bunk after turning off the lights when Janey's whisper sounds over my head.

"Yeah?"

"Do you think Raj will come back?"

I glance over at the single bed on the other side of the

room, barely visible in the dark. Up until two months ago, Raj would sleep there. The three of us arrived here at Transition House within a few months of each other and shared this room for the past three years.

Raj was a year older than Janey and me, but the three of us became close. As close as sisters, something none of us had ever known. As the eldest, she'd looked after us as best she could, comforting us with the promise of better times ahead.

I miss her soft voice in the dark room as she would talk to distract us from the dark thoughts that inevitably crept in with nightfall. Especially on nights like these, when I could still feel unwanted hands on my skin.

She was simply gone one day, without so much as a goodbye. It was the day after she turned eighteen and was of legal age.

"I don't know," I lie, secretly convinced we'll never see Raj again. "Anything's possible, I guess."

"I can't do this anymore..." I can barely hear Janey's voice, but the desperation is clear and it scares me.

"Yes, you can. You will. Just like I will."

ONE

*O*PAL

"...are you there?"

Janey's voice crackles through my earpiece.

I slide my hand under my hair and push the tiny button behind my ear twice for yes. If I wasn't in the middle of a group of volunteers, waiting to be briefed by a search coordinator, I would've stepped away and used my voice, but I might draw attention to myself, which is something I don't want.

"Keep an eye on James Genzel, one of Ricky's teachers. Fifty-one, five foot nine, glasses, dirty blond, and balding. No facial hair." My eyes immediately roam the crowd and zoom in on the slightly overweight man standing about twenty feet from me, at the edge of the search group, as Janey's voice continues to fill me in. *"School secretary says he left school in the middle of the day for a health emer-*

gency, and she didn't see him until yesterday when he showed up fidgety. Her words, not mine."

I hit the button twice more to let her know I got all that and start inching my way in Genzel's direction. It's not unusual for perpetrators to join the search for their victims. Some of those sick bastards feed off that, and they'll often spend more time observing everyone around them than actually doing any searching. It also wouldn't be the first time a perp tried to steer a search away from where they dumped their victims.

Either way, if the teacher had anything to do with thirteen-year-old Ricky's disappearance forty-eight hours ago, his behavior could give him away and I'll be watching.

"Can I have your attention please?"

The rich voice belongs to a tall, gray-haired man wearing sunglasses that obscure a large part of his face. A face, that from the lower half visible, is the kind that would earn him the moniker, silver fox. Luckily, I'm immune to appearances. A good thing, since I'm here to do a job.

As the man introduces himself as Agent Kenny with the FBI CARD team, I quickly return my attention to the teacher. He appears to be engrossed in the instructions the agent shares, nodding every now and then in understanding. Then we're split up in groups and I shuffle a little closer to Genzel, to ensure I'll be in the same group with him, when a hand taps my shoulder.

"Excuse me, ma'am," the deep cultured voice sounds behind me.

I turn to find a pair of intense, hazel eyes focused on me. His shades are shoved up into his hair, and at this proximity, I can see faint freckles dotting his face. Definitely a silver fox.

"Yes?"

"Were you planning on joining the search?"

My feathers are instantly ruffled, I hate being underestimated, but I remind myself this is exactly what I hope for when I'm in the field. The terrain we're supposed to search is a stretch of wooded area along the Potomac River, just a mile or so from the middle school Ricky went missing from the day before yesterday. A rugged stretch with ample undergrowth, fallen limbs, and dense trees.

I've been in much worse terrain, but he wouldn't know that.

"That's why I'm here. This isn't my first search," I can't resist adding.

Agent Kenny raises an eyebrow, clearly not convinced, but he doesn't press the issue and points me to the group that started forming a few feet away. Fortunately, my target is in that group.

We line up about six feet apart, most of us carrying a stick or a pole, and start slowly moving into the trees, occasionally calling out Ricky's name. I'm right beside the teacher, glancing his way from time to time, while still scanning the ground in front of me for any signs of Ricky.

It takes us a couple of hours of inching our way through when the trees open up and we hit the bank of the river. Kenny orders a small break before we retrace our steps downriver from where we ended up. I pull a bottle of water from the small backpack I have strapped on. I notice Genzel didn't bring any so I take my second bottle from my pack and hand it to him.

"Thanks," he says, twisting the top off and taking a swig. "I'm clearly not that well prepared. This is my first time doing anything like this. It's a little unnerving."

"Are you family?" I ask innocently, hoping to keep him talking.

He shakes his head. "No. I'm a teacher at Springfield. Ricky is in my math class. You?"

"Just a concerned citizen."

I don't detect any subterfuge in the man, but he could be a good actor.

He opens his mouth to say something when Agent Kenny's voice calls us all to attention. A few minutes later, the two groups are lined up with our backs to the river, and we start working our way through the next stretch of dense growth.

We've barely hit the trees when someone down the line calls the boy's name and I hear a sound from up ahead. I stop in my tracks.

"Hold up!" I yell out before cupping my hands around my mouth. "Ricky!"

Again, I can hear what sounds like a whimper and turn to glance at Genzel, who is looking at me, surprise on his face.

"I heard that."

"Keep calling out to him," I tell the teacher, as I start moving forward, trying to pinpoint where the sound is coming from.

Five minutes later I find him, the FBI agent close on my heels. His skinny body is mostly hidden by the large trunk of a felled tree. His leg sticks out at an unnatural angle.

Keeping my back to the man behind me, I mumble in the microphone tucked into my cleavage.

"Found him. Looks like an accident."

"Ten-four," I hear Janey's voice in my ear.

"Hey, buddy." I kneel down beside the pale boy and grab his hand. "You're gonna be okay."

Behind me I hear yelling down the line of volunteers, and Agent Kenny's voice barking our coordinates into his radio. I ignore them and keep my eyes on the child, digging up my water bottle so I can give him a few sips. The kid must be dehydrated.

It takes another hour and a half for EMTs to find us, stabilize Ricky, and carry him out.

"Glad for this outcome."

I'm watching the stretcher being loaded in the back of the waiting ambulance when the agent steps up beside me. I glance over at him and grin.

Mitch

Wow.

She definitely should smile more.

It would seem I underestimated this woman on more than one front.

I'm not sure what drew my eye to her in the first place, but something about her looked out of place in the group of volunteers. I guess she looked almost too innocent. I've been at the occasional search where a volunteer would not be prepared for the kind of scene we found and ended up more trouble than they were worth. Maybe I was afraid this woman would be like that.

Don't think anyone was as surprised as I was when she took control of her group and, without hesitation, walked ahead to discover the injured boy. She stayed with him, talking to him quietly, and keeping him calm until the medics arrived.

I didn't believe her when she said this wasn't her first search, but it's clear I was wrong. I also thought she looked unremarkable, but now that I've seen her smile, I realize I was wrong about that too.

"We should grab a sandwich before they're all gone," I find myself saying.

I point to the crowd at the back of a van belonging to a local restaurant kind enough to provide lunch for the volunteers. She looks over and seems to hesitate for a moment before she makes up her mind.

"Sure. I could eat."

She's made herself comfortable sitting on the open gate of a maroon pickup truck when I return with a couple of bottles of water and some sandwiches.

"Yours?" I indicate the late-model Silverado, trying to hide my surprise at her choice of vehicles.

"It is," she says, her mouth tilting up at one side. "Hop on up."

I set the food and water down before hoisting myself up beside her.

"Nice." I settle in with a bottle and unwrap one of the sandwiches, sneaking a glance at her. "Name's Mitch Kenny." I wipe my hand on my jeans and hold it out.

"Nice to meet you, Mitch," she says, firmly gripping my hand with her smaller one. "I'm Opal."

The name seems a bit frivolous. She strikes me as unpretentious and simple, but then she pulls the ball cap from her head and a wealth of hair drops down to her shoulders. Thick, wavy, russet-blond hair you'd want to bury your fingers into. My body involuntarily responds and I quickly focus on my sandwich before I give myself away.

"So, Opal," I start, after swallowing my bite. "What brought you out today? Are you local?"

When I turn to her, she eyes me with a hint of suspicion.

"Nope. I'm a Kentucky original, but I happened to be visiting Hagerstown when I heard about the boy's disappearance. I thought I could help."

"And you certainly did."

She opts not to respond to that and instead takes a decent bite of her sandwich. Even that suddenly seems appealing. I like a woman with a healthy appetite. One too many times I've taken someone to a nice restaurant, only to sit across from them while they play around with a few lettuce leaves on their plate. It's annoying as hell.

"How long have you been with the Child Abduction Rapid Deployment team?" she asks in between bites, turning the tables on me.

"2006."

"Wow," she says, surprised. "You're one of the original ones, then."

She clearly knows more about CARD than most, which I also find intriguing. Few people know what CARD is, let alone the year of its inception.

"I was already with the Crimes Against Children Unit so it seemed like a logical step. Never looked back."

"Really?" She looks at me dubiously. "It's gotta take a toll on you, dealing with young victims day in and day out."

There's a hint of an edge to her voice.

"That part eats away at you, but each sick bastard we bring down makes it worth it," I admit.

She nods as if she gets what I'm saying. I'm not sure how she could, since she doesn't know me from Adam. Even my ex didn't understand and she knew my history.

"Excuse me?"

One of the guys in the search party—he looks a little like George from *Seinfeld* but older—walks up, his eyes flitting between Opal and myself.

"Oh, hey. I'm sorry," she says with a kind smile for the man, "I'm afraid I never got your name."

"James. Look, I don't mean to interrupt, but I just wanted to thank you again for the water."

He avoids looking at me, which is probably good because I'm afraid my annoyance at the interruption may be showing. A sharp whistle draws my attention and I look up to see one of my teammates wave me over. Reluctantly, I slide off the tailgate and turn to Opal.

"I've gotta run." I hold out my hand to her and she places her palm against mine. "It was a pleasure to meet you, Opal. And thanks again for your help today."

I give the guy a nod and just as I start walking toward my team, I hear him say, "Opal, care for some company?"

It's probably for the best. Despite my initial impression of a plump, somewhat frumpy-looking woman, Opal managed to surprise me in ways that had my libido sit up and take notice. Apparently, I'm a sucker for smarts and confidence, and this woman has both in spades. The truck, the abundance of hair, and the sharp gray eyes only add to her appeal.

Any more time spent with her might've proven to be a distraction, and I have a job that requires my full attention.

"We need to roll out," Matt Driver informs me when I join the group of men. "Just got a call. We caught another one. Sixteen-year-old female in Huntington, West Virginia. Left work at the local Walmart last night around eight thirty, but never made it home. Feed from one of the store's surveillance cameras caught her being forced into an old cargo van in the rear parking lot."

I check my watch. It's one thirty, she's been gone for seventeen hours; it'll take us at least another five on the road.

That's a lot of fucking hours in the hands of a predator.

"Let's go," I confirm, swinging my pack on my back and jogging to the black, Bureau-issued Expedition.

Right before I climb behind the wheel, I throw one last look over my shoulder and catch a glimpse of russet-colored hair.

Then we roll.

TWO

Opal

"We need more people."

"We've been over this."

I grin as Raj rolls her eyes at me.

Our boss, Jacob Branch, is right; we have been over this more than once. That doesn't mean Raj will let it drop. If anything, it will make her push even harder. Rajani Agarwal enjoys going head-to-head with the boss, and to be honest, I think she'd be disappointed if he ever gave in.

"Look..." She leans into the speakerphone. "I don't think any of us had a day off in the past two months. None of us are spring chickens anymore, and pretty soon the bodies are gonna start falling apart, then where would you be?"

"Hey, speak for yourself," Janey pipes up, looking

away from her computer screen for the first time this morning to throw Raj a dirty look.

Raj makes a good point though. We may not be old—just starting our forties—but we also don't bounce back as easily as we once did.

"Nowhere without the three of you," Jacob admits, *"but we're still not hiring. Now, can we get back to the list of potential cases?"*

The cases he refers to are those of missing children.

Two years ago, Jacob Branch founded GEM, which stands for Gather, Evaluate, and Mobilize. The group's objective is to search for, rescue, and recover missing and exploited minors. Our focus is mainly on disenfranchised kids, the most vulnerable ones, who often slip between the cracks. The runaways, street kids, those bounced around the foster system, or from unhealthy home lives.

Having lived a childhood like that myself—and still carrying the well-hidden scars—I didn't have to think long when offered a chance to join the crew. An opportunity to stand up for forgotten and vulnerable children, the way I wish someone had stood up for me.

Jacob had been convincing; despite the fact I never met him in person. The first time he called me I almost hung up on him, but then he mentioned the names of the other two women I'd be working with. Names I hadn't heard in two decades. He offered assurances in the form of high-ranking law enforcement officers he suggested I contact for references, including my commander at the Kentucky State Police Academy, where I worked as a firearms instructor. I took that to mean he was law enforcement too. Whoever Jacob Branch was, he had friends in high places.

With the promise of being reunited with Janey and Raj, the offer of a salary I never thought I'd see in my lifetime, and a chance to seek justice for the powerless using the skills I'd honed these past twenty years, I jumped.

"*Opal!*"

Jacob's sharp voice snaps me to attention.

Opal is the code name he's given me. Janey is Pearl and Raj, Onyx. It all seemed a little over the top to me at first, until he pointed out some of the work we do might put a target on our backs and it was safer to create alternate identities.

We use the code names in communications, but when it's just the girls and me in the office, we tend to forget.

"Sorry, what was that?"

"*I asked if you are ready for a case that may be a little close to home.*"

I look over at Raj, who eyes me with concern. Clearly, I missed something important.

"Close to home? What do you mean? Hebron or Dry Ridge?"

Hebron is where the GEM office is located, conveniently close to the airport. I have a place about thirty miles south, just outside the small town of Dry Ridge, only I rarely get to spend time there. I'm mostly on the road, staying in hotel rooms.

"*Neither. I'm talking about Lanark.*"

Janey rolls her chair away from her desk and closer to

the conference table, her eyes holding the same concern as Raj.

"Lanark?" Even just the name of the town I grew up in has me swallow hard. I left when I was eighteen and never went back. I take a deep breath and force myself to ask, "What've you got?"

"Got a call from a volunteer at The Youth Center in Lanark. She's concerned about a girl who suddenly stopped showing up about a week ago."

"It's a youth center, don't kids come and go all the time?" Janey points out.

"Maybe, but according to the woman, this girl was a regular. Showed up religiously for the after-school home-work program and she always stayed for a meal. Sally Kendall, the volunteer, said she'd been in touch with the girl's mother, who confirmed she hadn't seen Melissa in five days, but didn't seem to care much. She admitted the school had called and she'd lied, telling them her daughter was sick, just to get them off her back. According to Sally, the mom's a meth head whose only worry is where her next hit is gonna come from."

I start jotting down information on my notepad.

"Melissa, what is her last name?" I ask.

"Romero. Fifteen years old, five foot two, slight build, dark, shoulder-length hair, brown eyes, pierced nostril and earlobes."

"Why is this Sally woman calling us?" Raj wants to know. "Why doesn't she contact local law enforcement? And why is a volunteer sounding the alarm on this anyway and not the center's program manager or director?"

Jacob explains the woman apparently did go to management but was cautioned not to cause waves for the center. It was a conversation she indicated 'left her feeling uncomfortable.' She found our name when she scoured the internet looking for information on how to find missing children.

"Sounds fishy," Janey comments.

"The volunteer or the situation?" I direct at her.

"The situation. Management at the center. The mother. Lanark," she clarifies. "It's all fishy to me."

"I agree, which is why I want to move on this. It could be just a coincidence, but what if it isn't? What if something is still happening in Lanark?"

None of us respond. We don't need to because what he suggests is already worming its way into our thoughts. I don't even have to look at the others to know their minds. We were all victims, and Jacob is aware of this.

I asked him once how he knew about what went on at Transition House, to which he cryptically responded the house may have burned down, but the ghosts linger. I always assumed that to mean he perhaps knew someone there, or lost someone connected to the group home. He never clarified, but it's clear—just like the rest of us—he's never been able to let go.

It's why Jacob picked us for GEM. Our common trauma.

It's what ties all of us together.

It's what drives us to do what we do.

Mitch

"It's a camping trip, Sawyer, not an extended stay at a luxury resort," I mutter at no one in particular, lugging her massive suitcase to the truck. The damn thing is going to take up half the space in my tent.

She comes bouncing down the porch steps, wearing short-shorts, a skintight tank, and her feet in the new Birkenstocks she just had to have, but are no match for the kind of terrain we're heading for. Sturdy hiking boots would be more suitable for the rocks and sandstone cliffs. I give her a stern look, but she grins back, her blond hair framing her happy face, and as usual, I cave.

Sawyer owns me and she knows it.

"Can we stop at Starbucks on the way out?" she pleads, pushing her luck. "Pretty please?"

"You know a Keurig pod costs less than fifty cents, right?" I grumble.

She's heard it before and laughs at me, the happy melodious sound a balm to my dark mood.

We just closed a case earlier this week that won't let me go. The sight of that small, broken, and violated body in a farm field north of Greensboro, North Carolina, is one that will stay with me forever. Just like many others before.

It gets to you: this job, the predators, the innocent victims, the level of depravity, and lack of humanity. It eats at you. Which is why taking an occasional few days away is so important. Time to rebalance all the ugliness in the world with some beauty and the company of loved ones.

That is the plan for the upcoming long weekend with Sawyer. An hour-and-a-half drive to Daniel Boone National Forest, setting up the tent at the campsite, and then three days of nothing but the sound of nature, fishing, hiking, and hanging out with my girl.

Sawyer isn't new to camping, which is why the size of her suitcase annoys me. She knows better, having joined me on camping trips since she was just five years old. My daughter was always a bit of a spitfire, her fearlessness something that terrified me as much as it made me proud. This past year she went from a fifteen-year-old tomboy to a sixteen-year-old young woman.

Let's just say it's an adjustment for a father. Where before she was happy as a clam hanging out and watching Sunday football on the weekends she was with me, now she's more interested in hanging at the mall, endlessly chatting with girlfriends, and leaving her makeup all over my damn bathroom because 'the light is better.' At least she still got excited when I asked if she wanted to go camping with me for the weekend.

"Starbucks is coming up on the right," she reminds me when we head out of town.

I respond with a grunt, but still pull into the drive-thru. I don't even bother ordering; I never get it right anyway. Instead, I move back as Sawyer leans across my body, spouting off what sounds like an entire Italian menu to get a couple of measly coffees that takes them almost ten minutes to make.

The caffeine hits the spot though. One thing I'll say, they know their coffee. Dark, rich, with a hint of bitter, and a whole lot of punch.

"Better?" my smart-ass daughter grins over the rim of her foamy, frou-frou drink.

"Much," I admit.

Four hours later, when I finally cast my line in Cave Run Lake, I'm feeling even better. I look over my shoulder at our campsite, where Sawyer is hanging in one of the folding chairs reading a book. She wasn't even that upset to discover cell phone reception here is spotty at best, and she wouldn't be able to chat on her phone all day long. Thank God she loves reading and snapping pictures because, apparently, fishing no longer holds appeal.

This is the kind of quality family time I remember from when I was younger, before life took a drastic turn. I tried to find it again when I met Sawyer's mom, Becky, but she never was one for camping, definitely not outdoorsy, and the few attempts we made ended in disaster.

So did our marriage, eventually. In the end, we weren't compatible at all. She didn't like the amount of time I spent on the job, and I didn't like the amount of time she spent with her fitness instructor. It could've been ugly, but I don't think either of us had the heart to invest that much energy. We've gotten along a lot better since our divorce, which works out well for everyone, our daughter included.

"Good fish, Dad," she mumbles around her last mouthful.

It's our second night here and I finally managed to land a couple of nice-sized smallmouth bass. Enough for a meal. Sawyer likes my beer batter fried fish, so I made that while she was in charge of the roasted veggies.

"Have some more," I tell her, grabbing for the cast iron pan holding two more fillets, lifting one on my plate.

"I'm full. You finish them," she says, as she gets out of her chair. "I'm gonna fetch some water for dishes."

I watch her grab the bucket we use for that purpose and head down the trail. There's a water tap by the outhouse on the other side of the inlet we're on. It's the only place you'll occasionally see other people, which is why I suspect Sawyer so easily volunteers to get water.

I quickly finish the last two pieces of fish and walk down to the lake to rinse the pan when my phone rings in my pocket. The number on the display is familiar, and with it comes a feeling of dread.

"You're lucky you caught me where I have some reception," I tell Matt.

"Fuck, man, you know I wouldn't call unless it's an emergency."

"I know. What've you got?"

"More cases than teams. I just sent Lampert, Punani, and Byron to Delaware this morning, and now I get a call about the abduction of a ten-year-old boy right outside his home in Frankfort. I'm stuck in Cincinnati, I'm gonna need you on this, Mitch. A neighbor watched the kid get off the school bus on the opposite side of the street. He started crossing the road when an SUV stopped in front of him, blocking the neighbor's view. When the vehicle drove off, the kid was gone."

"How long ago?"

"We're already two and half hours behind," he tells me, and I curse under my breath.

The memory of the last victim, about the same age, is still too fresh in my mind. He hadn't been gone that long either. By the time I pack up, drive home, and drop Sawyer off at her mom's, it'll be dark out.

"Give me three hours," I tell him before I hang up and run back to the campsite.

When Sawyer returns a few minutes later, I've already taken down the tent.

"Let me guess, duty calls?"

I bristle at the words I so often had tossed at me by her mother. It's the first time I've heard them from my girl and it stings even worse. I drop the tent poles with a clatter to the ground.

"Yes, a ten-year-old boy already missing for more than two hours. Do you know what can happen to him in only a couple of hours? A child stolen right outside his house. I see the fucking damage done by sick perverts every goddamn day."

I don't even need to see the tears start rolling down my daughter's face to regret every goddamn single word that came flying out of my mouth. There's no amount of soul-deep fatigue that justifies taking it out on her.

"Jesus, Pumpkin," I mutter, walking up to her to apologize, but she neatly ducks under my arm.

"Come on, then. Let's get packed up," she says, grabbing the poles off the ground and shoving them in the bag. I'd rather she kneed me in the nuts.

Thirty minutes later, she's beside me, quiet, as we leave the campground behind.

"I'm sorry. I can't even tell you how wrong I was to lay that on you."

She turns her face to me.

"I'm sorry too. It wasn't fair of me to say that thing about duty. I was being a brat."

I grab her hand and kiss the back of it before she easily slips her fingers between mine.

"Nah, this was on me. Sometimes it just gets to me."

"I know, Daddy, and I'm sorry for that too."

Christ, don't know how I got this fucking lucky.

"Love you, kiddo."

"Love you more."

We don't say another word until I drop her off at her mother's place, but the entire drive her hand firmly holds on to mine.

THREE

*O*PAL

"Morning, Opal."

I lift a hand and smile at one of the center's social workers walking through the small cafeteria.

It's been a frustrating couple of days.

Sally has been wonderful, managing to get me a volunteer position as kitchen help, and I've been able to chitchat with some of the staff and kids, but it hasn't really given me a chance to ask many questions. I would've preferred a job where I'd be in closer contact with the kids, but the program director apparently decides on those, and he's supposed to be back from vacation today.

Most of what I know comes from Sally, who apparently didn't stop poking around after she called GEM. She was able to tell me Melissa had not been the only kid who stopped showing up all of a sudden. She found three others who dropped off the roster in the past year. One of them, fourteen-year-old Georgia Braxton, a kid from a broken home and a regular for a meal and counseling with one of the social workers at the center, has apparently missed her last few sessions.

Sally talked to the counselor, who reported trying to get in touch with the father without any luck. Sally was ready to go knock on his door, but I immediately told her to cease and desist her sleuthing. If there's any truth to the disturbing pattern she paints, she may well be putting herself in danger.

I passed the information on to Janey right away, with the additional name to look into. She messaged me this morning to let me know the girl's mother had contacted law enforcement. Knowing my team is on the case, I can focus on my job of gathering as much information as I can on this end.

The backstory we're working with is simple. I'm an old friend of Sally's from her college days at Ohio State in Columbus, new to town. My fictitious twenty-year marriage just ended and I'm looking for something meaningful to fill my life. The center's volunteer coordinator swallowed it whole and fit me in to the kitchen rotation on the spot.

I put the last of the muffins for the kids' after-school snack in the basket and carry the baking tray back into the kitchen. Brian is sitting on a stool at the long stainless-steel counter, peeling a bucket of potatoes for dinner.

The center has two cooks on rotation and I'm one of a handful of kitchen volunteers. Brian is one of the cooks, a sixty-seven-year-old former restaurateur, who retired two years ago and passed his restaurant to his son. Widowed only eight months later, he quickly got lonely and ended up at the youth center for something to fill his days.

Why people spill their stories to me without much prompting, I don't know, but Brian sure had me up to speed on his life fast my first shift with him. He's a nice man, adores his children and grandchildren, and deeply grieves the loss of his wife. If there is a connection to be found between the center and the disappearing kids, I have serious doubts Brian would turn out to be in any way involved.

"Need a hand with those?" I offer, slipping the baking tray in the large double sink.

"Grab a peeler and pull up a stool."

So far, I've let Brian initiate all conversation, something he does naturally, but today I plan to probe a little.

"So I hear the program director is back from vacation today," I start, as I pick up a potato and start peeling.

The only response I get is a snort. I wait to see if more is forthcoming but he remains silent, so I push a little.

"What? Is he not nice? Sally seems to like him."

"Oh, the women like him just fine," he mutters under his breath but doesn't expand on that. Instead, he seems lost in thought.

I toss the potato in the big pot and put my peeler down, touching my hand to his arm.

"Brian? What do you mean?"

His eyes flick up. "Just be careful with that one. That's all I can—" He stops talking abruptly, his eyes focused over my shoulder.

"Brian, I see you're keeping our new volunteer busy."

The voice seeps like ice water in my veins, freezing me on the spot.

I know him.

It feels like minutes go by, when in fact, it's a fraction of a second before my training overrides my paralysis. I'm not the same person I was then and besides, I've altered my appearance for this assignment. The wig I'm wearing is a mousy brown bob, barely able to contain my own hair, and the glasses I have on conveniently distort my eyes. On top of that, I carry around an extra fifty or so pounds I didn't have back in the day.

I'm also not afraid. Not anymore.

I square my shoulders and turn around, expecting to be confronted with the familiar handsome face that haunted my nightmares for years. Instead, I find a stranger. A man I would've sworn I've never met in my life if I hadn't heard his voice.

Then he looks at me, the cold blue eyes staring back at me, familiar in a stranger's face.

"Ms. Berry, I believe? Welcome to The Youth Center."

"Opal, please, Mr. Kramer," I respond, placing my hand in his offered one. I fight against the shiver of revulsion his touch triggers in my body.

"Opal it is. What a lovely name. Please, call me Mason." I resist the temptation to rub my palm on my pants when he finally lets go of my hand. "Why don't we have a chat in my office. Brian? You can spare her for a few minutes?"

The look he throws the older man is everything but friendly.

"Of course," Brian answers, adding, "you're the boss."

"Yes. I am."

With a last look at Brian, I follow Mason down the hall to the offices in the back of the one-story building. As he waves me into his office and closes the door, I wish I'd at least had the foresight to wear a wire. I sit down in the chair he indicates on the other side of the desk and wait for him to speak.

I don't have to wait long.

"So, Opal, Sally tells me you're new to Lanark?"

"I am. I've only been here a week." I try hard not to fidget in my seat.

"What made you come here?"

I dive into my role as a recently jilted wife, and even manage to squeeze out a few tears for authenticity as I share my recent woes. As expected, the man looks uncomfortable and quickly changes direction.

"Why The Youth Center?"

"I've always wanted to work with children," I gush. "I've always worked administrative jobs but when Sally mentioned volunteering at the center, I thought perhaps it might be a good way to test the waters."

He leans his elbows on his desk and tents his fingers under his chin.

"I see." He purses his lips in a way that has bile surge up my esophagus. "Well, I don't have openings on any of the programs we run at the moment, but we could use some help in the office. Filing, correspondence, scheduling, those kinds of things. You wouldn't be working directly with the kids, but you'd interact with them daily."

That might work. The closer I can get to what this sick bastard is up to now, the better, and maybe I can sneak a peek at his files when he's not around. He wants me to come in from one-to-five daily during the week, because those are the high traffic hours.

"I need you to look into someone," I tell Janey when I step outside the center to make the call.

"Who?"

"Mason Kramer. The program director."

"I already did, along with the rest of the staff. Clean as a whistle. The man doesn't even have a parking ticket to his name."

"Check deeper. It's an alias."

That silences her, but only for a minute.

"How do you know?"

Her question is sharp, almost a challenge. For a moment it rattles me and I hesitate, but there was no mistaking that voice, or those cold eyes.

"I know," I tell her firmly before adding, "I recognized his voice."

"Recognized? From where? Who is it?"

I take a deep breath before I share the name of a man I believed to have been dead for the past twenty years.

"Josh Kendrick."

I can hear the phone clatter to the desk on the other end.

Mitch

Jesus, what a mess.

Cases like this make me grateful my ex and I were able to keep Sawyer as our priority, even after we split.

Hard to believe just three days ago, I was sitting around a campfire with my daughter, roasting marshmallows to celebrate the start of our mini vacation. Two days ago, I was racing to join the search for a missing ten-year-old in Frankfort, who turned up at a local arcade where he was forced to sell dime bags of pot by a gang of teens.

Then this morning I get a call from local law enforcement in Lanark about a fourteen-year-old girl gone missing. She was last seen five days ago. The parents are in the middle of an ugly divorce. The girl wasn't getting along with Mom and chose to live with Dad, who is a long-haul trucker. The man is gone from home days at a time and left the kid to fend for herself.

It wasn't until early yesterday they discovered her gone.

Unbelievable. Some people are seriously messed up.

"Did you get anything more?" I ask when Matt climbs into the passenger seat.

"Not much. Get this, she ate most of her meals at the local youth center," he says, his disgust evident. "Two damn parents living in the same town, not five blocks from each other, and somehow between them they can't manage to feed their own daughter?"

I grunt in agreement. Sadly, Georgia Braxton is not the only kid who slipped through the cracks while the parents were busy fighting with each other.

"Local cops talk to someone at The Lanark Youth Center yet?"

"They plan to meet with the director today. I told them we'd go instead."

"Good. Bring up the address in the GPS."

It's forty-five minutes after noon when I pull the SUV into the almost empty parking lot of a large, one-story building, just steps from Lanark's downtown. I wait for Matt to get off the phone with the local detective in charge, to let him know we arrived, before getting out.

"Any new developments?"

"They tracked down the father in Reno," he says in a grim voice as we approach the front doors. "Killing time at the slots while waiting for a load to haul back to Louisville. He's looking for a replacement driver so he can fly back."

"What a prince," I mumble, as I open the door and walk into a large space.

On the right side of the entrance is a wall of lockers and to the left what looks to be a large rec room with tables and chairs, a small bar with an industrial-sized coffee maker and a vending machine. The opposite side of the room holds two pool tables, a foosball table, and a few pinball machines.

The place is empty.

Straight ahead a man steps into the narrow hallway running to the back of the building and walks toward us.

"Gentlemen, can I help you?"

Matt and I both flip open our FBI badges when he approaches and I keep a sharp eye for any reaction. I'm guessing he's five ten or eleven, about my age, maybe a little older, judging from the lines around his eyes, and in decent physical shape. The most remarkable things about him are his piercing blue eyes and the skin graft covering the entire right side of his face and down his neck into the collar of his shirt.

"Agents Kenny and Driver," I take the lead.

"Mason Kramer, I'm the program director. How can I help you?"

"We're hoping to ask you a few questions about one of your young patrons, Georgia Baxter?"

Not a muscle on the man's face moves, in fact, I'd say he looks almost bored but that could be the result of his obvious burns.

"Ah, Georgia, yes. I understand she may have run away?"

"Actually, we're not at all sure about that, which is why we'd like to talk to you."

"Of course," he says with a flat smile. "Please follow me to my office." He leads the way and sits down behind his desk, inviting us to sit on the other side. "I'll do whatever I can to help, gentlemen."

"We understand Georgia came into the center regularly?" Matt gets to the point.

"Yes, she did. Usually after school, she'd come in for a meal and hang out with some of the kids in the rec room."

"What about counseling? I believe she was seeing one of your therapists?" I take over.

"Yes, quite possibly. I'd have to check—" He suddenly looks at something behind. "If you'll excuse me just a minute, I'll find out for you."

He shoots out of his chair and heads for the door. I twist in my seat in time to see him usher a woman into a room across the hallway. A few minutes later, he's back with a large planner.

"We keep all our scheduled appointments in here. It looks like she saw one of our counselors two days a week; Wednesdays and Fridays."

"What does this mean?" Matt points at the letters NS in red marker across Georgia's name both on Wednesday and Friday of last week.

"That's a no show. Apparently, she missed her last two sessions."

"Would that not have sent up any red flags?" I ask pointedly, poking a little.

"Not necessarily," Kramer responds easily. "The kids here come and go. It's a walk-in center."

"I understand. However, you admitted earlier Georgia was a regular. Surely if that was noticeable, her absence would've been as well?"

I know I got under his skin when his nostrils flare slightly.

"I'm afraid you'll have to check with her therapist on that. I was away on vacation and only returned yesterday.

As you can imagine, even a short week away means a pile of messages waiting, I've been busy processing those and haven't had a chance to check in with staff."

Matt doesn't skip a beat as he pulls out his notebook and pen.

"Then let's make this easy for you. If you could give us names and numbers for anyone on your staff, who would've been in contact with Georgia, we can check for ourselves."

Kramer is clearly reluctant but provides the information, and twenty minutes later we stand up to leave.

"Thank you so much for your time. We'll find our own way out," Matt says, shaking the man's hand.

"If we have any more questions, we'll let you know," I add with a fake smile before I follow Matt into the hallway.

I pass an open door and glance inside; spotting the woman I glimpsed earlier pulling open the drawer of a filing cabinet. She must've sensed me, because she turns around and her eyes widen when she sees me. Immediately she presses her finger against her lips and sharply shakes her head no.

I keep walking and it takes me a second to let it sink in.

The hair is different, but even behind the ridiculous glasses I recognize those gray eyes. I've thought about them often enough over the past few months.

What the hell?

FOUR

Opal

Shit.

I saw he was with someone in his office and backed away from the door immediately, without looking too closely. I should've; then I could have stayed out of sight until they were gone.

Catching Agent Kenny peering into the room where I was supposed to start on the filing backlog was a shock. I'm lucky he didn't call me out right there and then, but I guess he was as surprised as I was and kept walking after I silently pleaded with him. I have no doubt this'll have a follow-up though.

For the past hour or so, I've been wracking my brain trying to come up with some kind of excuse for being here, but there's nothing plausible that would have me show up in two different states on two different cases. From his perspective it must look pretty damn suspicious.

"Opal?"

I look up, from yet another stack of paperwork, to find Sally sticking her head around the door before she slips inside, closing it behind her.

"Hey, aren't you early? What's up?"

"Did you know the FBI is investigating?" she whispers with half an eye on the door.

"He left fifteen minutes ago," I assure her. "Something about an appointment he had to keep. And yes, I saw them when I came in."

"They called and asked me to meet them at the police station. I'm on my way now, what am I supposed to tell them?"

"The truth," I tell her, pulling my phone from my pocket. "At least about your suspicions, about Melissa and the others, and even your phone call to GEM, but you have to know the moment you identify me..."

"They'll pull you," she concludes correctly.

"More than likely."

Unless I can convince Agent Kenny I can be useful to his case. I don't want to have to walk away from a chance to bring down Josh Kendrick, aka Mason Kramer, and I'm not about to alert the FBI to his true identity without the go-ahead from my boss.

"I can tell them I'm waiting to hear back," Sally offers.

"I can't ask you to do that."

"You're not," she responds instantly. "I'm offering." I look her in the eye, giving her a chance to back out, but she squares her shoulders and lifts her chin. "I care about those girls. I want to believe you can help find them."

"I promise I'll do everything I can."

She grabs for the door, gives me a little nod, and disappears down the hallway. I immediately dial Jacob direct.

"Hold on," he barks before I can say anything. A few seconds later, he's back on the line. "Sorry about that. Had to find some privacy. Something wrong that you're calling me and not the office?"

"Maybe. We're about to be outed to the FBI."

I explain my situation, Sally's little visit, and the distinct possibility my cover will be blown by a federal agent.

"How can you be so sure he recognized you? After meeting you only once? You have a way of blending in with the wallpaper, that's why I hired you."

I could tell him I'd felt an instant connection with the man when we first met, or I could read it from the look in those hazel eyes, but Jacob doesn't deal in flights of fancy. He deals in concrete terms.

"I'm one-hundred-percent positive," I assure him with as much conviction as I can muster.

"Very well," he concedes after a pregnant pause. "I'm taking your word for it. I'll get in touch with Onyx, let her know what's up, and we'll deal with it on our end. You continue as you are until you hear otherwise."

"Yes, sir."

I tuck my phone away and dig back into the stack I was working on. I scan every piece of paper carefully before I file it away, hoping something will jump out at me, but so far, I have nothing.

Unfortunately, that doesn't change the remainder of my shift and when five o'clock rolls around, and Kramer hasn't returned to the office, I grab my bag because my eyes are gritty. I stop by the kitchen to say hello to Brian on my way out.

"How'd you make out?" He wants to know when I walk in.

"Okay. Familiar territory for me, paperwork, but it was quieter than I expected. I hardly saw another soul," I share.

"Yeah, I saw the boss beelining it out of here a couple of hours ago. What crawled up his ass?"

I bite off a grin at his barely contained dislike for the man. I wish I could tell him I share the sentiment, but I have a role to play.

"I have no idea, one minute he was there, the next gone. Does he disappear like that often?" I ask innocently.

"Not that I've noticed. Mind you, most of the time I'm back here and try not to pay too much attention to what goes on out there."

"I thought you liked it here?" I point out, determined to get him to elaborate on that last telling comment.

He looks at me, a little guilty. "Like most of it; cooking, especially for the kids, doing something useful with my time, and I get along with almost everyone."

"Except Kramer," I boldly prompt.

"Yeah, except him." He turns back to the two ginormous pans of mac and cheese he's topping with breadcrumbs. My mouth is watering and I wonder if I could beg for a taste. "Look, I'm sure he's a good man. He has to be, right? To do this kind of work?" he asks no one in particular, but I answer anyway.

"I guess. Some people can just rub you the wrong way, I suppose."

He hums in response and stays silent as he slides those pans into the oven. I guess he's said all he's going to. For now.

"Well, as delicious as that looks, I should probably be heading home."

"You found a place?"

He pins me with a smile, his eyebrows high. I'd mentioned I literally rolled into town and was still looking for something more permanent than the mini suite at the Creekside Inn on the other side of town.

"Not yet. I'm still at the motel."

"So what'll you do for dinner? You may as well stay and eat here. At least you'll have some company." He tilts his head in the direction of the cafeteria, where a couple of kids are already wandering in looking for food.

He's right. I may as well. It'll be a good opportunity to get to know some of the kids.

"You twisted my arm." I nudge him with my elbow and he snorts out a laugh.

"Please," he chuckles. "You were drooling so hard; I was about to tie a bib on you."

It's almost seven by the time I finally get into my truck.

Dinner was as delicious as it looked, and although most of the kids were wary of me, there were a couple who called out goodbyes when I walked out.

As soon as I turn toward the motel and notice the sun slowly going down, my thoughts go to the missing girls. Out there somewhere, maybe alone, scared, watching as yet another day comes to an end, and waiting for someone to come rescue them.

I should probably call in but end up driving to the motel in silence, my heart suddenly heavy. Pulling into the spot outside my unit, I dig into my purse for the key before I get out. I'm so focused on getting in the shower and changing into my pajamas, I jump at the sound of my name.

"Opal!"

Mitch

"Where are you off to?"

Matt catches me snagging the keys from the dresser in our hotel room.

So much for sneaking out while he's on the phone. He has it pressed against his chest waiting for my answer.

"Just gonna drive around a bit. I won't be long," I blow him off, as I dart out the door.

We've spent the afternoon talking to a few potential witnesses, briefing with the local detective on the case who'd been trying to retrace Georgia Braxton's last known steps, and strategizing our next move. But by far, the most productive talk this afternoon was with Sally Kendall, a volunteer at The Youth Center.

She shared how she had become worried last week—even before Georgia disappeared—when another minor had failed to show for days on end. Melissa Romero, a fifteen-year-old girl from the wrong side of the tracks, by the sound of it.

The woman raised a flag with not only the girl's mother, but also with management at the center. No one seemed particularly concerned, but Sally persisted and ended up contacting GEM, a victim advocacy organization. Matt seemed to know of them, having worked an abduction investigation they assisted with, but I've only heard of them in passing. When asked if GEM had taken the case, Sally looked decidedly uncomfortable when she said she thought so, but was waiting for someone to contact her.

That seemed off, just as seeing Opal at The Youth Center seemed off, and I can't help wonder if the two are connected. It would explain why the woman shows up at two separate child disappearance cases.

What it doesn't explain is why she was suddenly wearing a wig and glasses and basically begged me not to say anything, which is why I have a few questions for her.

Finding her proves easier than I thought it would be.

I'm about to turn right toward the center, in hopes I could track her from there, when I spot a new maroon Chevy pickup truck heading in the opposite direction. I quickly slip into the left-hand lane and turn as soon as I see an opening in traffic.

I stay a couple of cars behind her, until I see her turning into a motel almost across from the college grounds. She doesn't even seem to notice when I pull in behind her and for some reason that pisses me off. I'm already standing beside my vehicle when she gets out and moves toward the motel room she parked in front of.

"Opal!"

She comes to a dead stop and swings around, her hand already reaching in her purse. She may not pay much attention to her surroundings, but at least she has good reflexes. She clearly carries.

The moment she registers me, her head drops down and I catch her swearing softly.

"We need to talk."

Instead of responding, she turns her back and fits a key in the door, leaving it open as she disappears inside. I'll take it as an invitation.

"Close the door," is all she says, standing in front of the mirror next to the bathroom as she pulls the ugly wig off her head.

The thing gets tossed carelessly on the dresser, while her fingers make quick work of the bobby pins in her hair. Then she bends over, groaning as she shakes out her tresses, her rear sticking up like a big red flag waving in my face. I force myself to turn away.

"So talk." Her voice is soft and tired, and I turn back to find her staring at me with her hands on her hips. The glasses are gone and the luxurious waves of gleaming hair fall about her round, pale face.

"GEM," I force myself to say.

"Yes," she confirms without further explanation, as she grabs some clothes from a bag on the floor and slips inside the bathroom, locking the door.

By the time I hear the door open ten minutes later, I've worked up a good head of steam after a fruitless search of her stuff. But once again, she surprises me when she walks into the room wearing a pair of silky men's pajamas and a towel wrapped around her hair. There isn't a trace of makeup on her face and she doesn't seem to care one single iota. She completely takes the wind out of my sails when she flings herself on one of the beds, folding her arms behind her head.

"Are you gonna stand there, or do want to deep search my bathroom too?"

Sharper than I may have given her credit for earlier.

"Will I find anything?"

"Aside from dirty clothes, toiletries, and feminine products? I hope not."

I stifle a grin at her smart-ass comment, and sit down on the foot end of the second bed.

"Is Opal even your real name?"

I'm not sure why it's the first thing out of my mouth but now that it is, I'm curious for her answer.

"That's what you're going with?" she asks incredulously. When I nod, she rolls her eyes. "Fine. It's the name I use when I'm working and I have the paperwork to back it up.

"And I guess you're not about to give me your real name?"

"You'd guess correctly."

Yeah. This lady is definitely not as soft as she looks.

My anger forgotten, I kick off my shoes and scoot with my back against the headboard, crossing my legs in front of me on the mattress.

"Comfortable?" she sneers.

"Gettin' there. Now, what were you doing at The Youth Center?"

She raises an eyebrow.

"You haven't contacted GEM?"

I shake my head. "Not yet. My partner is making phone calls tonight." I lean forward a little and pin her with a glare. "Besides, I'm asking you."

"Oh for fuck's sake," she suddenly blurts out, shocking the hell out of me.

She jumps off the bed, and with impatient hands she yanks the towel from her head, and shakes out her hair like a wet dog.

The whole situation suddenly strikes me as funny and I can't hold back the chuckle. Instantly her head comes up with fire in her eyes, which quickly fizzles out.

"I've been assigned to dig up information on Mason Kramer," she finally admits, but before I have a chance to open my mouth she adds, "We have reason to suspect he may be involved in the girls' disappearance. Anything more you'll have to get from my boss; Jacob Branch."

"Kramer checks out. There's not a speck of dirt on him," I share.

"That's because you're not looking for the right man. Call Jacob," she urges.

I stare at her for a beat and then I pull my phone from my pocket and dial the number she recites.

"Agent Kenny, I was waiting for your call."

The voice is smooth, confident. Belonging to a man of some authority, I have no doubt.

"The name's Mitch. So tell me, Jacob, who is Mason Kramer?"

"You spoke with Opal," he says with a chuckle.

"Hmm."

"Is she there?"

"Quit beating around the bush," I snap, no longer in the mood for games. There are at least two young girls missing and we desperately need leads.

"Very well. His real name is Josh Kendrick. If you look up the name, you'll find he was supposedly killed in a fire at a group home that burned down in Lanark, some twenty years ago. The home was a front for the trafficking and prostitution of minors."

Jesus. The burn and graft scars.

"You're saying he's not dead."

"That's what I'm saying."

"Have proof for any of this?"

The quiet following my question is charged.

"Witnesses...victims," he finally clarifies and my gaze finds Opal who is looking back, her face almost impassive. *Fucking hell.* "We're committed to gettin those girls back, Agent Kenny," he continues, "first and foremost, and through whatever means possible."

"So am I," I growl.

"I have no doubt, which is why I propose it would be in everyone's best interest for us to pool our resources."

"You want me to let her go back in undercover."

"Got it in one."

"That's what I was afraid of," I tell him, my eyes never leaving Opal's face.

FIVE

OPAL

"Can you pull me the files on Jesper Olson, Jamie Lyons, Chantel Staffman, and Bryonne Taylor?"

As it has for the past week, my boss's voice sends shivers down my spine. It's an ingrained response I can't seem to shake, even after over two decades.

I don't turn around—worried something of my revulsion for the man might show, having been caught off-guard—and instead start rifling through the file drawer of the cabinet I already had open. I can feel his presence behind me though.

The temptation is great to do the world a favor and pull my Glock G42 Slimline from my belly band holster and blow him to kingdom come, but that won't bring back those missing girls. I can't chance tipping him off in any way or—provided the girls are still alive—I might as well be signing the girls' death warrants.

The only chance we have to find them is for me to act like I've never acted before. The request for files is not unusual, but for him to ask for Chantel's file—one of the four girls in total who've gone missing in the past year—has every nerve in my body on high alert.

Locating the four file folders, I plaster on a smile and swing around.

"Here you go. I don't think I've seen those names before," I mention innocently, all but batting my lashes.

Mason Kramer narrows his eyes briefly as he takes the file from my hands.

"Lots of kids coming and going at the center, no way to know them all."

"Of course," I quickly respond.

"Besides," he adds, smacking the stack on the palm of his hand. "These ones are old, and scheduled for disposal."

Then he turns and walks out of the office I've been assigned to.

The Kentucky Board of Social Work requires maintaining files in the case of minors for at least five years after termination of service, or until the client reaches the age of twenty, whichever is longer.

I don't know about the others, but Chantel was only seventeen when she went missing eight months ago so meets neither of those parameters. Not that there's anything I can do about that without drawing attention to myself, but at least I had copies. I jumped on the opportunity when Kramer was out of the office for the day yesterday and made sure I took copies of the files for all four girls: Georgia Braxton, Melissa Romero, Bobby-Jean Lark, and Chantel Staffman.

I'm curious to see if he actually destroys the file, which would be an interesting development. I wonder if there is something in the file he's hiding. Chantel's the one who has been missing longest according to Sally Kendall—eight months—although no one has filed a missing person report for her since she was listed in the center's paperwork as homeless.

The girl had landed in the foster system and was apparently known as a frequent runaway. I guess no one but Sally had been too concerned about her lot thus far, which makes Kramer's interest in her file even more suspect.

Maybe I should finally dial that new number on my phone I've been staring at for the past week, ever since I watched FBI Agent Mitch Kenny walk out of my motel room.

I hate to admit it, but the man left an indelible impression, which does not make me happy.

For years, I've harbored revenge fantasies should I ever end up face-to-face with the likes of Josh Kendrick. Except, I was convinced it would always remain a fantasy, something that would stay forever unresolved. I thought Kendrick was dead, had perished in the fire along with the others, so my heart nearly stopped when I heard his voice.

Now, an opportunity has dropped in my lap to bring

down the man who still haunts some of my nightmares and I can't afford to lose my focus.

Last thing I need is a hot-as-fuck fed distracting me from my objective.

Still, I should call him.

Jacob negotiated with the agent, assuring him I was well-trained and more capable than I looked, and already had a foot in the door at the center which could save the Bureau valuable time. Time the girls may not have.

When Kenny agreed to leave me to do my part and would keep GEM in the loop, I, in turn, was made to promise I'd pass on whatever valuable information I could dig up.

The sudden request by the center's program director for Chantel's file would definitely be of interest to him.

Last week Mitch Kenny had only been interested in Georgia Braxton, until I told him there were more girls missing. He was supposed to look into them as well but I haven't seen him back here at the center, nor have I heard from him outside of it.

If this is to be a collaboration, maybe it's time for us to talk.

"Opal," Brian calls my name when I walk by the kitchen on my way out the door.

I backtrack and stick my head in the door.

"What's up?"

"Hate to do this, because I know you're supposed to be off tomorrow, but I just got this sprung on me this afternoon."

"Had what sprung on you?" I ask, walking inside and joining him by the large stainless-steel counter.

He appears to be kneading dough.

"Fucking Kramer. He's got a bunch of dignitaries coming in tomorrow to have breakfast with the kids. Is expecting a full goddamn breakfast buffet and I only have two hands."

"Dignitaries?"

"Yeah, something about raising funds for the center. Wants to make it look like we're feeding the kids gourmet food, when any other day the measly budget he's given me won't allow for much more than a goddamn bowl of oatmeal. I swear, since that man took over, my joy in working here has all but disappeared."

Brian has hinted at his dislike for Kramer, but this is the first time he's actually given me some background.

"What time do you need me here?"

The look of relief on his face is instantaneous. "God bless. Five thirty?" He's wincing as he says it.

He doesn't know I don't sleep much on my best days.

"Five thirty is good, but don't talk to me unless you have a pot of coffee ready."

"You betcha," is his immediate response, which is paired with a wide grin. "You're a lifesaver."

I give him a little wave as I leave him to his dough and head outside.

Maybe tomorrow morning I can get him to open up a bit more about his beef with Kramer.

Mitch

"What have you got?" I ask a little more abruptly than necessary.

It's been a fucked-up week. I've seen and talked to more unfit parents this week than I cared to and have gotten exactly nowhere.

Because of Opal Berry's presence at the center, I decided to avoid going back there, not wanting to risk either of us giving away her involvement in this investigation. We've kept close tabs on Kramer, especially after discovering his real name and history, but that turned up nothing either. Then yesterday, he somehow managed to slip past our surveillance.

Gone for the entire day without his car, until he finally came walking down the street at nine thirty at night, letting himself into the front door to his tidy bungalow without a care in the world.

He may as well have flipped us off.

So I am clean out of patience today.

"Where are you?" Opal snaps right back.

She makes it clear again she's not a woman to be messed with, despite her appearance of an almost nondescript, middle-aged housewife. The woman is hiding a steel core under that soft body, which makes me even more curious about her.

I've conferred with Jacob Branch a few times this

week but every time I tried to find out more about his operative, he's shut me down. The only lead I have to her real identity is her suspected connection to Transition House, a privately funded group home for teenagers which burned down under questionable circumstances nineteen years ago. Three people supposedly died in that fire, of which, Josh Kendrick, aka Mason Kramer was one.

Any and all records burned right along with the group home, which made that another fruitless pursuit for me this week.

"Heading out to grab some dinner. Why?"

"Because I may have something and I could use a second pair of eyes."

Well, shit.

Wouldn't that just take the cake, if this woman turns up something while we've been spinning our damn wheels all week.

"Gimme thirty minutes and you'd better be okay with Indian food."

I don't give her a chance to answer and end the call.

Matt volunteered to be part of the surveillance team on Kramer tonight, but I promised to drop him off dinner. We were able to gain access to a house for sale across the road, only two doors down from the director's place. It has a good view of the front of the bungalow, but clearly, we needed to upgrade our surveillance after yesterday's fiasco. Matt is in a van parked on a side street with a view of the rear of Kramer's property, supporting the local law enforcement team until more FBI enforcements arrive tomorrow.

We're throwing a lot of manpower at this case at the behest of the Lanark Police Department, but as it turns out, Georgia Braxton is related to Chief of Police Dennis Furmont. Her mother is his niece. The chief apparently has friends in high places.

My order is ready by the time I get to Tandoor and I'm glad I ordered plenty, it smells amazing, taunting me on the way to meet up with Matt.

"Everything quiet?" I ask when I hand him his order.

We're standing behind the van so Matt can stretch his legs for a few minutes while still keeping an eye on the house.

"He got home twenty minutes ago and haven't seen a move since."

"Let's hope he doesn't slip past us again."

Matt turns to me with a grin.

"Oh ye of little faith," he mocks before turning serious. "We've got a good setup here. I was able to mount a couple of motion sensor mini cams, covering the front and back of the house, I can monitor from the van. Anything moves, I'll know. I just hope we're not wasting our time with this guy."

Even though Matt Driver is our team leader, because of my previous run-in with Opal Berry in Maryland he's asked I be the forerunner in this case. The rest of the team —Joe Lampert, Phil Dresden, John Punani, and Adam Byron—are set to arrive tomorrow morning. Phil just came off family medical leave after the birth of his twin sons three months ago, and the other three just finished up a case in Delaware—the abduction of an infant from a hospital in Wilmington—which took a fuck of a long time to untangle.

His point is valid; pulling everyone in on this case may prove to be a waste of resources that could be of more value elsewhere, but somehow, I don't think so. My gut says this case is bigger than one missing teenager.

Hope to hell my gut is right.

Matt opens the bag I handed him and takes a sniff while I gather my thoughts.

"Given the information Branch at GEM gave us, I don't think so. According to him, while Kramer worked at Transition House, he was neck-deep involved in the recruitment and grooming of kids in a sex exploitation ring. It would be a bit of a stretch to think he might not be involved in the disappearance of these girls."

So far, we know of four girls who've disappeared without a trace, even though the only case we're officially investigating is the missing Georgia Braxton. At this point, our best bet is to keep the fact we're looking into the other girls under wraps. If we start asking too many questions, it might tip Kramer off and he could disappear, leaving us without any way to track the girls down.

"It's the only lead we've got," I offer.

"I know. It's just frustrating, feels like we're spinning our wheels."

I don't disagree, usually our CARD team is more actively searching for missing or abducted kids, but unfortunately in this case we've got nothing else to go on.

I also understand Matt's reluctance to buy into Branch's claims of an underage sex ring. Even though we found evidence of some rumors going around at the time of the fire—in particular an article in the local newspaper the week following—no reports were ever made or investigations ever launched. The story died right there.

Still, it was enough to give some credibility to Branch's story. It also didn't hurt GEM—and Jacob Branch in particular—came highly recommended by none other than the chief of FBI's Violent Crimes Against Children program, Ian McCraig. He'd been able to tell me GEM was an acronym for Gather, Evaluate, Mobilize, and although the team is small—only three operatives from what I was able to gather—they'd apparently worked several cases with VCAC in the few years they've been in existence.

Maybe I'll have a chance to pick Opal's brain, see if she'll be a bit more forthcoming. The woman is intriguing, to say the least. You'd never guess she's an undercover operator and I'm more than curious to find out how she came to be one. I know next to nothing about her background, but I intend to find out more.

After all, I should at least know who I'm working with.

Or so I tell myself.

"I'm heading out."

"Going back to the hotel?"

"After I check in with Opal, yes. She has something she wants me to look at."

"I bet she does."

I ignore his grin and start walking toward the rental, relieved when I hear the van door slide shut behind me.

Despite having been married for seven years with three kids right on top of each other—or perhaps because of it—Matt Driver can't seem to shake his preoccupation with my love life since Becky and I got a divorce. Not that I've had much of one, nothing lasting anyway. I like sex as much as the next guy, but not enough to get drawn in by another set of long legs and a pretty smile.

Been there, done that, and although the daughter we made will always be the best part of my life, I'm not willing to go down that path again.

SIX

Opal

I try to stay pissed at his high-handedness earlier on the phone, but the man found my Achilles' heel without even trying.

Indian food.

Thus, when I notice headlights of a car pulling up to my motel room, I'm on my feet and have the door open before he can even exit his vehicle.

The plan had been to heat up a can of soup in the small microwave the motel supplied, so the prospect of a decent meal was a welcome one, even though the offer left a lot to be desired. It doesn't stop me from almost ripping the brown paper bag from his hand when he walks up to the door.

What can I say? I'm starving.

I quickly clear the papers I've been staring at from the small table so I can spread out the containers.

The fragrant aromas fill the room. It smells delicious, although I'm not so sure I'll still feel that way tomorrow or the days after when the potent scent of spices lingers.

Mitch closes the door behind him, an amused expression on his face.

"I did bring cutlery," he comments when I toss the paper bag aside.

"I've got real."

I turn and open the top drawer in the dresser where I store a couple of mugs, plates, and silverware. I can't stand using paper or plastic. It's bad enough I don't have a proper kitchen to cook in but am dependent on takeout or canned food. At least I have the mini fridge to store some fresh fruit and dairy, and some bottles of water.

Mitch pulls up an eyebrow when I slide a plate and cutlery in front of him.

"I don't like plastic," I explain, before asking, "Anything to drink? I'm afraid all I can offer is water, tea, or coffee."

"Water is fine, thanks."

While I grab a couple of bottles, he peels the covers off the containers. My mouth was already watering at the smell of food, but now I'm virtually drooling. Sitting down across from him, I take in the spread covering the small table. Aloo gobhi, spinach paneer, beef korma, vegetable biryani, butter chicken, a container of raita, and a tinfoil packet I'm sure contains naan.

"This looks so good," I mutter as he urges me to serve myself. "Not often I get the chance to eat Indian food."

"How come?" he asks casually.

"Dry Ridge isn't exactly a hotbed of world cuisine. Until a Chinese restaurant opened a few years ago, Taco Bell was the closest thing we had."

His deep chuckle startles me. He'd been in such an obvious foul mood on the phone, I wasn't expecting the warm, pleasant sound.

Sparkling hazel eyes meet my own drab gray ones.

"Dry Ridge? That where you live?"

Shit.

Rookie mistake, with food and casual conversation I let him lull me into revealing information connected to my real identity. Information I'm normally so careful to guard.

I narrow my eyes on him.

"Underhanded."

It was intended as an insult, but Agent Kenny appears unaffected and shrugs off my comment.

"Seems fair to me. If our collaboration is going to work, there has to be mutual trust. Hard to do when one side keeps their identity a secret. Can't blame me for wanting to know."

"Why not?" I fire back. "I don't see you volunteering your life history."

"My life is not a secret. In fact, you can probably easily find out anything you'd like about me online."

I press my lips together so I don't inadvertently let slip I already did this past week. The information I found gave me a little insight into the man and a better understanding of what drove him.

Mitchel James Kenny, forty-four, only remaining

child to James and Phyllis Kenny formerly of Huntington, West Virginia, now residing in Mesa, Arizona. His only sister, Valerie, fell victim to a sexual predator, whose arrest and trial were widely covered by the media. A lot of information available there. However, the simple and concise obituary I found dated only eighteen months after she was violently assaulted, didn't reveal a whole lot.

Not that I needed it spelled out, I can pretty much guess what happened to her.

I also found out Mitch had been married and was now divorced, and has a teenage daughter.

All of this only made the man more difficult to dislike, something that would've made life a hell of a lot easier. Instead, I find myself more drawn to him.

Dangerous.

His point is valid though. Trust goes both ways, but I'm not ready to lay myself bare. I've never told anyone. The girls know, because they lived the same history I did, and Jacob Branch does, but not from me.

Our boss is no more than a name with a voice. None of us have ever laid eyes on him so it's a mystery how he came by the information, but I have my suspicions.

"My name is Kate," I finally decide to share, figuring the name is common enough it's not telling him a whole lot, but it at least shows some goodwill on my part.

"Thank you, Kate," he says, sounding sincere. "I'm not going to betray your trust."

"Appreciate it," I mumble, a bit stunned by his promise.

For the next few minutes, we eat in silence and I

struggle not to groan with every bite. It's so damn good, I have to resist the urge to stuff myself.

"What did you want me to look at?" he asks after we pack the leftover food in my mini fridge.

I grab the four files I copied and spread them out on the table in front of him.

Then I tap a finger on Chantel Staffman's records.

"Yesterday, Kendrick was out of the office and I was able to make copies of the missing girls' records. This afternoon he asked for a bunch of files, including Chantel's, mentioning they were old files and slotted to be destroyed."

Mitch looks up with an eyebrow raised.

"Old?"

"Bogus, I know."

"Why now? The girl's been missing for eight months."

"Maybe your visit last week got him nervous," I suggest.

"We didn't even have Chantel Staffman on our radar then."

"Still, it may have spooked him and he decided to cover his tracks."

He seems to contemplate that before asking, "By chance do you remember the names on any of the other files he asked for?"

"Jesper Olson, Jamie Lyons, and Bryonne Taylor," I rattle off.

"Good memory," he observes.

"Not really." I hold up my phone and show him the

list of notes I've been keeping, recording details of any and all interactions I've had at the center.

"I'm supposed to help out with breakfast tomorrow morning, starting at five thirty. It'll just be me and Brian Tapper, the cook. I can see if I can get into–"

"Absolutely not," Mitch barks. "Not only is it too risky, but anything you might find will effectively be unusable as evidence. Besides, what if you blow your cover? We'd lose any advantage we have."

It irks me that he's got a point. Still, he's concerned about proper legal procedure when my singular objective is to stop predators by any means available to me.

The only reason I'm not going to fight him on this is I don't want to risk any more harm coming to those girls.

That is, if they're still alive.

Mitch

The idea of Opal getting caught snooping around the director's office has the hair on my neck standing on end.

"Can you forward me your notes?" I ask. "I'll look into those other names, see if I can find anything. What about the other three files?"

"You mean has he taken them? No, they were still in the filing cabinet when I left earlier."

So, he takes one but leaves the others. It doesn't really make sense.

"Why one and not the others?" I muse out loud.

"Timing? From what I can tell, Chantel stopped showing up at the center about eight months ago. The others were more recent. Bobby-Jean went AWOL three months ago, and Melissa and Georgia only in the last couple of weeks. Maybe he's afraid those more recent files going missing are more likely to be noticed?"

Possible, although I'd almost wonder why bother doing away with Chantel's?

"But that's not all I was calling about," she continues as she shuffles through the copied files in front of me.

Four girls, four sets of copies held together with a paperclip, and Opal flips each of them to the last page, displaying four portrait pictures.

I recognize Georgia; her mother provided us with a recent picture. Melissa is also easy to pick out, thanks to her social media presence which abruptly ended a few weeks ago. But I haven't seen recent pictures of the other two girls.

What we'd been able to find out about Bobby-Jean Lark isn't much. After losing her parents at eight years old, she ended up in the care of Child Protective Services, getting bounced around in foster care. I tracked down her social worker yesterday, who hadn't even known the girl hadn't been seen by her fosters in three months. Of course, the couple had been content to stay quiet as long as they received their monthly stipend for her care.

Turns my fucking stomach.

Even the social worker seemed less than interested, unable to provide us with more than the girl's six-year-old photograph attached to her file.

The picture Opal is showing me is of someone who looks way too mature for a fourteen-year-old.

Same for the fourth girl, Chantel Staffman. According to the volunteer, Sally Kendall, who first contacted GEM, Chantel was a street kid who had showed up to the center almost daily for a meal before she stopped coming abruptly. Her picture shows an African American girl, looking much older than her reported seventeen years, but that may be partially due to her hardened expression. Her face betrays a tough life.

Four pictures, four pretty girls.

What am I looking at?

"Do you see it?" Opal asks, leaning so close I catch the scent of some kind of soap or shampoo wafting in my direction.

Something light and a bit fruity.

Appealing.

So much so my body responds.

I glance sideways to find her face partially obscured by a curtain of her hair falling forward as she bends over my shoulder, focused on the images on the table. She turns her head slightly and I catch a glimpse of her gray eyes.

"The pictures, are you seeing what I see?" she prompts, and I dutifully turn my attention where she wants it.

I look at them in order of disappearance. Chantel,

Black, pretty, seventeen. Bobby-Jean, Asian, pretty, fourteen. Melissa, Hispanic, pretty, fifteen. And finally, Georgia, fourteen as well, pretty, and an all-American blonde.

Studying them I notice each of their images appears to have the same background.

"These pictures were all taken in the same place."

Opal nods, a small smile pulls at her lush lips.

Fuck.

I instantly avert my eyes.

"See the corner of that frame?"

I hum affirmatively. The same frame is visible in each of the pictures.

"It's from a print hanging in the director's office. It's on the wall across from the desk."

"Is that standard? For Kramer to take pictures for the files?"

Seems odd to me.

"I haven't noticed, but that'll be easy to check. It's not the only thing that struck me about those photos though," she prompts and I take another good look.

It takes me a moment because I'm looking for similarities, but then it occurs to me.

"They're all a different ethnicity."

"Bingo," she says softly as she sits down at the table across from me, taking a drink from her bottle before continuing. "At Transition House there were rarely more than twelve kids housed at a time. Among other things, Kendrick was responsible for interviewing new kids. Presumably to make sure they'd be a good fit with the rest, but in reality, he was handpicking by merit of gender and/or ethnicity. Creating a diverse offering. Something for every palate."

It's impossible to unsee it now and her words give me a sick feeling in the pit of my stomach.

Looks like a portfolio for a modeling agency.

Except I don't believe it is.

I think it's a fucking menu for sick, sexually depraved bastards.

SEVEN

OPAL

"These can go in."

Brian pushes another tray of cinnamon rolls across the counter and I slide it in the hot oven.

He's had me on my toes since I got here an hour ago. Already the sideboard in the dining space next door is getting full. Three kinds of muffins, Danish, and cinnamon rolls, and we haven't even started with the actual breakfast yet.

I've been waiting for an opportunity to slip into my office while it's still quiet to have another peek at the files. This time to see if I can find any other files that include pictures, but it may have to wait until I can find a quiet moment later.

It makes me wonder about those other so-called 'old' files slotted to be destroyed. Would they have had photos in them too? Did those kids go missing?

"You've been here a while, right?" I ask Brian, who is cracking eggs in a massive bowl.

He glances up at me from under bushy brows.

"About a year and a half or so." He points at a pile of potatoes at the far end of the counter. "Those need dicing."

I look for a knife and find one hanging from a magnetic strip on the wall. He nods his approval when I hold it up.

"Why?" he asks when I start cutting the potatoes down to the size of home fries.

I shrug, feigning indifference. "Oh, just wondering what kind of turnover of kids you see on average. Are most kids here frequently? I mean a lot of the ones I've met so far appear to be regulars, but I've also seen some names on files that aren't familiar."

"What names?"

I look up at his brusque tone. He's leaning forward, both hands planted on the counter and his eyes are narrowed on me.

"Well, one I remember is Chantel..."

"Staffman," he finishes for me. "What about her?"

"So you know her? That's weird, I swear the director said hers was an old file."

"She never missed a day until late last year. Then she stopped showing up from one day to the next."

His eyes are no more than slits now, scrutinizing me.

"What's this about her file?"

I turn my attention back to the potatoes and answer casually, "Oh, Kramer was asking for a few old files he said were slotted to be destroyed. Hers was one of them, but maybe I misunderstood."

"Whose were the others?"

I already knew Brian didn't particularly care for Kramer, but now I'm starting to wonder if perhaps this is more than simple dislike. Could it be he harbored suspicions of his own?

I decide to take a chance.

"Jesper Olson, Bryonne Taylor, and Jamie Lyons."

Jumping a foot when his hands slam down on the counter, I almost sever my finger in the process. Blood starts welling from a nasty cut on my left index finger. I drop the knife and quickly cup my free hand underneath so I don't contaminate the food, before turning to the large sink.

"Shit. I'm sorry," Brian mumbles, rushing around the prep station to my side to survey the damage. "Dammit. You got yourself good."

He dives under the sink and surfaces with what looks like a tackle box but appears to hold a well-stocked first aid kit.

"Jamie was a good kid," he mumbles while tending to my finger with great care. "Reminded me of my grandson, David, always hungry. Hung out in here a lot and actually helped me get familiarized with the kitchen when I first started. I asked Kramer once if he knew why the boy stopped coming around. He said something about all these kids being one step from a life of crime and he wouldn't be surprised if Jamie had gotten himself in trouble. Couldn't believe he'd say that, someone in his position. Hated the guy ever since. That benevolent, holier-than-thou attitude he puts on is as fake as can be."

I try to keep my mouth shut so I don't interrupt the unexpected flow of information. Better he volunteers than be prompted by me.

Interesting though, just like Chantel's file, Jesper's wasn't old enough to justify destruction.

Brian doesn't mention the other two but they could've easily predated his time at the center. Hopefully, Mitch can find out some more on them today.

His departure last night had been rather abrupt again. I can't quite get a bead on the man. One minute he looks at me with what I would swear to be heated interest, and the next he's marching out the door without so much as a glance back.

Maybe I'm imagining things, I've spent so many years intentionally cultivating an unremarkable persona, it's been a while since I've received any interest from the opposite sex.

"Now one of these hobnobbing sessions again," Brian continues his rant. "Parading those kids in front of a bunch of do-gooders like circus animals looking for hand-outs. Every couple of months he does this. Turns my stomach."

Do-gooders.

Yesterday he called them dignitaries. Fundraising is typically done once a year, but apparently this happens every few months? Something feels off about that.

I'm starting to wonder who'll be showing up for breakfast.

"Has Sally been filling your ear?" he suddenly asks, taping down the thin layer of gauze he wrapped around my finger.

"Sally?"

He hands me a glove to wear over my bandaged hand.

"I know she raised concern about one of the girls; Melissa. Took it to Kramer, who shot her down. Next thing I know, the FBI is here looking into another girl's disappearance. Somewhere in all that you show up, a friend of Sally's, asking questions. It all seems a bit coincidental. Doesn't take a brain surgeon to figure out something is going on."

Busted.

Now the question is whether to play innocent, or come clean. At least partially, since I'm not about to divulge the extent of this investigation. I think he can be trusted—he seems genuine enough in his dislike of the director and concern for the kids—but you never know, so I'm remaining cautious.

Still, it could be handy to have someone like Brian on board. Clearly, he has good instincts, connects with the kids—probably better than I have—and has been here long enough for staff to relax around him.

"Sally asked me to help," I simplify. "She felt she wasn't getting anywhere with her concerns and asked me to look into it."

One of those heavy eyebrows lifts slowly.

"And you're qualified, how?"

The sarcasm is thick. I don't blame him—I want

people to underestimate me—but now I have to come up with a believable story.

"I'm an investigative reporter. Sally hoped I could dig up enough to do a story, get attention that way."

I go back to cutting potatoes, resisting the temptation to watch for his reaction, which would make my lie too easy to spot.

He's quiet for a long time before he finally speaks, making it obvious I haven't fooled him one bit.

"I guess we'll go with that."

Half an hour later, the director bursts into the kitchen.

"How much longer? There's not even coffee out there," he barks.

Brian doesn't even turn away from the scrambled eggs he's finishing on the griddle.

"Ten minutes. Opal will bring out the coffee shortly."

He never noticed me until Brian mentioned my name, and even then, I barely get a glance.

"What is she doing here?"

It's like I'm not even here. I resist the urge to assert myself, which would be counterproductive to keeping a low profile.

"Helping me. Since I didn't know until late yesterday you were bringing guests for breakfast, I needed an extra pair of hands to get it done."

For a moment, it looks like Kendrick, aka Kramer, is going to say something but changes his mind. I resist reacting to the shudder running down my spine when he turns his eyes on me.

"Hurry up with the coffee."

———

Mitch

"Holy shit."

Matt is hanging over my shoulder as I pull the pictures Opal sent me earlier up on my laptop.

"Is that Congressman Melnyk?"

"Yup. And check this out."

I scroll to the next picture, which is of everyone at the table. I'm guessing Opal recognized the congressman, but may have missed the significance of another man at the table.

"Whoa, Paul Krebs?"

Figures Matt would recognize the former NFL player turned sports anchor. The man religiously follows the scores on his phone when work keeps him away from his games.

"And that guy is, Russel Germain, a Lexington council member and real estate lawyer. I had to look him up."

Fourth at the table is the object of our investigation.

"Interesting combo. Do we know what they're doing there?"

"They're all rich. As far as Opal has heard, this is a push for funding for the center," I relay.

"But you're not buying it," Matt prompts, taking a seat on the edge of the hotel bed.

"Neither is she. According to the center's cook, this isn't the first time this year he's invited a group of bigwigs for a meal."

"Granted, it's odd, but I'm not sure how it relates to Georgia Braxton's disappearance."

I shake my head, thinking about the conversation I had last night with Opal. One that had me up half the night, scouring social media to see what I could find on the other three names on those files Kramer requested.

"Not just hers. Don't forget Melissa, Bobby-Jean, and Chantel, and we may have more than that."

I toss the notepad I've been scribbling on half the night to him. Information I was able to find on two of the three names.

Then I repeat Opal's words from last night.

"Something for every palate."

I've had no success so far with Jamie Lyons, but I got lucky for both Jesper Olson and Bryonne Taylor. Jesper had an active Instagram account until just after Thanksgiving last year when the posts abruptly stopped. Bryonne's name showed up when I was scrolling through his feed. A picture posted in early August, with the caption; *'Me and Bryonne hopping the next train.'*

I pull up the image I downloaded and turn the screen to show Matt.

The two are standing in front of what looks to be an older railway coach. A good-looking, lanky kid with blond curly hair, his arm curled around a petite girl with long black hair and striking light blue eyes standing in front of him. The top of her head barely reaches his shoulder. Both kids are smiling at the camera. Behind them you can just make out the word 'Bluegrass' on the side of the train car.

It's clear someone else took the picture.

"That's that scenic railroad, isn't it?" Matt comments.

"Bluegrass Scenic Railroad and Museum. Yes, it is."

The museum is in Versailles, a town just outside Lexington, probably a twenty-five or thirty-minute drive from here.

"Okay. Joe can dig into that," Matt says. "We need to know where they're from and if someone's missing them. The rest of us need to focus on finding Georgia. The family and Chief Furmont are putting the pressure on."

I don't blame them. We've been here a week and have come up with little more than suspicions and theories to show for it. Normally, we'd use local law enforcement offices for a center of operations, but because of the chief of police's personal connection to the case, Matt made the decision to stick to our hotel to operate from. More often than not we find a family member or close family friend is involved in the disappearance of a child and, although there is no indication the chief is in any way involved, we're running this by the book.

For the most part, anyway. Working with a private organization like GEM is certainly out of the norm. Something I definitely am finding my way around in.

Because I'm the one who recognized Opal from our earlier encounter, I was assigned as her contact and have my focus on the center. Matt, as team leader, is responsible for keeping the larger picture in view, handing out assignments as needed to the rest of the team.

"What about Kramer's guests this morning?" I prompt.

"We'll have to be discreet looking into them. Don't want to raise any suspicions. See if Opal can find out if they were the same guests at previous occasions or whether the players are different each time. For now, other than they're all wealthy, prominent members of the community, there is little else to connect them. Maybe if we can identify more players, some kind of pattern becomes visible."

He gets up from the bed and heads for the door before turning to face me.

"Our resources are limited though," he cautions. "Finding Georgia, and the other missing kids, has to stay our priority."

It's my opening to make a suggestion I've been toying with.

"Agreed, and I know we need to minimize local law enforcement involvement, but how about GEM?"

"What about them?"

"From what I gather from Jacob Branch, there are two more operatives currently in Lanark. Why not utilize them as well?" I propose. "Chances are, they're working on much the same things we are, which is a waste of time if you ask me."

"Maybe, but what can they do that we can't?"

"They're a private organization without the same procedural parameters."

It's a careful way of saying they don't necessarily have the boundaries of the law to hold them back. Especially checking into Kramer's three breakfast guests. It may come in handy to be able to skirt the legal limitations and circumvent the loops our CARD team would have to jump through.

"It wouldn't produce any evidence we could use to build a case."

"Maybe not," I agree, "but what if it helps us find Georgia Braxton and the others?"

I can see the struggle on his face.

Matt is a by-the-book kind of guy for the most part and is good at managing all aspects of an operation, which is why he is well-suited to the role of team leader. However, it also means he doesn't like what he can't control, and getting an independent agency like GEM involved would mean easing up on those tight reins.

"I want to talk to Branch myself," he finally concedes.

So far, I've been the point of connection with Jacob Branch but I get Matt wants to set the parameters for any further collaboration with GEM. After all, as team leader it'll be his ass on the line.

"I'll give him your number."

He nods and goes to open the door when the sound of a phone ringing stops him.

"Driver," he answers after checking his screen.

He listens for only a moment before his eyes meet mine, his lips compressed into a tight line.

"Understood. We're on our way."

When he ends the call, I know I'm not going to like whatever news he just received, but I still have to ask.

"What was that about?"

He draws in a deep breath and slowly releases it through pursed lips.

"This morning a farmer clear-cutting a swath of land on the bank of the Kentucky River discovered a body."

EIGHT

Opal

The knock on my door doesn't really surprise me, but the sudden rush of nervous anticipation I feel does.

I'm not prone to fussing or fidgeting, and vanity has not been part of my emotional makeup for decades, but still I find myself glancing in the mirror over the dresser, patting down a few strands of wild hair before I reach for the door.

Maybe it's because I shared my real name with him yesterday, but for some reason this time when he steps into my motel room it feels different. More personal...intimate, even.

"Hope you like Mexican," he says, plonking a brown paper bag on the table.

Another shared meal.

I wince when I'm hit with a flash of guilt. I'd just blown off Janey and Raj, who asked me along for a quick bite, and if I'm honest with myself, it was because I'd secretly hoped Mitch would show up again.

Guilt doesn't stop me from taking two plates and cutlery from my drawer and sitting down across from him though. But it does propel me to talk about the case over dinner instead of asking him about the dark shadows I catch in his eyes.

"I wasn't able to safely go through the files today," I tell him. "I was hoping to look for more photos, but there was a lot of traffic out in the hallway and closing the door to the office would've raised questions."

Mitch takes a bite of his burrito as he attentively listens, while I'm trying not to get distracted by the flexing of his stubbled square jaw.

"A couple of girls were helping out in the kitchen with cleanup and I overheard them whisper about the football player. Apparently, it wasn't the first time he'd been there. Couldn't get them to tell me more."

I'd pretended to be a fan of his and asked them if he came often, which resulted in a mumbled, *"sometimes,"* from one of the girls. But when I probed further to see if they knew why he was visiting, they clammed up, Kaylie —the older girl—looking nervously behind them to the hallway visible beyond the propped-open door.

"I'm willing to bet one of the girls, Kaylie Bentevigna, knows something. I want to try and catch her alone, away from the center, to see if—"

"No."

For a moment I'm stunned, but then just as fast anger takes over.

"Excuse me?"

He puts his burrito down on his plate and leans forward.

"Absolutely fucking not. You'll do nothing right now."

To think I found this arrogant asshole attractive. Should've known better. If it looks too good to be true, it probably is.

"Do I need to remind you I don't work for you?" I snap.

"Oh, trust me, I'm well aware I'm dealing with a civilian."

That sticks in my craw.

My snort is loud as frustration has me surge up from my chair and jab a finger in his direction.

"Twelve years in the armed forces and nine years at the Kentucky State Police Academy say differently," I blurt out without too much thought.

His mouth falls open, eyes wide, as he sags back in the chair.

Well *fuck*.

Now I'm really mad.

Mostly at myself for letting him get me rattled enough I'm volunteering information I wasn't willing to part with.

Blowing out an annoyed breath, I slide back down in my seat, purposely not looking at Mitch as I pick up the burrito on my plate and start unwrapping it. I feel his eyes on me as I take a bite, not really tasting a thing.

It's not until I've worked down half the burrito Mitch speaks.

"What's your story, Kate?"

The fact he's using my real name, instead of my alias, throws me. It feels too close all of a sudden. Too personal. He's pulling the barriers down and it makes me uneasy.

"Already told you."

"Kentucky State Police?"

I sigh, dropping the remainder of my dinner back to the plate. At this point, it's not like I'm handing him information he wouldn't be able to easily obtain on his own.

"Firearms instructor at the academy."

He holds my eyes as he slowly nods.

"You're a surprise. How did Branch find you?"

That's a good question, one I've asked myself enough but haven't quite confirmed an answer to yet.

Oh, I have my suspicions. Given he found not only me but my two childhood friends, and he knew enough about our history, I'm positive it has to do with Transition House. However, the who, how, and why are still a question mark.

Jacob Branch is still a mystery.

"Ask him."

"I will, as soon as I tell him to have you stand down," he persists.

Exasperated, I throw up my hands.

"Oh, for Pete's sake, I can handle myself."

His face twists into an angry scowl.

"Is that so? Let's see if you can handle this."

He pulls his phone from his pocket, seems to look for something, and then turns the screen to me.

"She was found this morning on the banks of the Kentucky River."

He takes the wind out of my sails with the snapshot of a crime scene, and I immediately understand the dark shadows I saw in his eyes earlier.

She?

I try not to react to the gruesome picture he shows me. I know I'm looking at a dead person, but any distinguishable features have been obliterated.

I start asking a question but no sounds come out. Clearing my throat, I try again.

"Is it—"

"Georgia?" Mitch guesses. "Hard to tell. Hopefully the autopsy scheduled in the morning will give us more answers."

All the fire drains from my limbs as I sink back in my chair.

I've seen things I'd rather not remember during my career, but nothing as scarring as being faced with the ravaged body of a child. Twice before, since joining GEM, have I experienced this crippling sense of failure.

Limbs heavy with the weight of responsibility, the heart raw and open to absorb all the pain surrounding you, and a mouth so dry and bitter, it's hard to swallow.

"Hey..."

I look up to find him watching me intently.

"It may not be her," he offers, leaning over the table to brush his thumb over my cheek.

It doesn't really matter though, does it?

The unexpected tears are for a child whose death didn't come easy, judging from the state of her naked body.

I can't even bring myself to be upset I'm showing him weakness.

This entire case is hitting too close to home.

Mitch

"Hey..." I repeat, trying to draw her eyes to me.

Beautiful gray eyes, luminous with the sheen of tears betraying an appealingly sensitive side to the tenacious and uncompromising woman she presents as.

Funny, I can't even see the rather plain woman I first encountered a couple of months ago anymore. Or more like I can't *un*see that luscious, strawberry-blond mane, the full lips, and those pretty eyes.

Maybe it's guilt for shoving that picture in her face but something drives me out of my seat. Before I consider what I'm doing, I'm crouched beside her chair, sliding my hand under the weight of her hair, and pulling her head down.

Anything to erase the look of defeat from her eyes.

Except, the moment my mouth touches hers, every excuse becomes meaningless. Who cares what drove me here, the only thing that matters is the feeling of her lips surrendering to my kiss.

There are things in life that feel like they happen in a vacuum. Good *and* bad.

Moments indelibly seared into my soul.

The birth of my daughter was one of those.

So was the death of my sister.

For a long time, I thought maybe I could count watching Becky walk toward me on my wedding day among those moments, but the memory faded quickly when the love died.

Never in my wildest dreams would I have thought that kissing this stubborn, unyielding woman might evoke similar feelings of timeless buoyancy.

But it does.

I mark every sensation; the inviting wet heat of her mouth, the combination of spice and honey when her taste hits my palate, the tentative touch of her tongue to mine, and the firming grip of her fingers as she latches on to my shirt.

There isn't a thought of self-recrimination or doubt strong enough for me to pull away.

But a sharp knock on the door does the trick.

"Kate? You up?"

"*Shit,*" she whispers, wiping her hands over her face.

My knees creak when I straighten up. I move back to the other side of the table as she sends me a flustered glance before opening the door. Yet, when she greets the small Asian woman in the hallway, she looks perfectly composed. Other than the slightly swollen lips, you wouldn't be able to tell she'd just been kissed within an inch of her life.

Kate, aka Opal, is a formidable actress.

I'm afraid I don't fare so well, still feeling a bit

disjointed as she invites the woman in, and struggling to pull myself together.

She briskly introduces us.

"Agent Mitch Kenny with CARD. My friend, and colleague at GEM, Pearl Han."

Another alias, I'm sure, especially since I'm pretty sure she used another name in her greeting when she first opened the door.

"Agent Kenny."

The woman may be tiny but she has a grip like steel when she clasps my hand. I have trouble not wincing under the intense scrutiny from those near-black eyes. I get the sense this lady doesn't miss much.

"Ms. Han."

She finally lets go of my hand and eyes the leftover dinner, holding up the takeout bag in her other hand.

"And here I was taking pity on you," she aims at Kate. "I brought you a sub."

"I take full responsibility," I intervene, taking my seat. "I barged in on Kate unannounced."

I realize my mistake when Pearl's eyes narrow on her friend.

"Kate? You told him your name?"

A slight blush stains her cheeks, but Kate seems to shake it off as she grabs the takeout bag.

"I did. Now let me put this in the fridge, I'll have it for breakfast tomorrow."

"It's Italian meatballs."

"I'll heat it up in the microwave."

These two are entertaining, like an old married

couple, and I bite back a laugh at the disgusted look on Pearl's face.

"It'll be soggy."

Kate puffs out an annoyed sigh.

"Then I'll eat it with a spoon," she mocks.

Pearl has had enough of the banter and turns to me.

"So what brings you here, Agent Kenny?"

"Mitch, please," I tell her as she takes the chair Kate was occupying moments ago, leaving her the edge of the bed to sit down on.

"Mitch," she corrects herself, looking at me expectantly.

But before I can answer, Kate beats me to it.

"They found a girl's body this morning."

The shock is clear on her friend's face.

"Georgia?" she guesses, immediately followed by, "I monitor the scanners. How come I didn't hear about this?"

I repeat what I told Kate earlier, that we won't know more until tomorrow's autopsy.

"As for not hearing the call, it was decided to keep it off the radar for now. The Anderson County sheriff was called in and—knowing about the missing girl's connection to the chief—he contacted us directly. The scene was pretty brutal and we didn't want to risk Furmont showing up."

Pearl pulls a phone from her purse.

"There's been a development. Kate's room," she snaps before adding, "Bring a chair and my laptop."

Then she looks at her friend.

"Onyx is on her way. We need to get Jacob on the line."

We're crammed inside Kate's room.

Onyx is propped on the edge of the bed next to Kate. A striking woman with long black hair in a braid down her back, one single white strand woven through. She smiled and nodded when we shook hands but she never said a word.

I called Matt to join us as well and he's leaning against the wall by the door. The rest of the CARD team is either surveilling Kendrick or back at the hotel. We wouldn't have been able to fit them in anyway.

Jacob's disembodied voice comes from Pearl's laptop.

"What does your gut tell you?"

I assume the question is directed at Matt since he just finished describing the scene, and what we could see of the victim.

Matt glances my way in a silent communication before responding.

"It's her. It's Georgia."

A muffled curse sounds from the other end.

"If I might venture a guess."

This from Onyx, whose cultured, rich voice is a surprise. Matt gestures for her to go ahead.

"Perhaps whomever took her didn't realize she was the chief of police's grandniece. Not until your team started asking questions. Our perpetrator could've panicked and killed her."

The thought occurred to us. Matt and I mulled it over on our way back to town from the crime scene.

"Possible," I tell her. "Especially since someone went through a whole lot of trouble to make identification a challenge. Not impossible, mind you."

"As soon as we get confirmation from the medical examiner, we'll get a warrant for the center," Matt fills in.

"Wait...hold one second." Kate holds up a finger and gets to her feet, starting to pace in front of the dresser. "Kendrick went AWOL a couple of days ago. What if what we suspect is true and he had a hand in her disappearance? He could've killed Georgia then. The next day he started destroying files, trying to erase evidence of the other missing kids. He doesn't know we know who he is. He doesn't know Georgia isn't the only kid we know is missing. He thinks he's scot-free, otherwise, he wouldn't have invited his buddies for breakfast at the center this morning. Right now, we have the advantage, but if you walk in there waving a warrant, you're tipping our hand. What if he decides to harm the other kids? Melissa, Chantel, Bobby-Jean, and who knows how many more?"

"What if they're already dead?" Matt suggests.

Kate stops in her tracks and whips around to him.

"We don't work on assumptions," she snaps. "Until they're lying on a cold slab next to Georgia in the morgue, we're going to assume they're alive. We can't afford to push him in a corner or we'll never find those kids."

"So what do you suggest we do next?" I ask her carefully.

Her eyes are large and shimmering when she turns to me.

"What I suggested earlier. I want to approach Kaylie Bentevigna away from the center. I'm positive she knows more, and I may be able to get her to talk if I can catch her alone and off guard."

"You'll run the risk of exposing yourself," Jacob cautions.

"I know," Kate answers, her eyes never leaving mine. "But it's a risk I'm willing to take."

NINE

OPAL

"Can you get her to meet with us?"

We met up with Sally in a small coffeeshop around the corner from my motel after days of trying to catch Kaylie Bentevigna away from the center. The girl turned out to be slick as an eel, finding ways to avoid me like she knew I was trying to catch her alone.

Sally looks from me to Mitch.

"Kaylie won't talk to a man."

I almost feel Mitch bristle and under the table and I squeeze his knee in warning.

"Has she been…" I let my words drift off.

Sally shakes her head. "I can't talk about that."

It's as much of an admission as I can expect. Sally may be a volunteer counselor but she is equally bound to maintain client confidentiality. Still, it's clear the girl has some cause to be mistrusting of men.

"I'll meet with Kaylie alone," I promise, ignoring Mitch's annoyed huff beside me.

Other than my shifts at the center, he has been sticking close, insisting it was for my own safety. Since my boss agreed with him when Mitch first voiced his concern a few nights ago, I didn't really have a choice. Not that it made me happy.

I'm putting my foot down now though. We desperately need a good lead if we're going to find those kids. Hell, all we need is a place to start looking from. I'm keeping my fingers crossed Kaylie can help with that.

"I'm supposed to be meeting with her tomorrow afternoon. Let me talk to her. Maybe I can get her to meet me somewhere."

Mitch doesn't speak until Sally has left.

"I don't like it."

"That can't be helped," I respond curtly, sliding out of the booth.

Three days since he laid that kiss on me and it's as if it never happened. He's been surly, and I've been annoyed as hell myself. The latter mostly because I let my guard down.

That kiss, relatively chaste as it was, sure packed a punch. One that had me forgetting all the reasons why kissing Mitch was not a good idea. Although, technically it was him who kissed me, so why he's acting all bent out of shape now is beyond me.

Oh hell, who am I kidding?

Sure, I'm upset with myself for indulging, but only

because Mitch now looks at me like dirt under his damn shoe.

My ass is butt-hurt.

The sun has started to set when I step outside. There's a definite chill in the air tonight and I pull my light jacket tight. My eyes fall on the small neighborhood deli across the street. On one of my first nights in Lanark, I went in for a quick sandwich and saw they also offered soups and stews.

With the temperatures dropping outside, I'm really craving a hearty bowl of goulash or something. Comfort food. Lord knows I could do with some of that as well.

"Can I help you?"

The pleasant, gray-haired woman behind the counter speaks with what I'm guessing is an Eastern European accent.

"Yes, could I have a bowl of goulash? For takeout?"

"I'll have the same."

My shoulders tense when I hear Mitch's deep voice rumble behind me.

Dammit, of course he had to follow me inside.

I don't bother arguing when he takes over, ordering a couple of sandwiches and drinks as well. To my annoyance, he tells her everything can go in one bag and whips out his wallet to pay for it all.

I don't want to create a scene in front of the woman, so I save my comments for when we get outside.

"I don't recall inviting you," I snap over my shoulder as I start crossing the street.

Of course, he's only two steps behind me.

"We need to talk. We may as well do it over dinner," he responds curtly.

"Nothing to talk about."

"There's plenty," he promises ominously.

I get the sense he's not only referring to things work related.

Great.

When we get to my room, I walk inside, leaving the door open for him to sort himself out while I duck into the bathroom, needing a few minutes to compose myself before I face whatever he feels he needs to discuss.

I walk out a few minutes later, having quickly changed out of my stuffy, uncomfortable 'work' clothes and into yoga pants and a long-sleeved shirt, my itchy wig discarded on the bathroom counter. Mitch is already sitting at the table getting a head start on dinner and, apparently, took the liberty to grab cutlery and plates from my dresser drawer. Sucking back the snide remark that wants out, I sit down across from him and start eating as well, trying to enjoy the spicy stew.

"When you talk to the girl, I want you to at least go in miked up," he finally says, shoving his empty bowl to the middle of the table.

I lower my spoon as I lift my gaze.

"Please," he adds with a look in his eyes I can't quite place.

"Or...you could simply trust I know what I'm doing," I suggest with a healthy dose of sarcasm.

"Trust has nothing to do with it."

"Oh, really? Would you tell Matt, or anyone else on

your team, the same thing?" I ask indignantly. "I would think my training and years of experience should give me at least *some* credibility."

"Fucking A, I would. With this case especially. It has nothing to do with your training and everything to do with the fact we're working on mostly theory here. Kendrick clearly has connections in high places, so anything concrete we can get—any information we turn up, any witness statements we collect—it all needs to be watertight. Otherwise, this guy could slip through our fingers like that."

He snaps his own fingers for emphasis.

Damn. I hate he's being reasonable.

"Fine. *If* Sally can arrange something with her, I'll wear a wire, but I don't need anyone yammering in my ear," I concede ungraciously.

Then I bend back down over my stew, trying to hide my flushed face. Evidence of my embarrassment at behaving like a petulant child.

"Kate..."

"What?"

"There's something else we need to discuss."

I know in my gut what is coming and lower the spoon I had halfway to my mouth, mentally bracing myself.

"That kiss. It was a mistake."

Ouch.

I figured he had some serious regrets, but to hear him say it out loud stings unexpectedly. Not that I'd give him the satisfaction of knowing how his words sting.

"Trust me, I'm well aware," I return defensively, looking up at him with my chin in the air.

For a brief moment his eyes narrow and he gives his head a small shake.

"That kiss should never have happened," he adds salt to the wound before clarifying. "Not when our focus should've been on finding those kids. Now that I've had a taste of you, it's even more difficult to keep my head in the game since all I can think of is doing it again."

Oh.

Wow.

So not what I expected him to say, and a small frisson of excitement has my heart flutter in my chest.

"I see," I mutter stupidly.

"I'm glad you do because it can't happen again," he states resolutely as he stands up.

Thunk.

Both my feet crash firmly back on solid ground.

Mitch

I turn my back as Kate hides the wire of the hidden microphone in her clothes.

I convinced her to wear it as backup since it wouldn't be the first time outside factors messed with reception of the wireless signal. With the small recorder on Kate, we're covered in case of a mishap.

We're in my vehicle a block away from the library where Sally said Kaylie would usually go to do homework after dinner. She didn't have a chance to prepare the girl for a meeting with Kate, but because of time restraint we can't afford to wait to slowly win Kaylie's trust.

Kate is going in cold and if the girl threatens to bolt or she can't get her to open up, Kate won't have a choice but to put our cards on the table to prompt her to talk.

"Ready," she says.

I straighten in my seat and glance over, noting the pang of disappointment when I find her put back together with all her parts appropriately covered.

Tonight, Kate purposely ditched the schoolmarm gear and dark bob wig in favor of a more casual look of jeans, a loose-fitting top, and a hoodie. The different look will hopefully give her a chance to approach the girl before she's spotted, and also, on the off-chance she's seen talking to Kaylie by someone else, she won't be easily recognizable as Opal, the soft-spoken center volunteer.

"I'll be here."

I'd feel more comfortable if I could keep her in my view, but my inconspicuous parking spot on the residential street behind the library will have to do.

My eyes are glued to her round ass as she gets out and starts walking to the end of the street, the well-worn jeans showcasing her ample curves. The moment she disappears from sight, I rub my hands over my face in an attempt to get a grip. Then I quickly don the small covert communications equipment that will allow me to listen in and talk to her in case of an emergency.

My earpiece crackles and then I hear Kate's voice.

"Heading into the library."

I'm starting to get restless when I have to wait for her to talk again.

"Kaylie? Can I sit down?"

A surprised, *"Opal?"* is followed by, *"You look so... different. You changed your hair."*

Kate's soft chuckle in my ear stirs my blood as well as my imagination. I can see her in my bed, that hair fanned out around her head, creamy skin and endless curves, as she smiles up at me.

Jesus, I need to get a grip.

Shoving the heel of my hand in my crotch, I force my hardening cock into submission.

Not the time, nor the place.

I focus back on the conversation.

"...a wig? Why?"

I listen to Kate explain how she purposely altered her appearance so she wouldn't stand out.

"I'm actually hoping to find some information about some kids that used to come to the center."

"I don't know anything about that."

Judging by Kaylie's immediate response, the opposite is likely true. Kate was right, the girl knows something.

"Look. I don't want to put you on the spot, which is why I wasn't going to push you back at the center, but Kaylie, the truth is, I need your help. More importantly, I

think Chantel, Bryonne, Jamie, Bobby-Jean, Jesper, and Melissa need your help."

Wow. Kate's voice may be soft and her words gentle, but she isn't wasting any time putting serious pressure on the girl.

There's quite a pause and I don't know if I would've had the patience to wait Kaylie out, but Kate does and it eventually pays off.

"Georgia too," Kaylie adds, and my heart sinks.

We received the medical examiner's preliminary report and Matt went with Anderson County Sheriff Allen to notify the family. I don't envy them that part of the job. Chief Furmont had been made aware already the morning of the autopsy, there was no way we could've kept it from him any longer, but at least we were able to spare him seeing his grandniece.

No way to spare him the details of her death however.

The ME concluded the girl had died from strangulation, but the extensive damage to her body had been done after she was dead. A small blessing but I'm sure it didn't make her loss any easier, especially since the ME found evidence of sexual assault in the form of abrasions and traces of semen.

The knowledge she'd been dead at least seventy-two hours by the time she was discovered, or that drugs were found in her system, didn't bring much comfort either. As far as we've been able to learn, Georgia wasn't known to have used drugs. The ME found a single injection site, but in a habitual user you'd expect there to be more track marks. Hardly conclusive, but it does make the fact she had heroin in her system suspect, to say the least.

Maybe heroin in her system was supposed to suggest she had gotten in with a bad crowd or something. But we figure whoever killed her definitely tried to buy some time by making her identification difficult. What obviously hadn't been known was Georgia had badly broken her leg when she was hit by a car a few years back. The state of the body had made identification through dental records nearly impossible. However, the autopsy X-rays taken of her body showed the metal plate left to fuse her bones matched the hospital X-ray perfectly.

"I'm sorry," I hear Kate tell the girl. *"Georgia was found dead a few days ago."*

Her death hasn't been made public yet. In part to give the family a chance to process the news, but also because this is still an active investigation with the lives of other kids at stake.

We know we can't keep it under wraps forever, which is why we're desperate for a good lead.

The girl's sniffles can be heard on the other end.

"Dead?"

"Kaylie, listen to me. If you know anything that could help us find—"

"I can't. Melissa said if I told anyone, I'd get her in big trouble."

"Melissa? You talked to her?"

"A couple of weeks ago, before she stopped showing up. She'd come to do her homework here at the library too. Sometimes we'd talk."

"About what?"

"Whatever. School, parents, sometimes the center."

"Kaylie, what were you two talking about last time you saw her?"

She doesn't respond immediately and I'm afraid she's shutting down when I hear her mumble, *"She said if I let on I knew anything I could get hurt."*

"It's okay," I hear Kate calm the crying girl. *"I can make sure nothing happens to you, sweetheart. I'm working with the FBI and I promise we can keep you safe. Was someone hurting Melissa?"*

There is no audible response but Kate's next question implies Kaylie must have nodded.

"Someone at the youth center?"

Fuck, we're finally getting somewhere.

"Sort of," she mumbles.

"Director Kramer?"

"No, he didn't hurt her."

Dammit. I guess that would've been too easy.

"He visits sometimes," she goes on to say.

I shoot forward in my seat and adjust my earpiece, afraid I'll miss something.

"Was he there a few days ago? When you were helping in the kitchen?"

Kate had mentioned the girl was nervous then.

"I've gotta go," Kaylie abruptly announces,

I hear some rustling, like the sound of papers being gathered, and then Kate's voice.

"Kaylie, wait."

More background sounds.

"Shit. She's spooked and took off."

I'm already turning the key in the engine as I break my promise to stay quiet.

"Kate, see if you can catch up with her. I'm coming around the front."

Unfortunately, I have to wait for a taxi blocking me in as they drop off a customer. While I wait for them to haul a few suitcases from the trunk, I can hear Kate's heavy breathing in my ear.

As soon as the taxi drives off, I slip out of the parking spot and head for the corner.

"Kaylie! Watch—"

Then I hear an engine revving, someone screaming, and a thud followed by the screech of tires.

"Kate! Jesus, Kate!"

TEN

MITCH

"It's just a scratch."

Exasperated, I ignore the stubborn woman sitting in the back of the ambulance and turn my attention to my ringing phone. It's my daughter.

"Hey, kiddo."

"Dad, when are you coming home?"

I immediately feel guilty. I'm only forty-five miles from Richmond, but I've only been home once to grab more clean clothes and that was during a school day.

We often opt to stay near to the center of our investigations, especially when we are keeping a close eye on someone. A situation can change in a heartbeat and we want to be ready to move if it does.

The difference between life or death is often a very thin margin of time.

Still, it's been almost two weeks since I've seen Sawyer.

"Not sure, Pumpkin. It's a complicated case." I hear her snort and tamp down on my annoyance before I continue, "Did you need me for something?"

She sighs dramatically.

"Mom is being a bitch."

"Sawyer..."

"Well, she is, Dad. This weekend is the last chance I have and she won't take me."

I pinch the bridge of my nose, feeling a headache forming.

"Last chance for what?"

"The dress for the athletic banquet at school next week. I told you," she adds accusingly.

"I thought you already had a dress?"

Somewhere in the back of my mind, I recall her mentioning something on the subject a few weeks ago.

"But it's green, Dad."

My head is still reeling with earlier events, which is perhaps why I find myself confused and more than a little irritated. Seeing Kate on the ground, against the curb in front of the library, when I tore around the corner had shaken me.

She was already trying to get to her feet by the time I got to her side and I may have barked at her to stay the fuck down.

The vehicle—according to Kate, a dark-colored SUV —was long gone, as was the girl it had apparently aimed for. She'd pushed Kaylie out of the way, then was able to jump on the hood of the moving vehicle, grabbing on to a windshield wiper, which she still had clutched in her hand when she'd been thrown off.

Kate was lucky, scraped up, a few deeper cuts, and probably black, blue, and sore by tomorrow, but without apparent broken bones or other serious injury. Still, when emergency services showed up, I insisted she get checked out.

One of the library's employees who'd come rushing outside at about the same time I got here had already called 911, so I quickly dialed Matt while we were waiting for first responders to arrive. I needed him to check and make sure someone has eyes on Kendrick since he was the first person to come to mind. He assured me the guy was in view of his detail, having dinner at a restaurant in Lexington.

With Kendrick accounted for, my first concern was finding Kaylie Bentevigna. I wanted to make sure she got away unharmed and asked Matt to get on it. Last thing we need is another girl missing.

"Dad!"

Right. Sawyer's dress.

"I thought green was your color?"

"But Kimberly's dress is green! Exactly the same green. I can't wear that one."

I have to bite my tongue not to go off on my daughter's conceived life crisis when there are kids out there in real trouble depending on me. The color of a fucking party dress is not what I should spend my time on.

"Sawyer, sort it out with your mother. I have to go."

As I move the phone away from my ear I can hear her whine, "But, Dad!"

I ignore the pang of guilt as I slip the phone back in my pocket, only to be almost knocked off my feet when I'm shoved in the back.

"You were supposed to keep an eye on her!"

Swinging around I find Pearl standing there, her stance wide and her hands on her hips, glaring at me.

"Where were you, huh?" she challenges, not giving me a chance to answer before she takes a step forward and shoves me again, this time with her hands on my chest.

I grab on to her wrists before she can manhandle me again.

"Janey! Knock it off!" I hear Kate call from the ambulance behind me. "I'm fine!"

I'm sure she doesn't mean to let Pearl's real name slip. Not that it tells me any more than the name Kate does, both names are common. If I put any energy into it, I'm sure I could find out more information, but that's not my priority right now. Besides, I'm sure there's a good reason they don't use their own identities.

Pearl quite easily breaks my hold on her wrists by abruptly rotating her forearms in and down. A move commonly taught in self-defense classes, but what is surprising is the strength in the small woman's arms. There's a lot of compact power packed in that petite little body.

Without saying another word to me, Pearl rushes toward the ambulance and starts questioning Kate at the rear of the rig. A police officer blocks my path when I try to follow.

"Sir, we need some information from you and the victim."

So far, the responding police officers have focused on the small crowd that has formed, but I knew it was only a matter of time for them to focus attention on us.

"Ask away," I volunteer.

With as much patience as I can muster, I do my best to answer his questions, knowing I don't have a hell of a lot to contribute. The officer is aware of the ongoing investigation into Georgia's murder and the other, still-missing children, and doesn't keep me too long.

Then he moves to the ambulance where Kate is being treated and I follow. I'm surprised to notice her colleague has already disappeared. It's a safe guess she's probably trying to chase down Kaylie, before the girl disappears as well.

My foot hits something and I notice I kicked the discarded windshield wiper still lying next to the curb. I'm doubtful any information can be gleaned from it but it can't be left lying in the street.

"...Can't be a hundred percent sure, but I think it may have been a Chevy. I only got a flash of the grill for a second before I jumped."

"And you're sure it was an SUV?" the officer probes, scribbling in a small notebook.

"Yes, I'm positive. I managed to see as much as it was speeding away."

"Were you able to catch the size? Chevrolet SUVs range anywhere from compact to large."

Kate nods. "Larger model for sure."

"About the size of a Tahoe? A Suburban?"

"Either one is possible, I guess."

He jots down another note when I tap him on the shoulder.

"Ten feet back you're gonna find a windshield wiper lying near the curb. Make sure to pick that up and have it processed. It came off the SUV."

"I pulled it off when I ended up on the hood," Kate clarifies.

The officer calls over a colleague and instructs him to collect the wiper as evidence before he turns his attention back to Kate.

"Any chance you saw what happened to the girl?"

"I honestly have no idea where she went," Kate answers. "One minute she was there and then she was gone."

"Is it possible she got into the SUV?" he asks, piquing my interest.

Kate's eyes find mine as I listen from the open ambulance doors.

"I hope not," I hear her mumble before she turns to the EMT. "Are you done with me?"

"I'd still recommend you go to the hospital to get thoroughly checked out," he suggests but Kate is already up and off the stretcher.

I offer my hand to help her down, which she takes without protest. My guess is the incident shook her more than she's willing to admit and she's downplaying her injuries. The slight hiss of air from between her teeth as she takes the last step to the ground confirms it.

"If you need anything else from us, get in touch with FBI Special Agent Matt Driver. He's the CARD team leader," I tell the officer as I wrap a steadying arm around Kate's waist.

"Where are we going?"

"My hotel, after we pick up some dinner."

"No. We need to look for Kaylie," she states with a stubborn lift to her scuffed chin.

"My team is already looking and if my guess is correct, so is yours. We need to eat and you need to take it easy. You'll be sore enough tomorrow as it is."

She's quiet for minute, probably considering how much she wants to fight me on this. To my surprise she concedes, proving once again she's hurting more than she lets on.

"Fine. But why your hotel?"

"Because we have a suite with a living room and two bedrooms." Matt has one, I have the other. It makes sense when more than one person is on a case to have an area we can use as a center of operations. "More space to facilitate a team meeting, which I'm sure Matt will call at some point tonight."

As soon as we're in my vehicle, I get him on the line again.

"I need you to check the DMV and see what Paul Krebs drives. Actually, while you're at it, check Doug

Melnyk and Russel Germain as well. We're looking for a dark—probably navy—large Chevrolet SUV."

"You've got it. Haven't tracked down the girl yet, but I'll let you know as soon as we've got something."

I end the call and start the vehicle, glancing at Kate to make sure she's buckled up. She's looking back at me.

"You heard," she comments.

"I fucking heard everything."

Opal

I watch him clench his jaw as he pulls away from the curb.

Pretty sure he refers to more than just my conversation with the girl. Experiencing almost getting run over was no picnic, but I imagine listening to it wasn't fun either.

"I'm fine."

"So you say."

His eyes flit in my direction before focusing on the road again.

I decide ignoring the comment is probably better for both our blood pressures and change the topic.

"What do you know about Paul Krebs?"

"I assume you're not referring to his athletic career?" At the shake of my head he continues, "The guy is a high-ticket customer. Aside from his job as a *Sunday Night Football* anchor, he has his fingers in a variety of businesses, and earns big bucks from a number of endorsements. That, added to whatever money he amassed during his football career, makes Krebs a very rich and influential man. Married twice already, with five kids to show for it. There were some rumbles during the time of his contentious divorce from wife number two, but those died down quickly after they settled for what was rumored to be a substantial amount of money out of court."

"What kinds of rumors?" I ask, intrigued.

"Initial reports of the breakup mentioned the possibility Krebs had been inappropriate with the kids' babysitter. There's no record of the babysitter ever confirming the allegations and the story died."

"With that kind of money, you can buy anyone off," I observe.

"Likely. Anyway, I think it was easy enough for people to brush it off as a vindictive story made up by wife number two for leverage in their divorce."

That may have been understandable at the time, but the story holds far more significance in light of what we know of this case.

"Think it warrants another look?"

"Not sure what we'll be able to find since I think this was five or six years ago, but it's worth a try."

We stop at a McDonald's drive-thru, not my favorite burgers but their fries more than make up for it. We place our orders and five minutes later pull up outside the hotel.

My body is starting to feel the impact as the adrenaline in my system lets down, so I don't object when Mitch comes around to my side and holds out his hand for me.

Matt is on the phone when we walk in. He looks up and his eyes scan up and down my body as if to see I'm still in one piece. Then he glances over at Mitch and lifts a finger.

"You can use my bathroom if you want to freshen up before we eat," Mitch whispers as the other man returns his attention to his call. "I can lend you a shirt and some track pants if you want a change."

I glance down at myself, noticing only now I'm a bit of a mess. There's a rip in my jeans and I have dirt and blood smears on the legs, as well as the front of my top. I have a few cuts and scrapes, damaged the heels of my hands and skinned my knee when I hit the ground.

"Sure, thanks."

Mitch points me in the direction of his room where I take a quick peek around.

Tidy.

Both double beds are made despite the do-not-disturb sign hung on the outside doorknob I spotted coming in. There is a well-read paperback copy of John Grisham's book, *The Fugitive*, facedown on the nightstand, along with a phone charger and half a glass of water. A partially-opened closet door shows a few shirts hanging neatly on hangers, and I'm sure if I'd open the dresser, I'd find neat stacks of T-shirts and jeans in drawers.

The bathroom looks much the same. A plastic cup holds his toothbrush and an almost depleted tube of toothpaste. A leather shaving kit holding an electric shaver, dental floss, deodorant, and a ratty old comb sits on the counter. One towel hangs on the back of the door, but there are a couple of neatly folded ones, as well as a couple of clean washcloths on the shelf underneath the sink. The faint scent of soap or shampoo hangs in the air, reminding me of Mitch.

Grabbing one of the washcloths, I turn on the faucet when a knock sounds on the door.

"Are you decent?" he asks, his voice muffled. "I've got some things for you."

I reach for the door and find him standing outside, holding a stack of clothes.

"Thank you."

I take them from his hands and watch as he turns his back, only to swing around again.

"Feel free to grab a shower. The food will hold."

"Thanks," I repeat as he walks away.

Already starving, I take the fastest shower in the history of womankind, liberally using the agent's shower soap which apparently doubles as shampoo. My hair will be a rat's nest tomorrow, but so be it, the rest of me won't fare much better.

Mitch's sweats are soft and thankfully fit over my large ass, although a tad tight. I'm grateful for the X-large navy T-shirt sporting the FBI logo on the chest, which is roomy enough and reaches the top of my thighs.

I roll up my dirty clothes and grab my shoes, padding through the bedroom in my socks.

Mitch is on the balcony talking into his phone, and

Matt is working on a laptop at one end of the small dining table.

"Feel better?" he asks.

Better is a bit optimistic. The shower felt good, but I felt every inch of my body by the time I toweled off.

"Cleaner, for sure."

He chuckles and points at the paper bag and large cup at the other side of the table.

"I think that's your food. I grabbed you some ibuprofen as well. Figured you might need it."

God, yes.

I sit down and immediately grab for the small white container, shaking out a couple of pills I wash down with the iced tea I ordered. I'm just unwrapping my cheese-burger when the sliding door opens and Mitch steps in, his head down.

"That was Branch. We have a—"

He stops abruptly when he sees me sitting at the table. I can tell from his expression he hadn't realized I was out here, and the information he was about to share was not meant for my ears.

Well, I'm here and I heard.

"What did my boss tell you?" I prompt him sharply. "We have a what?"

He sighs and runs a hand through his hair before walking over.

"Someone tossed your room."

ELEVEN

MITCH

"I'll go," Matt says, breaking the status quo.

I'm physically blocking Kate, who shot out of her seat and had been heading for the door. She's mad at me for not letting her through. Not that it would do any good, her car is still at the motel.

"I need to go."

"You may have been made," Matt tells her.

"We don't know that. It could be a coincidence."

"You don't really believe that," I point out.

She snaps her eyes at me.

"What did Jacob say?"

It's more a challenge than a question.

"I called Pearl when you were in the shower to stop by your room and pick up a change of clothes for you. She was going to drop them off here. When she got to your room, the door was open and the place tossed. She called Jacob, Jacob called me."

"Did anyone call the police?" Matt asks.

"No. Jacob is holding off on that until we can have a look."

"Then let's go," Kate says impatiently.

I place my hands on her shoulders and force her to look at me.

"Listen to me. Let's for a moment assume you've been found out. Do you really want to broadcast you've been working with the FBI? It would send anyone who may be watching scrambling for the woods. We might lose any headway we've made." I give her a gentle shake when I still see doubt in her eyes. "What do you figure would happen to the other kids then?"

I know she heard me when her head drops and her shoulders slump under my hands. Over her shoulder, I nod at Matt, who grabs his phone off the table, shrugs on a jacket, and picks up his keys.

"I'll call you when I get there."

Kate lets me move her aside so Matt can get out the door, but when it closes behind him she twists out of my hold. She moves to the glass sliding door and stares out into the night. I let her be for a moment and busy myself making a pot of coffee in the tiny kitchen. I have a feeling we're going to need it tonight.

"Does someone have eyes on Kendrick?"

I look up at her question. She's facing me from across the room, her arms wrapped around her midsection. Only now do I notice she's wearing my clothes. Her hair still wet and unruly from the shower, a soft flush on her face, it's like she just got up after a hot night in the sack. With me.

Fuck.

I'm staring. Not much I can do about my dick's response without making it even more obvious so I turn back to the coffee maker.

"Lampert and Punani are on him. They would've called if there was a problem."

"Is there any way they can make sure?"

"I'll call."

While I get hold of our team, I watch Kate walk into my bedroom.

"What's up?" John Punani answers.

"Whereabouts are you?"

"Outside the Cheetah Club in Lexington."

I shouldn't be surprised, Cheetah is labeled as a gentleman's club, otherwise known as a strip club. Classy.

"We've had some developments on our end," I inform him. "You guys still have eyes on your target?"

"Affirmative. Kendrick was joined by a couple of friends and moved into a private room with a steady flow of bottles and women going in. Looks like a party. He'll be a while."

"Any idea who the friends are?"

"Lampert got pictures. I'll forward them to you. What developments?" he asks, changing tracks.

"Our contact inside the center was targeted. Was run down in the street tonight and we just found out someone broke into her motel room. She may have been exposed."

"She okay?"

I glance over at the door to my bedroom.

"Yeah, should be. We've got her here."

My phone pings with incoming messages. I assume the pictures John promised.

"Byron and Dresden are relieving us in thirty minutes. I'll check in with you then."

"Sounds good."

I end the call just as Kate walks back in, her own phone in her hand.

"Kendrick is at a strip club," I let her know, chuckling at the expression of disgust flashing over her face.

I pull up the pictures John sent me. One of the men I recognize as a local real estate agent, whose face I've seen on the side of transit buses and billboards across the city. Another high roller. I'm not surprised to recognize another as councilman Russel Germain, but I don't know who the other two are.

I show Kate the pictures.

"Either of these two guys look familiar to you?"

She barks out a harsh laugh.

"Marshall Browning."

She taps a finger on the image indicating a large, bald man with a goatee, my guess would be mid-forties, maybe fifty.

"Who is he?"

She glances up from under her lashes, a pinched look on her face.

"The son of one of Lanark's former chiefs of police, George Browning."

"No shit?"

"Not a single one. He was a few years ahead of me in high school."

I make a mental note to look into Marshall. See what he's up to now and how he may be connected to Kendrick. This is becoming a virtual who's who of prominent figures. People in positions of power.

The whole thing gives me a foul taste in my mouth.

"By the way, I just talked to Pearl," Kate informs me, changing the subject. "She says she was able to rescue some of my clothes, my phone charger, and my toiletries, but everything else is a loss. My laptop was taken, but she wiped it remotely as soon as she noticed it missing so the bastard won't be able to access any sensitive information."

"Good to know."

"Yeah, but my truck is missing. It holds my gun safe. All my weapons are gone as well."

"Weapons?"

I shouldn't be surprised. The woman already showed me she's tougher than she looks, but I'm having a hard time imagining her handling a gun, let alone owning several of them.

"Yes, my weapons."

She rattles off an impressive arsenal of guns that have my eyebrows disappear in my fading hairline.

"Wow," is all I manage.

She sighs deeply before moving to the table to pick up her drink, and takes a sip.

"I was a marksmanship master trainer for the U.S. Army and after some years took a job as firearms instructor at the Kentucky State Police Academy before joining GEM. Those weapons are my babies."

I'm shockingly turned on by the fact the woman obviously knows how to handle a gun. She continues to surprise me, and not in a bad way. At all.

Then my rational mind takes over.

No gun registration in Kentucky, but anyone can find the owner of a vehicle with a license number.

"What name is your truck registered under."

"Opal Berry."

"Home address?" I probe.

She shakes her head. "The address is for an empty farmhouse south of Louisville registered to a property management company, which is owned by a dummy corporation front for Jacob Branch."

Smart. I already knew GEM wasn't a mom-and-pop operation, but this added a whole extra level of sophistication. Knowing Branch went through such lengths to protect his employees made me feel a hell of a lot better.

"Jacob wants me to stay out of sight," she continues, looking like she bit into a lemon.

He'd mentioned to me earlier he didn't want Kate anywhere near the motel or the center, which is why I wouldn't let her get out of the door. I'm glad she heard it from someone other than me because it's clear she's not happy about it.

"You can stay here."

I try to make it sound like she has a choice, even though she doesn't. Even if Branch hadn't asked me to stick close for now, there's no way I would let her out of my sight. It may not have been Kendrick driving that SUV, but there's no way to know for sure he wasn't involved.

She mumbles, "Whatever," picking at her fries, which must be cold by now.

I take a seat across from her and catch her eye.

"We need to find Kaylie," she comments, changing the topic.

"Lanark PD is keeping an eye out."

"For what that's worth," she mutters.

"You don't think they will?"

Glancing up from her food, I notice her eyes look tired.

"She's not technically missing so it'll hardly be a priority. I'd rather be out there looking myself."

"You can barely keep your eyes open as it is."

I wasn't too far off.

About ten minutes later, while watching the late news as we wait for an update, she's curled up on the couch, zonked out. I could try and move her but that would likely wake her up, so instead I slip into the bedroom, strip the cover off the second bed, and drape it over her.

Then I turn down the volume on the TV, grab my laptop, and sit down in one of the chairs with my feet on the table.

But instead of checking my emails, I watch Kate sleep.

Opal

"Thank you."

I grab the takeout cup Raj offers me and take a sip. The potent brew going a long way to clearing the cobwebs from my head.

I woke up on the couch a couple of minutes ago when Mitch opened the door to Raj, who came bearing what is left of my belongings, and a tray of coffees.

"What time is it?"

"Four thirty," Mitch answers, his voice as scratchy as mine.

Sounds like maybe he got a few hours in as well.

My body feels like it's been run through an industrial dryer. Bruised, swollen, and sore as hell. A groan escapes my lips when I move to make room on the couch.

I'd love to tell Raj about Marshall Browning—I'm pretty sure she'd remember him—but I can't with Mitch here without revealing her true identity.

"So what's happening?" I ask her instead.

She sits down beside me.

"Kaylie's safe."

I almost spit out my coffee.

"Really? Where is she?"

"In Frankfort, at her aunt's place. Her father's sister. It took some time to track her down."

The girl's father had died in an industrial accident when she was only eight. From what I've learned, she lives with her mother.

"I had to find Mom first. She works the overnight shift at the Tempur Sealy plant in Lexington. She's the one who suggested to check at her sister-in-law's. Apparently, she and Kaylie have been fighting a lot and her daughter often looks to the aunt for support."

"I need to talk to her."

Raj smiles while at the same time shaking her head.

"Not at four thirty in the morning. Besides which, Jacob suggested, perhaps I could give it a try?" she cautiously formulates in the form of a question.

As much as Pearl is a bulldozer, taking no prisoners, Raj will always tread carefully around people's feelings.

"Of course," I answer, not in the least offended.

After all, Raj is the most qualified of any of us to get information from the girl. Not only does she have her master's degree in psychology, she also has years of experience working as a child victims' advocate.

"Kaylie implied one of the so-called center donors who were there at breakfast a couple of days ago hurt Melissa," I brief her. "I think it's Krebs, I overheard her whisper about him to another girl that morning."

Mitch jumps in to update Raj on the rumors about the former athlete.

"Wouldn't be the first time an athlete uses the power that comes with fame and fortune to hide anything from inappropriate behavior to flat-out rape," Raj responds fiercely.

"Sadly true," Mitch comments before announcing, "Ex-wife number two apparently lives in Glenview, I think I might take a drive out there today. See if she's willing to talk."

"I'm coming," I announce. "No offense, but she might be more forthcoming with a concerned center volunteer than she would with an FBI agent," I add when Mitch raises his eyebrows.

"She makes a good point," my friend offers, backing me up.

I may not be able to return to the center, but I'm not about to sit here and twiddle my thumbs.

"After, we should see if we can talk to Brian Tapper. The cook," I clarify. "He never said anything specific, but there's a reason he has a healthy dislike for Kendrick. Perhaps if I tell him why I was at the center to begin with, he'd be willing to substantiate his animosity toward the man."

Mitch doesn't even attempt to stop my ramble and continues pacing slowly around the room. It's starting to get on my nerves.

"Are you gonna sit down?"

Raj's eyes bulge at the snap in my voice, before a wide grin spreads on her face.

"Wasn't planning on it," he responds dryly. "Spent half the night sitting, I can't feel my ass."

Of course my eyes immediately drop down to the level of the indicated body part, but since he's facing me, I find myself looking at something else altogether.

I don't really have any complaints about my skin or coloring, but right now I'm vehemently cursing my pale complexion as I can literally feel the blush turning my cheeks beet red. I'm not one to get flustered easily these days but, apparently, Mitch's promising package does the trick.

I could kiss Raj when she gets up, drawing the attention.

"Well, on that note, I should get packing." At my confused look she explains, "Jacob is arranging to move us into an Airbnb five minutes from the motel. Roomier and more private."

And, knowing Jacob, I'm willing to bet the place has a good security system.

"We'll stay in touch and I'll text you the address when we get there," she promises, adding, "Oh, and he wants me to arrange a rental car delivered to the new location for you."

As driven and demanding as a boss he can be, he also takes good care of us.

"Try a warm shower," Mitch suggests when Raj is gone. "It'll probably hurt more at first, but will loosen up those muscles."

I haven't dared look him in the eye after ogling his crotch but now guardedly peer up at him. His hazel eyes almost appear calculating. My chin instinctively lifts in a silent challenge.

It doesn't escape me he never conceded to me coming with him to conduct interviews.

"And have you bail on me the moment I'm out of my clothes?" I confront him.

A smirk steals over his face as he stops in front of me. It's only then I realize I could've worded that differently.

"Not a chance in hell I'd walk out on you, naked."

An involuntary shiver ripples over my skin at his grumbled voice. Before I can embarrass myself more, I surge to my feet and—as fast as my aching body will allow —dart past him to the bathroom.

Yikes.

I only have myself to blame, I left that door wide open.

TWELVE

MITCH

"What do you mean, he's gone?"

I feel rather than see Kate's attention snap to me.

We didn't pick the best time to drive through Louisville to Glenview. It's rush hour, so gridlock, and people are fucking idiots on the road.

I'm having a hard time navigating this traffic while my mind is trying to process what Matt just dropped on me.

"Gone, as in his car is still parked in the same spot at the club, but he's not inside. Dresden was at the bar with eyes on the door to the private room when the place closed at five. One of the waitresses explained it wasn't unusual for private parties to continue past closing time. At least until the cleaning crew showed up at eight in the morning. Phil went out and waited, eyes on front and back exits. When the stragglers came out, Kendrick wasn't among them."

Shit. He slipped out on us.

I'm pissed, not sure where to direct my anger, but it's no use blaming the team.

"How did he get by us?" I ask instead.

"Dresden swears he wasn't among the departing crowd at closing time, and Byron had his eye on the rear the entire night. The only activity at the back most of the night was an occasional employee dropping a trash bag in the container, but there was a brewery delivery at four this morning and he said the truck blocked part of his view of the exit for a few moments until he found a better vantage point. No more than a few minutes."

"Enough time to slip out."

"Yeah," Matt confirms.

"You think he made us?" I ask.

"I don't think so—the guys were careful—but he may suspect someone is paying attention to his movements. We think he may have tagged Opal, but I doubt he can link her to GEM or knows she was working with us."

"I'll agree on the first, but have my doubts on the second part of that. If he had eyes on her, he may have caught us together. I was with her outside the library in full view."

I glance over at her and note she's paying close attention to my conversation, her lips tight.

"Are you saying he has help?" Matt inquires.

From the corner of my eye, I see Kate nodding.

"I think it's likely. Maybe it's time we start rattling some cages."

"What about the kids?" Kate speaks up for the first time.

I'm sure she's referring to the risk rattling anyone's cage might pose to the missing teenagers.

"Unfortunately, with Kendrick in the wind, I don't think we can afford not to," Matt soberly informs her.

My instinct is to turn around and join in the search for our suspect, but we've already come this far. My time is better spent following up on this lead.

Following the GPS instructions, I pull into a gated community in the affluent neighborhood of Glenview. A security gate looms up ahead.

"Gotta let you go. We're almost there," I tell Matt. "I'll give you a call after."

I pull my credentials from my breast pocket and roll down the window as I ease up on the security guard already stepping out of the small gatehouse.

The FBI badge does its job, and we're granted entry without a hassle.

Cassandra Hogan lives in a glass, wood, and steel mansion backing onto the Ohio River. The entire look is contemporary and reeks of big bucks.

"Yowza," Kate mumbles as we roll up to the three-car garage.

A mother-of-pearl Range Rover is parked in front and I pull in beside it.

Something tells me Cassandra did pretty well for herself in the divorce. The rumors of a substantial payoff may hold some merit. This place is worth millions. Hell, the SUV alone would cost a couple of hundred grand.

When we walk up to the house, the front door opens. Either someone saw us pulling up or they have some sort of security system alerting them. The woman in the doorway is tall, slim to the point of skinny, and is wearing some kind of pink yoga outfit, plastered to her skin. Her platinum-blond hair is piled on her head in a messy bun and her face is flushed.

"Can I help you?"

Her voice isn't exactly inviting, but more curious than challenging.

Once again, I pull out my badge, but it's Kate who makes the introductions.

"This is FBI Agent Mitch Kenny, and my name is Opal."

Cassandra Hogan barely pays Kate a glance until she adds, "I'm a volunteer at The Youth Center."

That gets her attention as her eyes suddenly zoom in on Kate and her face registers shock.

"You're kidding, right? The Youth Center? Listen, whatever that bastard is up to now, I want nothing to do with it. Our divorce was final years ago."

"Yet you seem to connect The Youth Center with your ex-husband instantly," I point out.

"I had no idea until a couple of days ago when that reporter cornered me outside my hairdresser."

"Reporter?"

That's the first I've heard about any reporter asking questions. Of course, we weren't able to keep Georgia Braxton's murder a secret from the media, but there'd been no word of other missing kids in any of the reporting, so I'm intrigued.

She looks behind me to the street and seems to come to a decision as she steps to the side.

"You may as well come in," she says with a sigh.

We follow her inside, down a hallway with gleaming, wooden floors. The stark white walls sport black-and-white photos of who I presume are her children. At the back of the house, we walk into a large open space spanning the entire rear of the house. Sparse, modern furniture in leather and steel is clustered in small groupings, keeping the focus on the floor-to-ceiling windows boasting a spectacular view of the river valley.

The design is not exactly my style, but I have to admit, it works against the vivid colors of the fall foliage.

"Have a seat. Can I get you a drink?" she asks, gesturing toward a large kitchen island with four barstools.

"Not for me, thanks," Kate answers, hopping onto one of the stools.

I grab the one next to her and shake my head at Cassandra, who then ducks into the fridge and pulls out a bottle of water for herself.

"He asked me how I felt about Paul's involvement with a youth facility in Lanark, given his history with teenage girls. I figured he was another one of those tabloid sharks, trying to blow some life into those old rumors. I brushed him off and got in my car." She takes a sip of her water before continuing, "I'm guessing there's more to the story when the FBI shows up asking questions about the same thing."

"There is," I volunteer. Then I ask her as an afterthought, "By the way, did you get the name of the reporter?"

May be good to know who is snooping around.

"I think he said Lee something, I was too busy trying to get away from him to pay attention."

"Was it a rumor?" Kate asks the woman pointedly, keeping the interview on track.

"Was what a rumor?"

"Well, you mentioned you thought the reporter was trying to blow life into *those* old rumors. I assume you mean the ones accusing your husband—"

"Ex," she snaps.

"Ex-husband," Kate corrects herself. "Of inappropriate behavior with your children's babysitter?"

"What was the question again?"

The woman is stalling, but Kate is not letting her off the hook.

"Was that a rumor or is that what happened?"

Cassandra turns toward the view.

"I can't talk about that."

"Can't or won't?" I intervene and her eyes land on me.

To my surprise they look tortured.

"Can't," she repeats.

Opal

"Good job drawing her out."

I'm ridiculously pleased with the compliment as we drive out of the neighborhood, Mitch lifting his hand to the security guard when we pass the gate.

Not that I needed the pat on the back to know that went well, or the confirmation I'm good at what I do, but it's the kind of thing you'd say to a partner.

An *equal*.

"Thanks."

It's good he knows I can handle myself. It'll make working with him a lot easier, because I don't intend to be pushed out of this investigation.

Full credit to him for taking a step back to let me take lead on the interview with the former Mrs. Krebs.

When she'd mentioned being unable to answer my question, I guessed she must've been asked to sign a non-disclosure agreement as part of her divorce settlement from Krebs. She confirmed and added she would risk losing custody of her teenage children if she talked out of turn. Then she surprised us by suggesting we ask questions about the time prior to her marriage, or post-divorce. Apparently, the NDA had been limited to any knowledge she might have gained during the time she was married.

Once we crossed that bridge, she turned out to be a fount of information, painting the former athlete as a nasty piece of work.

First of all, he was apparently a habitual philanderer,

cheating on her before they were even married. It was something the first Mrs. Krebs had warned her about, but at the time she'd been too in love to listen. She discovered his first infidelity twelve days before their destination wedding in Belize, when she was three months pregnant with their first child.

She confronted him, he claimed it had been a mistake, a girl he'd met at his gym, and it didn't mean anything. The girl had been underage—something he claims not to have known at the time—and if word got out not only would his life be ruined, but Cassandra's and their baby's as well.

She chose to let it go.

When I explained we're looking into the disappearance of several teenagers and the murder of fourteen-year-old Georgia Braxton, all connected to the center, the woman's face went hard.

"He has an unhealthy fascination with kids," she'd said, followed by, *"And I already know there isn't a price he wouldn't be willing to pay to keep his name clean and his ass out of jail."*

That was big.

When Mitch ended the interview, asking if she knew of any place Krebs might go if he wanted to get away for some R&R, she mentioned a vacation property in the hills of Daniel Boone National Forest south of Irvine.

"What've you got?"

Matt's voice comes over the sound system. I didn't even notice Mitch dialing.

Mitch updates him on the interview with Cassandra Hogan.

"The guy sounds like a piece of work," Matt comments.

"No kidding. I'm sure there's plenty more she could tell us, but she's bound by an NDA and scared she'll lose custody of her kids."

"An NDA won't stand if it prevents her from reporting a crime," Matt clarifies. "And it doesn't supersede the law, so she'd be compelled to testify if subpoenaed. Maybe suggest she get advice from a lawyer about that."

"We'll let her know," I volunteer, planning to give her a call after.

I get the sense the woman would be happy to talk if she could trust there'd be no repercussions from her ex.

"What about you?" Mitch asks. "Any luck locating Kendrick?"

"Nope. We're in the process of getting copies of security feeds from businesses around the nightclub, but that's going to take a while."

"Talk to Pearl," I suggest. "If it's server storage, you'd be surprised at what she can do."

"You mean hack?" Matt wants to know, sounding amused.

"I'd rather think of it as speeding up a process when urgency is a factor."

And urgency is definitely a factor here. Who knows what Kendrick is up to? For all we know he could be eliminating witnesses as easily as he eliminated their files.

"What about Kaylie?" I ask. "Have you spoken with Onyx?"

"Not yet. I'm waiting to hear from her. Are you guys heading back?"

"No," Mitch responds, surprising me.

I wasn't aware of any planned detours and I look at him with an eyebrow raised.

"I think we should go check out that property near Irvine. We now have two suspects in the wind, Kendrick and Krebs, unless you've been able to track him down?"

"No luck there either. We've got eyes on his house though."

The sports anchor has a place in the country about fifty miles south of Louisville and about the same distance west from Lanark. As soon as we found out one of the four vehicles listed in Krebs's name was a navy Yukon Denali, Matt called in for assistance from the Hardin County Sheriff's Office to do a check at his house.

"He could be anywhere," I point out.

"True," Mitch concedes before explaining, "But if I tried to run someone down and failed—getting my vehicle damaged in the process—I might opt to lay low somewhere. Especially if I had such a place readily available to me."

"No heroics," Matt cautions.

"Not planning on any. Right now, all I want to do is make sure we're on the right track. If he's there and I can get eyes on the vehicle to confirm it was his Yukon at the library last night, at least we know we're not wasting valuable time."

"Fine. You focus on Krebs. I'll stay on Kendrick."

"Call Pearl," I remind him.

"Will do. Stay in touch."

I'm processing all the new information, and I'm guessing Mitch is doing the same since it's quiet in the car. Until we turn onto the highway, then I speak up.

"How do you plan on finding this property?" I ask.

Cassandra had only been able to give us vague directions once we pass Irvine, involving mostly dirt roads, but she'd only been out there once and that was over a decade ago. So much can change in that amount of time, there's no guarantee everything is still as she remembered.

"He needs food and supplies. I'm guessing he's got someone local looking after the place, and—since I don't see Krebs walking into a grocery store himself—they probably stock up for him."

A fair enough assumption.

"So, we're going to hit up grocery stores in Irvine?"

"There aren't that many, but no, I just got a better idea. Most of the gas stations are on the north side of town. There's only one at the south end, right before we cross the train tracks."

"That's where Cassandra said to turn left along the river."

"Bingo," he says, grinning sideways at me. "The only thing he'll likely get himself is gas, and that Marathon station would be the last one before he hits the hills..."

"And the first one heading home," I finish his thought before concluding, "Sounds like you're familiar with Irvine."

"Drive through there whenever my daughter and I go camping," he answers. "I live only twenty or so miles up the road in Richmond."

Then he turns to me.

"I'm no stranger to the area."

My stomach does a little flip at the sight of his hazel eyes lit up with excitement.

The thrill of the chase, I'm sure.

It's a damn good look on him.

THIRTEEN

MITCH

When I drive into the Marathon gas station, I notice they have a full-service pump on the other side.

A young kid, maybe eighteen or nineteen, comes to the car when I pull up. I roll down the window.

"Fill'er up?" he says.

"Sure."

I wait for him to fix the nozzle in my tank but when he reaches for the squeegee to clean my windows, I call him back.

"Maybe you can help us. We're supposed to have dinner at a friend's house and I must've written the instructions down wrong. It said left on Miller Creek Road, take the first left, and then about five miles up the road, turn right onto a dirt road." I shrug and try to look sheepish. "I can't seem to find the dirt road and keep looping back into town."

"Who's the friend? I reckon I know most all the folks livin' up in those hills."

"Yeah, I don't know if I should. My friend values his privacy. He's a bit of a public figure, you see."

I glance over at Kate, as if I'm getting her input, when she reaches over and puts her hand on my arm.

"Don't be silly, honey, I'm sure Paul won't mind," she says, playing right along.

Then she smiles and leans over the center console, shaking her head at the kid.

"My husband is being overly cautious. We're looking for Paul Krebs. You wouldn't happen to know him, would you?"

"Mr. Krebs? I sure do," he grins back. "Saw him this mornin' when I got to work. He was my first customer of the day."

"Well, isn't that just perfect," she beams before she sits back, patting my knee. "See, honey? I'm sure this nice young man can tell us how to get there."

"It ain't hard," the kid says, falling for her performance hook, line, and sinker. "You got the first part right, heading east on Miller Creek Road, but you've gotta keep goin' for about five miles 'til you hit a T in the road. Turn left, and then you take the first right. No more 'n a dirt road is right, but it'll get you right up the hill to the house."

When my tank is full, I thank him, hand him thirty bucks, and tell him to keep the change.

"Husband? A little fast, don't you think? It was only one kiss," I tease, grinning as I pull away from the station.

"Hey, I was just playing along," she says defensively, but when I glance over I catch her smiling.

Good.

Spending a couple of hours on the road in very close proximity to this woman I could feel the tension build, and before I did something stupid—like kiss her again—I tried to defuse the situation.

Joking about that kiss takes some of the tension off.

Getting Kate to smile is a bonus.

Except now I want to kiss her even more.

The dirt road isn't easy to spot and I almost drive past it. Luckily, there's no traffic on the road so I'm able to back up a bit and turn in. Despite being largely obscured from the road, the path heading up the hill is somewhat maintained with gravel filling the worst of the ruts.

We make slow progress, my vehicle not exactly made for the rough terrain, until I notice the driveway narrowing even farther ahead.

"We'll have to walk up from here."

I don't like going in blind, and up ahead the trees are thick, crowding in on either side of what is no more than a trail. Safer to leave the vehicle down here, where I can pull in behind the brush and still have room to back out when we leave.

Kate gets out on her side and I inch up a little more to be completely out of view of the dirt road before exiting as well.

"Are you carrying?" I ask when I catch up with her.

She pats the pocket of her coat as she keeps moving,

staying off the trail and trudging through the undergrowth just inside the tree line. A path I would've chosen myself.

For now I'm quite content letting her take the lead—the view is enjoyable from back here—since I already know she can hold her own. But when I notice the tree cover getting sparser, I hustle to the front.

Up ahead the ground levels off to a clearing, revealing a substantial, rustic house nestled in the trees on the far side. The two-car garage is separate from the main building, partially obscured from view.

Holding up my hand, I stop Kate from moving ahead.

"No vehicles," she says in a soft voice beside me.

"Doesn't necessarily mean there's no one here," I return.

"Only one way to find out."

Before I have a chance to react, she's already walking into the clearing, aiming straight for the house.

"You could get shot at," I hiss when I catch up to her.

She turns her face and pointedly rolls her eyes.

"Give me a break. Unless he has a sniper rifle handy and is a highly-skilled shot, he'd have a hard time getting near me," she states while swiftly traversing the clearing. "And that's assuming he's here and trigger happy."

Then she points to the stone chimney emerging from the steel roof.

"No heat on and it's been chilly at night. Colder up here. I'm guessing if he was here at all, he's probably gone already."

She makes a good point, but I still don't like she turned herself into a potential target. If he was the one driving last night and got even the slightest glimpse of her, catching sight of that strawberry-blond mane heading toward his house could've panicked him.

Nothing like a man who feels trapped to ramp up the body count.

A shiver runs down my spine at the thought and I find myself darting past her up the steps to the front door. I knock, keeping an eye on the narrow pane of glass next to the front door to see if anything's moving.

Nothing. Not a sound either, so I try again with the same lack of result.

"I'm gonna have a look around," Kate announces, heading back down the steps.

I try the door—it's locked—before moving around to the side of the house, pressing my face up to windows to have a peek inside. The place looks like a hunting lodge full of leather, hides, and more than a few mounted animal heads on the white-washed walls.

When I come around the rear, I find a big deck with a built-in firepit, surrounded by rustic chairs. Wide glass sliding doors go to a dining area inside. I check to find the sliding doors locked as well before turning around to look into the woods beyond.

Shit. Kate is right, there's no one here. I fight a wave of disappointment. Somewhere in the back of my mind I'd hoped maybe we'd find the missing kids here, but there's no sign of life anywhere.

"Mitch!"

Her voice snaps me out of my thoughts and into

action, jumping off the deck and barreling toward the sound of her call.

I find her—luckily in one piece and alone—standing in front of what looks like an old barn, hidden under the trees behind the garage.

The doors are wide open and I notice a new-looking chain attached to one of them, an open padlock dangling down. I step up beside Kate and peer into the shadows to see a vehicle, covered by a dark green tarp.

"What do you want to bet there's a Yukon under there with a wiper missing," she suggests.

"I'd say those are some good odds," I mumble back, before stepping into the barn.

I'm not surprised when she proves right when I peel back the tarp. Not only is the wiper missing, but I wince at the sight of an ugly dent in the hood. A reminder of how different the outcome might have been.

Looking around, I note the only window is high above the barn doors.

"How did you know it was in here?" I ask, facing her.

"I didn't," she admits. "I'd hoped to find Melissa, or maybe one of the others." She turns and points at the padlock on the door. "A new chain and padlock on a building that looks to be near collapse suggested it had to be something important."

I walk over to the door and lift up the opened padlock.

"How did you get in?" I want to know, glancing her way.

She shrugs her shoulders and fails to hide her smile.

"Let's just say I tripped and bumped into the door to find it hadn't been locked properly. Or something like that," she adds.

I shake my head before flipping the tarp back down. The Yukon is evidence, but it would be easily dismissed if we had gained illegal entry—hell, I could lose my job—a fact Kate is evidently aware of.

Leaving the padlock dangling, I shove the doors shut, but not all the way.

Then I grab Kate's arm and steer her away.

"You are a woman of many talents," I mutter.

It earns me a wide smile.

"You have no idea," she teases, a sparkle in her eyes.

Have mercy.

This woman is going to be the death of me.

Opal

It's late, well after dark, by the time we head back to his vehicle.

We had to wait two hours for the FBI's crime scene investigators to get here with a flatbed truck.

I have to hand it to Mitch, he was a cool customer after my break-and-enter, spinning a story based on my transparent lie to try and preserve the integrity of the evidence. He wasn't questioned too closely, not when we're actively investigating a case of missing children, something no one in or outside of law enforcement takes lightly.

Upon closer inspection of the SUV, one of the crime techs found what he later confirmed was blood on the side panel behind the rear seat. Based on that, Matt had been able to arrange a search warrant for the entire property. Mitch went in with the CSI unit while I was told to wait outside. I wasn't exactly happy about it, but understood the need to stick to proper procedure.

I guess he's learning I'm not much of a rule-follower.

In hindsight, I'm glad I stayed behind.

They found a concealed room in the basement of the house, the door hidden behind a stacked washer and dryer combo. No one inside, thank God, but they found evidence of someone being kept down there for a length of time.

Hard to believe it's possible, but apparently the former football star is an even sicker individual than I already pegged him as.

From Mitch's description, whoever was down there was kept under the barest of conditions; chained to the wall, with only a dirty, thin mattress for comfort and a bucket to relieve themselves.

It's a good thing this place is out in the boonies, because if the press got wind of this, given Krebs's fame, the shit would hit the fan. I'm sure it would be the final nail in those kids' coffins.

The crime scene techs are going to be busy here for a while, but Mitch announced he wanted to get out of here, and I didn't argue. I'm wrung out, both physically and emotionally, and unless I get horizontal in a hurry, I'm afraid gravity and sheer exhaustion will do it for me.

Mitch opens the door for me when we get to the car.

"Thank you," I mumble, waiting for him to round the hood and get behind the wheel before I ask the question that's been burning on my mind. "Where could they've gone?"

Over the last hours we've learned a few more interesting details. Like the fact Kendrick was caught on the video feed of an all-night convenience store, coming out of the alley at the rear of the nightclub, at three minutes past four in the morning. There he'd been picked up by a large, dark Yukon, the plates listed to one Paul Krebs.

The two were together. Or at least had been early this morning. Another piece of information which will become valuable evidence once we have them in custody.

But we'll have to find them first.

"I don't know, but someone in this town must've seen something," he says, obviously frustrated. "Hopefully we'll be able to get some answers tomorrow when we meet up with the chief."

A Detective McCandles of the Irvine Police Department had shown up while we were waiting for CSI to get here. Matt had apparently contacted local law enforcement as a courtesy. McCandles was sent here to keep an eye on things but notified us the chief of police wanted a word first thing tomorrow.

"And what do we do until then? Drive back to Lanark?"

He glances over before returning his focus to the dirt road ahead.

"Nope. Richmond. We need food and rest, and I'm not about to drive all the way back to Lanark to get it, so we're going to my place."

His tone bears no argument, and I don't have the energy to object anyway.

Richmond it is.

I have to admit, I'm more than a little curious to get a glimpse at the man behind the badge.

FOURTEEN

*O*PAL

We drive into a fairly new subdivision on the south side of Richmond, lit by sparse streetlamps.

Mostly single-level houses on royal-sized lots.

Mitch's place is at the end of a cul-de-sac. A neat-looking bungalow from what I can make out. It has an attached garage and backs onto a ravine.

"This is home," he says a bit awkwardly as he parks his vehicle in the short driveway.

"Nice place," I mumble, not quite knowing what else to say.

I'm feeling a bit awkward myself. The quiet anticipation on the drive over here suddenly rages into full-on butterflies in my stomach. It's not like I haven't been alone with this man during the past few days, but that was mostly about the case. Although we've definitely had some private moments, this feels somehow more alone.

More loaded with opportunity and definitely rife with the promise of what has been crackling between us.

Mitch grabs the pizza we picked up on the way through town from the back seat and gets out from behind the wheel. As I follow him to the front door, I force my mind away from the mental images of Mitch naked, and back into safe territory.

"You realize both Krebs and Kendrick are going to be in the wind now," I point out when he opens the door and steps inside. "With the kind of money Krebs has, they could be on an island in the South Pacific by now."

"Maybe Krebs, but I have my doubts Kendrick is the type to run. He's bold enough to show back up in Lanark after he supposedly was killed in the fire at Transition House. That's pretty cocky, especially given the rumor he was involved in sexual exploitation of kids at the time."

I snort derisively before I can check myself, and Mitch stops in the middle of the spacious living room, turning to face me.

"Not a rumor. A fact," I can't resist correcting him.

He's given me some indication he suspects what happened at the home back then impacted me as well. I've kept the abuse hidden for more years than I suffered it. It's like it happened to a different version of me—a version I've long outgrown—but these past few weeks since discovering Kendrick's involvement in the disappearance of the teens have shown me the trauma continues to be part of me.

Yet I still can't seem to bring myself to talk about it. Old habits die hard, I guess.

"Fair enough," Mitch comments, not pushing me to elaborate.

He continues into the kitchen where he drops the pizza box on the counter and reaches into a cupboard for some plates. Then he heads for the fridge.

"Drink?"

"Just water, please."

I perch a hip on one of the barstools at the high-top kitchen table and glance around the open space. The decor is sparse. The most prominent feature—aside from the large, dark gray sofa with a chaise lounge on one side in the center of the living room—is a floor-to-ceiling wall unit. The shelves not only hold a decent-sized TV, but a virtual library of books.

Curious, I'm drawn to the books, where I'm pleasantly surprised to find some of my favorite authors represented. They're mixed in with autobiographies, reference books, some American history, and I even spot a few paranormal romance titles.

I slide a finger along the spines of the books by JR Ward, Nalini Singh, and Anne Rice, when I hear Mitch approach.

"My daughter's."

A tiny shiver runs down my spine when I hear his rumbled clarification inches away from my ear.

"Makes sense. Great books, but unexpected."

"Yeah, paranormal is not my thing. Reality is enough of a challenge," he comments.

"I would've thought it was the romance that seemed

out of place," I observe, turning to find him right behind me.

"I have no issues with romance. In fact, I think my shelves could use a little more of it."

Is he using his bookcase as a euphemism for his life?

The look on his face certainly implies as much, and my mouth goes dry at the heat in his eyes. The air crackles between us and my glance drops down to his firm lips. My heart rate ramps up and time suspends as I can almost feel the pressure of his mouth on mine.

A loud rumbling reverberates from my midsection, breaking the tension. I press my hands against my stomach, as if that will stop my body's hunger growls. My cheeks heat as Mitch's mouth spreads into a grin.

"Guess romance is going to have to take a back seat to pizza." He leans in and brushes the pad of a thumb over my cheek. "By the way, pink looks good on you."

I'm relieved when he heads back to the kitchen, missing my face flush an unflattering shade of beet red. I shake my head, annoyed I'm allowing myself to get flustered by this man. I hardly recognize myself.

Lifting my chin and squaring my shoulders, I follow behind, settling back on the stool I vacated.

"Tell me about your daughter," I ask as he carries plates and the pizza box over to the table.

"Sixteen going on thirty-six," he comments dryly, taking a seat across from me. "She's my light, and the reason I lie awake at night."

I may not have children but I can understand his

sentiments. I know only too well how dangerous this world can be to navigate for kids.

"That's her," he says, taking a bite of his slice as he indicates a picture frame hanging on the wall next to a hallway leading to, what I assume, are the bedrooms. "That's Sawyer."

A pretty girl, her dark hair in two braids, is sitting on an outcropping of rock, smiling wide at the camera. I can see the family resemblance; she has the same eyes as her dad.

"She's lovely. Bit of a tomboy?"

Not too much of a stretch, since the rock she's perched on is hanging precariously over the edge of a deep canyon.

"Used to be. Nowadays I'm lucky if she comes camping at all."

There's a wistful tone to his voice I imagine a lot of parents use when talking about their teenage kids.

"I hear they return to normal after a while," I offer to lighten the tone.

"Hope so," he responds. "What about you? Any kids?"

"Nope." I pop my P. "Not averse to kids, just wasn't in the cards for me."

He nods thoughtfully before returning to his pizza. I do the same. Good pizza too.

I'm wolfing down my third slice when Mitch suddenly slaps the counter.

"Almost forgot; what happened with Kaylie? Wasn't your colleague supposed to drive out to interview her?"

Onyx was, I forgot about that. I should probably check in.

"She was, I haven't heard anything though."

I fumble to get my phone from my pocket and check for messages, feeling Mitch's eyes on me.

This isn't like me. Normally I would have been in touch with my team every step of the way, but I realize they don't even know where I am.

This man is proving to be a bit of a distraction and I'm having a hard time keeping my head in the game.

Mitch

I clear the plates away while listening to Kate talk on the phone.

It's been a strange night.

Not sure what I was thinking when I invited her, but having her in my space there's only one thing on my mind.

Maybe I should feel guilty, but we've both been eating and breathing this case for weeks. We deserve a break, a decent night's sleep.

I watch as Kate ends her call and walks toward me.

Who am I kidding?

Sleeping is the last thing on my mind.

"Onyx is still in Frankfort," Kate reports. "Getting

information from Kaylie hasn't been easy and she's going to try again tomorrow."

I'm finding it hard to concentrate on what she is saying when all I can think about is kissing her pretty mouth like I was about to earlier.

"Mitch?"

"Sorry, what?"

Jesus.

Keeping my eyes locked on hers, this time I make sure I don't miss a word.

"I was saying that Onyx is still working on the girl, and apparently Pearl has been digging up information on Russel Germain and Congressman Melnyk. She came across something interesting. Two and a half years ago, both men attended some kind of professional development seminar on a large yacht in the Caribbean. Guess who else was there?"

I don't need time to think.

"Krebs," is my immediate response.

"The one and only."

"That has to be more than a coincidence. Who was putting on the seminar?"

"The yacht was chartered by a company by the name of *Glan Development*. Pearl is looking into it."

Excitement at this new lead is obvious on Kate's face, adding yet another attractive layer to the woman I'm already finding hard to resist.

"I should probably let Matt know," I mention.

I'm less than enthusiastic about spending more time on the phone, but he should be made aware. There are resources the Bureau has which might come in handy tracking down that company.

"Pearl already talked to him," Kate murmurs, taking a step closer.

Now only a few feet apart, facing each other, the electricity sparking earlier recharges the air between us.

Oh, what the hell.

Two steps, and my mouth is covering hers before my arms have a chance to close around her, pulling her soft curves against my body. Her hands go straight for my head, fingers twisting in my hair as she opens up and invites me in.

A groan surges up from my gut at the first deep taste of her mouth. A release of the barely containable restraint I've been holding on to for what seems like forever. Hunger rages through me as I voraciously claim her with my kiss. One she matches with every lash of my tongue.

The next moment we're moving, my body pressing hers backward toward my bedroom. Her restless hands in my hair still and she pulls back from my kiss.

"Is this okay?" I remember to ask, staring into her now almost silver eyes.

"I'm not sure," she whispers, and I can sense indecision war within her.

"For what it's worth, neither am I," I admit. "But it sure as fuck feels okay."

"This will complicate things."

Her words are almost breathless and her face is flushed deep. She wants this as much as I do.

"They're already complicated," I point out, firming my hold on her body.

She brings her hands down to my chest and for a moment I think she might push me away. But then her fingers curl into my shirt and she lifts her face, mumbling, "You're right," right before she presses her lips to mine.

With intent clear between us, my mind is blank and the pace almost frantic, mouths and hands claiming as clothes disappear. Full breasts fill my hands as I taste my way down the long column of her neck. The moment my lips close over a flushed pink nipple, she arches her back, pressing herself deeper into my mouth.

"Yesss..."

Her hissed encouragement has me go down on my knees, exploring the soft flesh of her belly. The scent of her arousal lures me to her center.

Everywhere I can reach I'm met with downy, fragrant skin; her breasts, the swell of her stomach, the globes of her ass, and even the firm muscles of her legs are encased in a layer of softness I can't seem to stop touching.

Peering up from my vantage point, I find her eyes dark with heat as she looks down at me. Magnificent and unapologetic. She's stunning; a picture of delicate strength and bold confidence.

I hook my fingers in her panties—her last remaining garment—and hold her gaze as I slowly pull them down her legs. Grabbing her firmly by the hips, I move her a step until the backs of her knees hit the edge of the mattress. She lets herself fall back and I groan at the sight of her.

My eyes zoom in on the neatly-trimmed, russet patch of curls between her legs and she doesn't resist when I press her wide open.

Fuck, so pretty.

When I drag a finger through her folds, slick with her arousal, the tangy scent of her makes my mouth water. My eyes flit up to hers, a silent request for permission, which is granted with a further widening of her legs.

It's fucking bliss; my face cushioned by her soft thighs as my lips and tongue explore her pussy. One of her hands grabs on to the back of my head as she slides the other between her legs, spreading her own lips to guide my tongue.

It's the hottest thing ever, having her take control of the way I please her.

When she lifts her ass off the bed, grinding herself on my tongue as she flicks her own clit, I almost lose it. I'm glad she hadn't managed to get my jeans off yet. The delicate balance between pain and pleasure it provides keeps my cock from blowing prematurely when she climaxes with a full body shiver and an elongated moan.

"My turn," she declares in a mumble, propping herself up on her elbows.

I run the back of my hand across my mouth and grin at her.

"Sweetheart, you even look at my dick, it'll go off," I point out, getting to my feet as my hands go for my fly.

"Surely, a seasoned federal agent like yourself is in full control of his body," she teases, her eyes following closely as I pull down my zipper.

I shove jeans and boxer briefs down, my angry cock slapping against my stomach as I kick my clothes aside.

"Not when I still have the taste of you on my lips," I warn her as I plant my fists in the mattress on either side of her. "Scoot up."

I enjoy watching her tits bounce as she wiggles herself up the bed.

"Nice," she drawls out, her eyes fixed on my dick when I climb over her.

Reaching out, she strokes her index finger from root to tip, eliciting a pained groan from me. Grabbing her hand, I stretch her arm over her head, wedging my hips between hers.

Her pussy is slick and hot as I rub the head of my cock against her folds. She tilts her hips to invite me inside when a thought hits me.

"*Fuck.* Condom. I don't think I have any."

I let go of her wrist and brace myself on my arms, preparing to lift off her when she wraps her arms around my neck, pulling me back down.

"For what it's worth, last time I tested clean and I haven't been...active since. Pregnancy isn't an issue since I lack the proper equipment," she informs me.

So that's what the faint scar right above her pubic bone is from. I was wondering.

"Haven't been with anyone since my last test either."

Still I wait, poised over her. It's her call to make, which she does with a sly smile and a sure hand that glides down my chest and over my belly, grabbing my cock firmly at the base.

"Then what the hell are you waiting for? Fuck me already."

I don't need to be told twice.

Poised at her entrance, I intend to gentle myself into her, but Kate has different plans. She moves her hands to my ass, plants her feet flat in the bed and lifts her hips, taking me inside her to the root.

The last conscious thought I have is, *damn, this woman is something else,* before my mind blanks and my body takes over.

FIFTEEN

MITCH

The muffled sound of a phone ringing penetrates my groggy mind, but it takes me a moment to orient myself.

The bed is familiar, but the soft body I'm wrapped around is a bit of a surprise.

Then it all comes back to me, and I have to bury my nose in her luscious strawberry-blond hair to make sure I didn't just dream one of the most memorable nights of sex in a long fucking while.

Her soft moan as she wiggles her butt back, brushing up against the one part of me that was apparently well awake, has me almost forget what woke me in the first place.

Then the ringing starts up again.

Fuck.

Pressing a kiss on her smooth shoulder, I reluctantly

release my hold on her. I roll over and blindly grapple for my jeans. The ringing stops before I can pull the phone from my pocket.

The screen indicates it's just after five and Matt is trying to reach me.

Swinging my legs out of bed, I return his call.

"Opal with you?"

"Yeah."

I glance over as she slowly rolls on her back, her eyes on me. Mine drift down to her exposed breasts and I feel a pang of regret. I had plans for those beauties.

"I need you both here ASAP."

"Where is here?" I snap back.

"Back to the cabin. We found Krebs."

Ten minutes later, armed with travel mugs of coffee—thank God for my Keurig—and a couple of granola bars, we're speeding back toward Irvine. Matt had been brief in his report, simply stating Krebs body had been found on the grounds, but there'd been no sign of Kendrick.

Our prime target is still in the wind.

Kate is quiet. I'm not sure if it's because of the news, or the early hour, or even regret over what happened last night. The latter concerns me most. It would seriously suck if she had second thoughts, because I'd hoped last night would not be a one and done deal.

"Are you okay?" I find myself asking as I glance over and meet her eyes.

"I'm worried. Kendrick is on the run and we have no way to know where he's heading. Assuming he killed

Krebs, what if he's tying off loose ends? We still have five girls and two boys missing."

I squash the flash of relief hearing it isn't regret that had her pensive. The point she brings up is valid and very concerning. If Kendrick was desperate enough to off a public figure like Krebs, he might not hesitate doing the same to those children.

One dead girl was bad enough.

"We'll find them," I promise her, hoping like hell I can live up to it.

She smiles wryly, nodding once before aiming her gaze out the windshield again.

There's frost on the ground when we drive into the hills. The moon reflecting off the layer of pale white clinging to every surface. A bit of magic on an otherwise dark drive.

I pull my vehicle in behind a few police cruisers and the coroner's van. Matt must've been on the lookout, he's already stalking toward us when we get out of the car.

"Where?" I ask.

He turns toward the house and points to a bare spot on the slope behind it, visible by what I assume are flood-lights illuminating the scene.

"See that rocky outcropping? We stumbled across his body at the bottom of the cliff when we were scouring the hill in the dark. There's a narrow trail—looks like it was used for ATVs or something—heading east into the woods. I sent a few guys to follow it up, see if they could find any sign of our suspects heading that way when they found Krebs."

"How was he killed?" Kate asks, voicing the question entering my mind as well.

Found at the bottom of a cliff could suggest an accident. In fact, if we hadn't found the video feed showing Kendrick getting into the former athlete's vehicle, it might well have been passed off as one.

"Coroner's up there now, so we'll know for sure soon enough. At first glance, it looks like he fell, knocked his head—he had a massive head injury—but there wasn't a lot of blood where he looks to have fallen. There was at the top of the rock though. We're waiting for daylight to do a thorough search up there. Don't want to traipse through possible evidence in the dark."

Probably smart.

The hike up to the scene is hefty but Kate doesn't even break a sweat. Fueled by only a coffee and granola bar, she's showing me up, making tracks ahead of me while I bring up the rear, panting already. I'm going to need to add some cardio to my exercise regime if I want to keep up with her.

"We're going to get some help from the Lexington office this morning," Matt says over his shoulder. "Wouldn't take much for Kendrick to have slipped across the West Virginia border. He's got almost a day on us. We need more eyes looking for this guy."

"I don't think he went far," I put out there, echoing what I suggested to Kate last night. "Something has kept him around here when it probably would've been smarter for him to set up shop somewhere else. His connections to big rollers in Kentucky might be the reason for it."

The congressman, lawyer, and real estate mogul may only be the tip of the iceberg.

"Possible," Matt concedes. "I wonder how he made those connections. We should be looking into the other men he was at that club with."

"Jacob is digging into links between those men and Transition House," Kate contributes from the front of the pack. Clearly there's nothing wrong with her hearing either. "I know for a fact his connection to Marshall Browning reaches back that far."

"Was that the son of the former chief of police?" Matt wants clarified.

"George Browning, yes. Although I think he was deputy chief at the time."

"We're gonna need to take time for a proper briefing," I propose. "We've had a ton of developments and we're bound to miss something if we don't compare notes. We can't afford to."

I hate taking the time from actively investigating but the reality is, with the added manpower coming in, we need everyone up to speed. We're going to have too many cooks in the kitchen otherwise. That's never helpful.

At this point it's not even clear whose investigation this is. Will the Lexington FBI office take over or defer to us?

If the death of Krebs is in fact murder, we're going to be dealing with a mess of jurisdictions stretching across Kentucky.

"Let's wait until we hear back from the Hardin County Sheriff's Office," Matt states. "I spoke to the sheriff earlier to rope off Krebs's property there until Lampert and Byron can get there. They're on their way with a warrant."

Wow, that's fast, but a good call. Hopefully Krebs was as sloppy with potential evidence in his house as he was at his cabin.

"What about Kendrick's place?" Kate asks from the front.

"Agents from the Lexington office will be going through it," Matt answers her.

Kate stops to look back at him.

"Any chance you could arrange for Pearl to have a look at any electronics they pick up?"

"We have an entire specialized department with highly capable agents to do that."

She tilts her head slightly, staring him down for a moment.

"That may be so, but I'm willing to bet Pearl is better than all of them put together. She knows Kendrick. She'll know what to look for."

As much as Matt is right—we do have some of the best computer techs at the Bureau—I do think in this case Kate makes a good point; it might be worth getting Pearl's eyes on whatever evidence they find.

"It's not a bad idea, actually," I voice my support, earning a surprised smile from Kate and a frown from Matt. "Can't hurt," I push on. "She already knows this case inside out."

He stares hard before lowering his eyes and giving his head a shake.

"I'll see what I can do."

Then he turns on his heel and continues toward the group gathered under the bright lights up ahead.

Kate waits for me to catch up.

"Thanks," she states simply, falling into step beside me.

I shrug it off.

"Your point was valid."

Then I put a hand in the small of her back and change the subject.

"It'll be an ugly scene."

The look she spears me with in response to my warning is hard as she moves away from my touch.

"Don't worry on my account. I've seen my share of those."

A good reminder not to underestimate this woman. She may be sweet sighs and soft curves in bed, but out here she's all business.

Opal

Holy shit.

If possible, the up-close images displayed on the large overhead screen in the Lexington FBI's situation room are even more disturbing than the actual scene itself. I already had a problem keeping a straight face there.

I was at a safe distance and only got glimpses of Krebs's body, which was mangled and deformed from the fall, but these shots are up close, showing every single one of his extensive injuries.

Not the least of which was his almost pulverized head.

The reason the FBI's Lexington Field Office was picked for a briefing was because it's central, and large enough to house the many different agencies now involved.

I was frankly surprised GEM was invited to sit in. I'm not sure whether it was at the CARD team's suggestion or if Jacob managed to pull some strings, but here we are. Pearl isn't here—she's cooped up in an office in Louisville with FBI techs—but Onyx is, sitting a couple of chairs down from me.

It sounds like we're to be part of an official, two-tiered task force.

The CARD unit, with GEM's support, is to concentrate on locating and recovering the missing children, while the Lexington FBI—with support and resources of the main FBI offices in Louisville—along with the various local law enforcement agencies, will focus on the criminal aspect of the investigation. Of course, the objectives will overlap in places, which is why Matt and SAC Greg Walker will be in continuous contact.

We've been listening to Matt relaying the early findings of the Estill County coroner, who was able to take away from the state of Krebs's body, which had been in full rigor, his death occurred at least fourteen, but possibly as long as twenty hours prior.

FBI agents confirmed a substantial amount of blood near the trail and found a tree branch in the underbrush nearby with evidence to suggest it was used as a club to bash Krebs's head in.

It's clear an accidental death is off the table.

"Homicide," SAC Walker confirms. "That makes two, that we know of anyway. The second one is Georgia Braxton, whose body was found last week on the banks of the Kentucky River in Woodford County. Let's make sure that count doesn't go up.

"We have a forensics team going over the property near Irvine, the house in Hardin County, and we're centralizing any and all evidence collected at the FBI lab in Louisville. Josh Kendrick, aka Mason Kramer, is our number one focus at this point. A profile of him—courtesy of Jacob Branch of GEM—is attached to your handouts. This morning we exercised a warrant on his house in Lanark and are in the process of assessing what we have in terms of useful evidence. Agent Driver and myself will be responsible for distributing any new information that becomes available to our respective teams."

The burly, older man shoves his glasses back up his nose and with a serious expression scans the room.

"I'm sure I don't need to point out the urgency of this case or the need to be discreet in our investigation. However, there are children missing, which always makes for a juicy front-page story. Already, this morning, our team at the Lanark house had to chase off a nosy reporter.

Frankly, I'm surprised there haven't been news vans parked outside The Youth Center yet, but I guess we've been lucky so far. The less media involvement, the more efficiently we can do our job."

"By chance were you able to get the name of the reporter?" I find myself asking, instantly regretting it when every eye in the situation room turns my way.

Walker peers at me over his dark-rimmed glasses, holding my eyes long enough to have me squirm in my seat before he pulls a notebook from his inside jacket pocket, flipping through the pages.

"Lee Remington," he finally says, his eyes coming back to me. "A freelance reporter. Any particular reason you're asking?"

I glance over at Mitch, who nods at me and I turn back to Walker.

"When we spoke with Krebs's ex-wife, Cassandra Hogan, yesterday, she mentioned being accosted by a reporter about Krebs's involvement with The Youth Center."

That seems to ramp up the interest.

"You don't say?" Walker comments.

I'm grateful when Mitch takes over.

"She was upset and blew the guy off. Krebs apparently had a bit of a history with young girls, and Ms. Hogan was forced to sign an NDA as part of their divorce to get custody of her children. She wasn't happy to find out he was involved with a youth center and decided to break the agreement when she discovered why we were there. All she was able to tell us about the reporter is she thought his first name was Lee."

"I think we need to have a word with Remington," Walker states. "I'd like to know why he is sniffing around."

SIXTEEN

OPAL

"I need a laptop."

I feel Mitch's eyes on me.

"You can use mine when we get to the hotel."

Right. His hotel, where the remnants of my belongings are. At least I'll be able to put on some clean clothes, maybe use his bathroom for the quick shower I desperately need. After last night's activities in Mitch's bed and this morning's trek in the hills, I'm starting to smell rank.

If I had my truck, I could whip home, check my desktop, use my own bathroom, and take a moment to gather my thoughts. So much has happened, I feel I need a moment to process it all and decide where to go from here. But, to my knowledge my Silverado hasn't been found yet, and for the time being I'll have to contend with driving around with Mitch.

Not that it's a hardship, necessarily, but after last

night the man is even more of a distraction, and if I want to find those kids, I'll need to keep my wits about me.

Also, I don't want Mitch looking over my shoulder when I try to dig up information on Lee Remington. SAC Walker was clear when he said he'd be looking into Remington's interest in The Youth Center himself when I offered to do it, but I'm used to doing things myself and on my own timeline.

Remington has to know something that prompted him to start looking into the center and Krebs in particular. I want to know what that is. Maybe he talked to one of the kids at some point. I should get in touch with Brian too, see if the reporter approached him at any time.

However, Mitch is a federal agent, he's going to want to play this by the book when I feel the need to go off-script. We're no closer to knowing where those missing children are than we were before, and God knows what they are being put through while we are juggling proper procedure and respecting jurisdiction.

Time is ticking.

"I can hear you thinking from here."

"Just wondering if there's any news on my truck."

A partial truth at best.

"That's all?" he questions, apparently not satisfied with my answer.

"Actually," I start, shifting in my seat so I don't have to crick my neck looking at him. "What is the plan once we get to the hotel? Where do we go from there?"

"Shower, change of clothes, touch base with the rest

of our teams to see what—if any—information they've uncovered. Then we draw up a plan of action."

Sounds reasonable enough, I guess.

"I think after the hotel we should head to the center. See the state of affairs there, talk to Sally and question Brian again. Maybe with Kendrick on the lam we'll be able to get some of the kids to talk."

"We could. Not sure how long it'll be until Kendrick's absence is noted."

"Unless he's been calling in, which I seriously doubt because he wouldn't be leaving a trail of crumbs like that. Kendrick is too smart."

"We've been monitoring his cell phone and there hasn't been any activity, but he could've used another phone."

Except he didn't, and I know that because one of the first things Pearl did since we arrived in Lanark was monitor The Youth Center's incoming and outgoing phone calls. I'm not going to tell Mitch that, since hacking is against the law, and that's how Pearl gained access to the account.

This is one of the reasons why—despite feeling all kinds of right—last night was probably a mistake. There are a few things I haven't shared with him about the way GEM operates. Mostly because they're not exactly legal, but one of the reasons our team is able to get the kinds of results we do is because our main focus is getting the job done, by whatever means possible. Even if it means crossing the boundaries of the law.

The kind of man Mitch is, he won't take being lied to kindly.

Even if it is only by omission.

I may have been limited in my movements since I basically ended up joined at the hip with Mitch—quite literally so last night—but I know behind the scenes my team has been gathering information on all the players in this investigation any way they could.

That's why it was imperative to get Pearl access to Kendrick's computer. I wasn't blowing smoke when I argued she'd know what to look for.

"You take a shower first," Mitch says when we walk into the hotel suite. "I'll check emails and then my computer is all yours."

"Thanks," I mumble as I move by him into his bedroom.

Grabbing a clean pair of jeans, socks, a sweater, and my last clean set of underwear, I dart into the adjoining bathroom, immediately turning on the shower.

Covered by the noise of the water, I quickly dial Raj, who I wasn't able to catch alone leaving the FBI offices in Lexington.

"Any word from Janey?" is the first question out of my mouth.

"Nope. Jacob says they probably made her leave her cell phone with security."

"Damn. Wish I could get a hold of her."

"I'll shoot you a text if I hear anything."

"Thanks. Any progress with Kaylie today?" I ask, changing the subject.

"She's cagey," Raj admits. "I get the sense that incident outside the library scared her. When I asked who had hurt her friend, she wouldn't say, but she eventually shared Melissa told her she was getting some help to take care of it. Kaylie didn't know what that meant and Melissa didn't elaborate."

Who would she have been getting help from?

An idea occurs to me, although it's little more than a shot in the dark. The timing fits, however.

Time for me to do a little digging, but maybe I'll pass on using Mitch's laptop. Not sure how far I can get with the browser on my phone, but I can see what a simple search turns up.

"Keep at it. I've got something I want to look into that may turn out to be helpful, but it's a long shot. I'll let you know."

I set a speed record for my shower and quickly vacate the bathroom so Mitch can get his. The moment the door closes behind him, I open the browser on my phone and type in; Lee Remington, journalist.

Oh, wow.

That generated more hits than I expected. Apparently, the guy has written quite a bit, his articles showing up in a large variety of newspapers and other publications. Most of them either social interest pieces or investigative stories.

I scan through all the articles, finding more than a few of his articles deal with things relating to disenfranchised or troubled youth. Drug use, street kids, crimes against and by children, and also sexual exploitation. The articles go back a good twenty years, and when I'm scanning down the third page of links, I spot it.

A social interest article published the end of last year in *The Woodford Star*, a small newspaper located in Versailles, Kentucky, and covering Woodford County. It wouldn't have a huge reach, which is probably why I had to scroll down this far.

The title caught my interest.

Lanark Opens a New Center: A Safe Haven for Youth or the Echo of a Dark Past?

Mitch

The scent of her shampoo still hangs in the air when I step out of the shower.

Tantalizing, like the woman herself.

I noticed her withdrawing a bit on our drive back here. The conversation was limited to the investigation without any personal references.

Mind you, I wasn't exactly turning on the charm myself. I was still processing the influx of information we received at the briefing, but none of it gives us a direct lead to where these kids may be. I understand the need to separate the investigation into two tiers, but it does mean waiting for the other guys to come up with something we can follow up on. That part is frustrating.

As I towel off, I wonder who I heard Kate calling earlier.

In an unguarded moment I'd found my way into the bedroom, entertaining thoughts of joining her in the shower. But when I got close to the bathroom door, I could hear her talking. Couldn't quite make out what she was saying and I felt a bit like a dirty stalker standing there with my ear pressed against the door, so I ended up backing out.

Moving into the bedroom, I quickly get dressed, except for my boots, I left those in the other room. Kate doesn't notice me when I walk in and I'm surprised to see she's not on my computer but sitting on the couch, her back to me, intently reading something on the small screen of her phone. I walk up behind her and catch a glimpse of what looks like a newspaper article.

"Do we have anything new?"

She almost launches off her seat and swings around, her phone pressed against her chest.

"Sorry, didn't mean to startle you," I tell her, holding up my hands in a gesture of peace.

"It's...I didn't hear you come in."

I wonder what she was looking at. She actually looks a bit guilty, and it makes me wonder if she wasn't using my computer because she didn't want me to see.

"Anything I should know about?" I prompt her, raising an eyebrow.

I watch her chest rise as she takes in a deep breath, fills her cheeks, and blows the air out all at once.

"Fine."

She hands me her phone and I scroll to the top of the article, noticing the title before I see the byline: Lee Remington. I glance up at Kate who now wears a stubborn expression, emphasized by the arms she folds in front of her.

"Why were you looking into Remington? Didn't Walker say he'd take care of that?"

She juts her chin out before she answers.

"I had a hunch."

"A hunch," I echo.

"Yes. It looks like Melissa had someone she thought might be able to help her. She mentioned as much to Kaylie, but never mentioned a name."

"Not sure how this lands us with Remington, but I'm waiting with bated breath."

There's an edge to my tone which is impossible to miss. Too damn bad, I'm annoyed. For no other reason than Kate clearly doesn't trust me. Hell, she hid in the bathroom to call her team when I've made an effort to include her in every aspect of our investigation.

I wish she would've given me the same credit.

"I knew you'd be pissed."

"Damn right I am," I confirm. "Not a fan of discovering you're trying to keep me out of the loop. So much for trust."

She shakes her head. "That's not it. You guys work

according to a set protocol, within distinct parameters. We're more...flexible in our approach."

"Flexible," I find myself echoing again.

"Yes. If I'd waited for Walker, I wouldn't know Melissa knew Lee Remington."

That piques my interest. I've only read the headline so far but find myself scanning the rest of the article. Four paragraphs down I find it.

One such example is M.R.; a mouthy, street-smart fourteen-year-old, whose mother is more concerned with her next hit than her daughter's whereabouts, and whose father is unknown. By her own admission, the new center spared her from sliding down that dark path to addiction herself. With other kids like her—from broken and neglectful homes, or in some cases home-less—friendships were easier to forge which, added to the daily meals the center offers and the counseling it provides, went a long way to make life a little more hopeful for M.R.

I lower her phone and look up.

"You think he was the one she turned to."

"It makes sense. He would've had to build some kind of rapport with her to get her to let him interview her. If she was being harmed at the center, who better to turn to than the same reporter whose article questions whether the center is a safe haven or an echo of a darker past. He's referring to Transition House. He must know something."

I take a minute to consider what she's implying. Remington knew what happened at Transition House?

"How would he know?"

"I have no idea. I don't remember his name from back then, and to be honest, I'm less concerned with that than I am with Melissa's whereabouts right now. We need to find Lee Remington."

I fish my cell phone out of my pocket, ready to call Matt, when Kate's hand shoots out, covering mine. When I look up, her eyes are pleading with me.

"It's a good lead. One that might help us find Melissa, who in turn might be able to help us find the others. Go in flexing our muscles and she may clam up. Kids like that don't trust authority, and often with good reason. I don't want her to clam up on us."

"So, what are you suggesting?"

She lets go of my hand and walks over to the table where I left my laptop open, and sits down in front of it.

"I'm suggesting we keep this between us for a few hours, try to find Remington and, hopefully, the girl ourselves," she says, already pounding away at my keyboard. "I want a chance to talk to her before your agency takes over."

I appreciate her honesty.

"Is that a fact?"

She hums, not even looking at me, she's too focused on the screen.

"What if you can't locate Remington? Or if the girl isn't with him?"

She looks at me over her shoulder.

"In that case: no harm, no foul."

A chuckle escapes me.

She's a bit of a ballbuster, and I'm surprised to find I don't mind it in the least.

SEVENTEEN

MITCH

"Is that him?"

Matt leans over my shoulder to see the photograph on the screen.

Lee Remington is a tall, Black man with short-cropped hair. According to his records he is forty-five, but he doesn't look it.

It wasn't easy finding this shot of him. The man is little more than a name, despite netting the byline on articles in a substantial number of big and not so big publications nationwide. He clearly doesn't like the spotlight for himself.

The picture was taken at an awards ceremony for some kind of social justice journalism award. Remington had been a nominee.

Matt, Joe, and Adam walked in twenty minutes ago to Kate's annoyance. I'm sure if I hadn't confronted her, she would've gone after the journalist herself. It's becoming obvious she's not a fan of red tape. However, what she doesn't realize is our team's main objective will always be finding the children. In that, we're no different than GEM.

Since we're all impatiently waiting for useful information to come out of the various searches over the past twenty-four hours, the guys were happy to have something to dig their teeth into.

Everyone is either on their laptop or phone. Kate, who took hers into the bedroom a few minutes ago to give Jacob an update, comes walking out.

"I have an address," she announces, adding, "In Lexington. And a phone number. Courtesy of Jacob."

"Good," I answer her. "And I found a picture of the guy."

Kate rushes over and Matt makes room for her as she leans over my shoulder, her fantastic tits brushing against me.

I haven't touched her since earlier today, our interactions nothing but professional since we rolled out of bed this morning. Still, my body doesn't make any distinction at her inadvertent brush against my shoulder. It responds with the same heat and passion as this woman invoked last night.

I shift slightly in my seat, trying to create a little separation before I make a fool of myself in front of the guys. I'll never live it down.

"Can you send that to my phone?" Kate asks, backing away.

"Sure. I'll send it to everyone," I tell my team.

"What's the next step?" Adam wants to know.

"I think we should—"

"Call the—"

Matt and Kate speak at the same time.

"I'm sorry," Kate mumbles. "Go ahead."

"I was going to suggest calling the guy rather than trying to chase him down." He glances at her. "I see you're not on board."

"No," she says, pulling her shoulders back. "I'd rather catch him off-guard. If we're working on the assumption he at least knows where the girl is, we don't want to give him the opportunity to warn her or disappear from sight himself."

"See, I don't get that," Adam interjects. "Working from your assumption, why not go to the authorities? I get the girl may be jumpy, but you'd think this Remington guy would welcome our involvement."

"Then why hasn't he contacted law enforcement already?" Kate counters, not about to back down.

She doesn't really look the part, but this woman is a force to be reckoned with.

"There's a reason he's been asking questions," she continues. "We just don't know what it is. Hell, at this point assumptions are all we have, which is exactly why we should be more cautious in our approach."

I watch as my teammates study her while contemplating her point. Again, it's a valid one, proving once again the woman they officially know as Opal is much more than she appears. Something I'm already well aware of.

"Fair enough," Matt concedes. "We'll do it your way. This address you have, is it an office or a home address?"

"Home address. He doesn't have an office to our knowledge. No permanent affiliation with any publication."

"Makes sense," I volunteer. "Being freelance, I imagine he'd likely work from home. Here," I address Kate. "Sit down and pull it up on the screen. We can check satellite and street view to get an idea of the layout."

She takes my place at the table and types in an address I recognize as Joyland, an area in Lexington just north of I-75 which once housed a well-known amusement park by the same name. It's a similar neighborhood to the one I ended up in Richmond, with mostly one-story houses, but they were built a lot longer ago, after the park was torn down in 1965. I actually checked out a place there when I was looking, but being much older, it needed a bit too much work. From what I recall, the lots are fairly big, and parts of the neighborhood have a rural feel because of the proximity of farm fields to the north and east.

"Not an easy surveillance," Adam, who joined us behind Kate, points out.

He's right. It isn't. The house Kate zoomed in on is a typical neighborhood bungalow, with attached garage, set back from the street, with a decent-sized front and back yard bordering a farm field in the rear.

"Won't have a lot of coverage," I note.

"Works in our favor too," Kate pipes up. "No way anyone could take off without being seen."

"So what's the plan?" I ask her.

"Simple. We wait until your team has eyes on the rear, then drive by, and if we see his vehicle in his driveway I walk up to the door and knock."

"You?"

She twists her head around and glances up at me, her eyes sparkling.

"Fine...*we*, but at least let me lead the way. I'm less threatening."

"You think I'm threatening?"

She smirks. "Have you seen that scowl you wear?"

I don't scowl. I look serious, we're in a serious line of work.

"She's got you there, buddy."

Joe, who's been quiet this whole time, chooses now to speak up. I send a glare his way.

"See? There it is," he confirms, pointing at my face.

Matt decides to get this conversation back on track.

"We'll take two vehicles. Opal and Mitch in one, Adam and Joe, you're with me."

Everyone jumps into action. The guys head downstairs to pull some surveillance gear together. Kate is out of her chair and disappears into the bedroom, presumably to grab her coat. Mine is hanging on the back of the chair she just vacated and I shrug it on.

"I never had a chance to say anything earlier," Matt starts, a smirk on his face which has me brace for what's coming. "But I hope I didn't interrupt anything when I called this morning."

"Don't know what you're talking about."

I refuse to look at him and concentrate on zipping up my coat. His chuckle grates on my nerves.

"This is me you're talking to," he says. "I recognized that loose-limbed gait of a man well-fucked."

"Bite me, Driver," I grumble.

"Nah, I'll leave that to someone more qualified."

"I'm good to go," Kate announces as she reappears.

That bastard is still chuckling when we take the elevator down.

Opal

We're parked around the corner from Remington's address.

We noted his black Toyota Highlander parked in the driveway so drove out of sight to give the rest of the team a chance to get in position.

I'm edgy, I badly want my hunch to be true, that Melissa sought out the reporter for help, but doubt is starting to set in. These agents decided to indulge me, but if it turns out I was wrong, I would've taken away valuable time they should've spent looking for these kids.

"Stop fidgeting," Mitch grumbles beside me. "Even if

the girl isn't there, we can still gain a lot from talking to Remington."

His hand goes to his earpiece, pressing on it with his middle finger.

"Ten-four."

Then he puts the car in drive and turns his eyes on me.

"Time to roll."

Too late for second thoughts now. I force my nerves into submission and by the time Mitch pulls his vehicle in behind the Toyota—effectively blocking him in—I feel confidence return.

We don't speak as we walk up to the front door, but I see Mitch notice the blinds moving in one of the smaller front windows. The door opens before we have a chance to knock, revealing the man I recognize from his picture.

"Lee Remington? My name is Opal Berry. I'm—"

"Feds," he interrupts, glancing at Mitch.

"Actually, I'm not a federal agent, Mr. Remington," I correct him. "Agent Kenny is, he works for CARD, which I'm sure you're familiar with. I, however, work for GEM, an organization—"

"I know about GEM," he interrupts again.

It's starting to annoy me and, if not for the sudden pressure of Mitch's hand in the small of my back, I would've let him know that in no uncertain words.

I'm here for a purpose.

"Exactly. I'm hoping you might be able to help us."

He folds his arms over his chest and looks down his nose at me.

"And how is that?"

"We are investigating the disappearance of a number of children who frequently attended The Youth Center. You wrote an interesting article on the center last year."

He doesn't give an inch, simply standing there like an unmoving object, an impassive expression on his face.

"In your article you talk about who we believe to be one of the missing children, Melissa Romero."

There is no reaction to the name whatsoever, which makes him even more suspect.

"Do you remember her, Mr. Remington?" I ask him directly.

"Vaguely."

He shrugs as he lies through his teeth, but his head snaps around when he appears to hear something behind him.

"Is she here?"

"Why the hell would she be here?"

His reaction is immediate and betrays an emotion he's been doing his best to hide, as he whips back to me, his eyes blazing.

He'd be a striking man if he wasn't so unpleasant.

"Because, Mr. Remington, I spoke with a friend of hers at the center, who indicated Melissa might have been in trouble and was turning to someone who could help."

He snorts derisively, sliding effortlessly back into his impassive persona.

"You're barking up the wrong tree, *Ms. Berry*," he mocks.

"Am I? You seem to have an interest in the goings on

at The Youth Center. You showed up at the house of the center's director and was asked to leave by law enforcement. And finally, you knocked on the door of the ex-wife of a well-known sportscaster and former athlete, whose name has been connected to the center and Mason Kramer, the man running it."

My mention of Cassandra Hogan seems to evoke surprise. He clearly wasn't expecting that. I decide to push my luck.

"Mr. Remington...Lee," I correct myself. "Whatever your motivations are to look into what is going on at the center, we are on the same side. We want these kids found and to stop what we've begun to uncover is happening at the center."

He doesn't look convinced, so I throw out my ace in the hole. My Hail Mary.

"I was fourteen when I was placed at Transition House and spent the next four years there. I'm guessing from the article you wrote; you are aware of what happened there."

For the first time, I read a hint of sympathy in his eyes.

"Those were supposed to have been rumors," he says, confirming my assumption.

"But we both know they weren't. I know because I lived through it, but I'm not sure how you know."

His shoulders suddenly slump and he drops his head. The pose gives off an air of resignation, and I wonder if I managed to break through.

"My mother was a member of the custodial staff at Transition House," he clarifies, glancing up at me. "She saw things. Heard things. Tried to talk to law enforcement." A dark glare is aimed at Mitch beside me. "No one would listen. She died in a single vehicle car crash shortly after, and two weeks later the place burned to the ground."

"And you think..." Mitch speaks for the first time.

"I *know*," Remington growls. "I saw the car. The front of the new white Honda she saved up to buy for years had been wrapped around a tree at the side of the road. You tell me why then her bumper was half torn off the back and blue paint was visible in a scratch as long as my arm running along the rear fender on the same side. Local cops wrote it off as damage done in the accident."

"You don't trust law enforcement."

"I don't trust anyone in positions of power," he corrects me.

"For what it's worth," Mitch says. "I may fall under that nomer, but like you, I have personal reasons driving me to do this work. Valerie, my younger sister, was the victim of a sexual predator."

Remington stares at Mitch for a beat before shaking his head. Then he steps back and to the side, motioning us inside.

"Give me a minute."

He disappears down a set of stairs in the kitchen, and a few minutes later leads a scared-looking Melissa Romero into the living room.

I walk up to her and take her hands in mine.

"You don't know me, but I'm so relieved to see you. I've been looking for you."

"You have?"

She seems surprised and it breaks my heart.

I sit down on the edge of the couch, pulling her down beside me. From the corner of my eye, I see Lee Remington motion for Mitch to follow him down the hallway off the living room, but I make sure to keep my focus on the girl.

"For you, Chantel, Jesper, Bryonne, Jamie, and Bobby-Jean."

Tears glisten in the pretty girl's eyes.

"I didn't believe her at first," she mumbles.

"Believe who?" I prompt her.

"Bobby-Jean. She warned me, before she disappeared, but he'd been so nice to me. He said I was pretty enough to get a job modeling. Said he could help me earn my own money, maybe even get a place of my own."

Rather than ask for clarification, I let her talk. I'm pretty sure she's referring to Kendrick, or Kramer, as she knows him.

"He took my picture, said he wanted to show it to a friend of his who had connections. Took me to see him, but..."

I squeeze her hand. This story is painfully familiar.

"He wasn't interested in taking your pictures," I fill in for her.

She shakes her head, her eyes downcast.

"The friend he took you to see? Had you seen him before?"

"At the center. I was so stupid."

I reach out with a hand to lift her chin so she has to look at me.

"Not stupid. You hoped, that's never stupid. You hold no responsibility in what happened to you, it's all on them. People prey on those of us who dare to hope for a better future, who are full of life and promise."

Her eyes slide to the side and I give her chin a little shake.

"Look at me, Melissa. Don't let them steal that life, that promise. Don't give them that power. It happened to you and nothing will change that, but it doesn't have to define you."

Her deep brown eyes stare into mine, perhaps recognizing a kindred soul. When I give her a little nod, she hesitates only for a moment before she nods back.

The clearing of a throat has me turn my head, to find Mitch and the other man standing in the doorway.

Both sets of eyes are on me.

EIGHTEEN

MITCH

I glance over at Kate, who is sitting ramrod straight beside me. The knuckles on her hands are white as she clasps them on her lap.

Her expression doesn't betray a thing, but I know the last hour and a half took its toll on her. It had to have. Hell, it impacted me. I had a hard time keeping my composure when all I wanted to do is let go of the rage and put my fist through something.

Lee Remington had briefly taken me aside while Kate talked with the girl. He wanted to feel me out, see how much we knew, but first he wanted an assurance from me we'd keep any information he or Melissa shared close to the chest for now. Given what he told us about his mother, I understood his mistrust.

Then, he added a warning that this sex ring involves

some very influential people with a long reach—something we already suspected—and we'd not only be risking his life and Melissa's, but the lives of the missing kids as well.

To show my goodwill, I shared the latest about Krebs, which has not yet been made public. He'd been shocked, but not exactly heartbroken when I told him we found the man dead.

Not really my place to give that information, especially with a journalist, but if I wanted him to share what he knows, I had to give him something in return.

I also shot Matt a text, telling him I had things under control and would catch up with him later. Last thing I wanted was for my team to come looking for us and freak Remington and the girl out.

Darkness has already set in, and I realize we've been on the go the entire day. More importantly, we haven't eaten a bite since that measly granola bar this morning. I need some fuel.

"Hungry?" I ask, my eyes peeled for a sign for some restaurant we can stop at.

"Not really," is Kate's muted response. "I need to talk to my team."

I understand why, given what we learned from Melissa, but especially Lee. The man had some serious suspicions that sounded valid but were lacking hard evidence. We had some digging to do and it would probably be better for GEM to tackle that task. Running it through the task force would require following official channels which—if Lee is right—could catch unwanted attention. We need to be cautious.

"You have to eat. *We* have to eat."

"Fine, but let's make it quick."

Quick turns out to be burritos at a Mexican restaurant a little down the road. While we wait for our dinner, Kate is sipping her sweet tea, while I toss half my Corona back. It's already past eight and it looks like the dinner rush is over, which hopefully means we don't have to wait long.

"What are you thinking?" I ask her, setting my bottle down.

My question is purposely nonspecific.

I don't like the walls I could feel going up all day, but more so these past few hours. I'm guessing it's probably her ingrained self-preservation to be guarded, but I don't like being on the other side of the barriers she's throwing up.

My hope is she won't feel pressured and maybe is willing to open up a little.

She gives me a glimpse at her gray eyes, which betray some of her inner turmoil.

"I'm just trying to catch my breath," she says.

I give a nod, keeping my mouth shut. Silence is a simple but effective technique to get someone to talk and at the top of the list for a successful interview or interrogation. Not that this is either, but the objective is the same.

"I hope she can get over the guilt," she finally caves.

She's referring to Melissa, who was devastated to find out Georgia Braxton lost her life.

She brought the other girl up, asking if we knew how she was. When Kate gently filled her in, we discovered Lee had kept the news of Georgia's death from her. That fact is public knowledge by now, although the manner of death had been listed as an 'unfortunate incident' at the behest of the chief of police. The reporter had obviously put two and two together and guessed how that news might impact Melissa.

When asked what made her worried about Georgia specifically, she admitted she hadn't been the only girl the director took to what we now know was Krebs's place in the hills outside Irvine. As it turns out, Georgia had been there as well.

We'd assumed Krebs had been the one interested in Melissa, but that wasn't the case. According to the girl, Georgia had been the focus for Krebs, but the 'friend' Kendrick had mentioned to Melissa had been another man. Someone she'd recognized visiting the center a month or so prior.

She mentioned trying to approach Georgia about what happened after, but the other girl didn't want to talk and ended up avoiding Melissa altogether.

It had been torture trying to listen to her account of events while keeping a straight face. Especially when she recounted how the man had threatened her when she put up a fight, told her he'd know if she talked because he had friends in law enforcement.

It went a long way to explain why Melissa opted to seek help from the journalist instead of going to authorities.

When prompted to describe the man, she'd become

distraught. The agent in me wanted to press on, maybe show her pictures of some of the folks we already know are associated with Kendrick. However, the father in me —who could too easily imagine his own daughter sitting across from him—decided Melissa had been traumatized enough for today.

Maybe I could've suggested to her it wasn't her actions that caused Georgia to be killed, but more likely the news the missing girl was related to Dennis Furmont. It's not too far-fetched to think Krebs panicked realizing the Lanark police chief himself would be looking for the girl he was by then holding prisoner at his vacation home. But I don't think she would've heard me at the time.

Perhaps there will be a better moment—when she's not quite so traumatized—sharing that information is helpful to her.

"The truth will help. Exposing these sick bastards too. As will finding the other kids," I suggest, reaching for Kate's hand across the table. "And just maybe it'll provide a modicum of closure for you too."

Her eyes are down, but at least she doesn't pull away from my hold on her hand.

"I thought it was over when that place burned down," she scoffs. "Imagine my shock when I discovered it wasn't. Not by a long shot."

With only a few words, she offers me a glimpse at something I hadn't stopped to consider. How difficult and traumatic this investigation must be on her. Yet she never lost her composure, never lost her focus, which has stayed firmly on the recovery of those children.

Another testament to the woman's strength and tenacity.

Before I can tell her as much, the server is back at our table with our dinner.

Opal

"Pumpkin, I need you to listen to me."

I'd be lying if I said the nickname he has for his daughter doesn't make me feel a little mushy inside. I hope his girl knows how lucky she is to be loved like that.

The only nickname I remember having was crybaby. My grandmother called me that when she took me in after the house fire. I was eight and dragged from our home by a neighbor who had seen the flames. Sadly, it spread so fast he wasn't able to go back for my brother and my parents.

I think my grandmother always blamed me for having survived when my dad—her only child—didn't. She certainly made me feel it the two years I lived with her before she died.

For four years after, I bounced around the foster system, which didn't exactly make me feel loved, and at fourteen I was finally placed at Transition House.

Oddly enough, as much as it was the worst time of my

life, it also ended up being the best. It's where I met Janey and Raj, who became like family to me.

I listen to Mitch's conversation with half an ear while I type out an accounting of the interview with Melissa, while it's fresh on my mind, at Jacob's request.

We ended up back at Mitch's place in Richmond, by my suggestion. He didn't object and simply contacted Matt to let him know where we'd be, and we'd catch up with the rest of the CARD team in the morning.

He didn't even ask for an explanation, but seemed to instinctively understand I needed a little more time to fit myself back into my professional persona, Opal Berry.

Right now, I'm all Kate Jones, which makes me far too vulnerable.

I'm working on Mitch's computer when I hear him curse under his breath behind me. I swivel around to find him with his hands folded on top of his head.

"Problem?"

He barks out a laugh that doesn't exactly sound happy.

"Yes," he confirms, turning his eyes to me. "Her name is Sawyer."

"I'm sorry."

I smile at him sympathetically.

"Oh, you will be," he cautions. "She's probably on her way here."

A sudden rush of anxiety has me out of my chair in a hurry.

"What? Now?"

"What can I say? She's stubborn. I shouldn't have told

her I was home. I tried to tell her now wasn't a good time, but it's doubtful she listened."

Of course he wouldn't want his daughter to see me here. God, how embarrassing. We should've just gone back to the hotel.

While I'm having a panic attack, Mitch walks into the kitchen, casual as can be, and grabs a beer from the fridge. He holds it up to me by way of an offer. Still half in shock, I shake my head.

"Something else? I think I have a bottle of wine somewhere, or I can make you some tea?"

"I'm...I think I should go."

Fuck. I don't have a vehicle.

I'm already heading for the door, grabbing my coat off the hook, when Mitch catches up with me. Firm arms wrap around me from behind as his breath brushes my ear.

"What are you doing?"

"I have to go."

"How?"

I twist around in his hold and glare at him.

"I know how to call a taxi," I snap ungraciously, before moderating my tone and adding, "It makes sense for me to be with my team anyway. I have a perfectly good room waiting for me at the Airbnb."

He drops his arms, and for a moment it looks like he'll let me go. But before I can shove my arm in a sleeve of my coat, his hands are cradling my face and his mouth is hot on mine.

The kiss is brief and hard, almost punishing, but

when he lets me up for air, his eyes are warm and his voice soft.

And my resolve melts at his words.

"What if I don't want you to go?"

Then he kisses me again.

This round is sweet and seductive, but quickly heats up. In no time at all I'm pressed up against him, my hands curved around his neck, and I've completely forgotten why I was heading for the door to begin with.

My coat is on the floor at my feet and when Mitch turns me up against the wall, and if we hadn't been clinging on to each other—almost desperately—I would've tripped.

Unfortunately, as Mitch deftly works his way up on the buttons of my shirt, the door flies open, followed immediately by a loud crash and a loud curse in a young woman's voice.

Shit.

"Dammit, Sawyer," Mitch grumbles as he disentangles from me and bends over to haul the dark-haired girl, sprawled on the foyer floor, to her feet. "When are you going to stop barreling in here like a herd of buffalo? Look where you put your feet."

I'm still fumbling to rebutton my shirt when I hear the girl respond.

"Well, sue me for not expecting someone stripping right inside my front door."

My hands freeze and I peek up, catching a flash of angry hazel eyes. The same color as her father's.

In fact, the girl is a clone of her father, except more delicate and less hairy. She's also a lot less welcoming.

"Behave, Sawyer," Mitch growls at his daughter. "This is Opal. She's a friend. We also work together," he adds.

The girl's expression turns from pissed to incredulous as she takes me in, head to toe, before turning back to her father.

"Sure doesn't look like any FBI agent I've ever met."

"That's enough!" Mitch barks.

Okay, this is getting really uncomfortable.

I bend down to grab my coat so I can slip out the door while these two have it out, but once again I'm stopped before I can get an arm in when it's ripped right from my hold.

With my coat in one hand and his other hand curved firmly around his daughter's neck, he marches both of us into the living room.

"If you can't behave like the grown-up you tell me you want me to treat you as, why don't you tell me what was so fucking important it couldn't wait?"

Then he releases his daughter, tosses my coat on the couch, and stalks into the kitchen where he snatches his beer from the counter, pops off the cap on the edge, and takes a deep draw from the bottle. The girl is watching him with her fists planted on her hips.

I use the moment to ease into the living room, aiming for my discarded coat.

"Don't even think about it!"

My head snaps up and I find him glaring at me over his daughter's shoulder.

He doesn't just sound angry, he looks it as well.

Too bad he's directing it at the wrong person.

"Excuse me?"

My own anger has the pitch of my voice go right up the scale.

Our eyes throw daggers across the room and a different kind of heat builds between us as his daughter stands between us, almost forgotten.

A sniffle fills the loaded silence as suddenly the girl's shoulders slump, changing her posture from defiant to defeated.

Her voice sounds brittle when she speaks.

"I wanted to see you. You haven't been around for three weeks. I missed you."

The last is said on a sob as she turns on her heel. With her eyes down, she heads for the front door, mumbling "Sorry," to me in passing.

Such a contrast to the angry teen only moments ago, my heart breaks a little.

"Fuck! Pumpkin, wait up!" Mitch yells after her, but she's already out the door as he chases after her.

Curious, I peek out the front window to see him catch up to her at the sidewalk where a little red car is parked along the curb. There's no one behind the wheel.

I watch him swing her around, wrapping her in a bear hug.

By the time he comes back inside, I'm back at the computer finishing the report for my team. He's alone.

"Where's your daughter?"

He stops beside me.

"On her way home."

"Didn't you tell me she's sixteen?"

You may be able to drive at sixteen in Kentucky, but only with a fully licensed person, twenty-one or older, in the passenger seat beside you. It didn't look like there was anyone waiting in the car for her.

He rubs the back of his neck and looks a little guilty.

"She is. Her mom and stepdad let her drive alone, and I didn't feel like getting into yet another argument. There's been too many of those as it is."

It's clearly a sensitive subject so I decide to drop it. Not really my business anyway.

"Is she okay?" I ask instead.

"She is after I gave her the hug she needed and explained I would've like to have been the one to decide when and how she meets the woman I'm seeing."

Oh. Wow.

I'm not sure what to take away from that but my stomach is in knots.

Especially since his expression is stern and his eyes intense on me, but this time I'm not so sure it's from anger.

"You almost done?" he bites off.

"I just need to email this."

"Do it."

My hands are shaking a little as I type in Jacob's email address, which only gets worse when Mitch closes in on me. I have to correct a typo first, then I attach the file, and the moment I hit send, he reaches out, snags my hand, and pulls me up from the chair.

The next thing I know, I'm dragged down the hallway to his bedroom where he kicks shut the door.

As his mouth descends on mine and his hand shoves down the back of my jeans, grabbing on to my ass, he mutters.

"God, woman. How you stir my blood."

NINETEEN

MITCH

"Will you tell me about your sister?"

This time it hadn't been the phone waking me before the sun had a chance to rise, but a hot, wet pair of lips, wrapped around my cock.

I can't remember the last time I had a wake-up call like that, probably sometime at the onset of my marriage to Becky, since I made it a rule after my marriage disintegrated to make sure I'd wake up alone in my bed. Mostly because my job is unpredictable—I could get called to a new case any time of day or night—and it was simply easier not to have to explain.

With Kate it's different. She already understands what's at stake. Hell, we're in the same boat; she faces the same challenges.

But that's not the only reason.

For the first time, I feel like I've met my equal on every level. She not only approaches her job with the same depth of passion, but has a mind that never stops working, and she matches me pace for pace in the bedroom. As evidenced by the spectacular sex, which left us both boneless last night, and again by that gorgeous mouth sucking me dry minutes ago.

It doesn't hurt Kate is a beautiful woman, lush from her hair to the tips of her dainty toes.

All of those things combined compel me to open up a painful wound which never quite closed.

Her head is on my shoulder—a few strands of her hair tickling my cheek—and her body is half-draped over mine.

I stroke my hand from the small of her back over the pronounced curve of her ass.

"Valerie was six years younger. She was one of those rare people everyone seemed drawn to. Everyone was her friend and she was absolutely the center of our family."

I take in a deep breath, emotion starting to clog my throat when I realize how long it's been since I allowed myself to remember the person she'd been before.

Kate's fingers skate over my chest, prompting me to continue.

"MSN Messenger was in its heyday back then, before social media became a breeding ground for predators. Valerie told my parents she was meeting up with a friend and they assumed she meant one of her school friends."

I need another deep breath to get through the toughest part.

"I was enrolled at Penn State at the time. My father called after she hadn't come home the night before. He had her for almost two weeks in a cabin in the mountains of West Virginia, and despite her injuries, she managed to capitalize on a moment when that fucking sonofabitch was distracted. She spent two days hiding in the woods when a motorist spotted her naked body lying on the side of a mountain road."

"I'm so sorry," Kate mumbles, her lips brushing my skin.

"She survived the ordeal but was never the same. She became obsessed, making sure no other girl would have to go through what was done to her. She was like a robot when she testified at his trial. Her testimony was the nail in his coffin.

"Then, less than two weeks after his conviction, my mother went into the garage and found her body. She'd hanged herself from the rafters in the garage."

Her softly mumbled, "Jesus," and the way her body presses closer is surprisingly comforting.

If anyone gets it, it's this woman, having gone through a similar ordeal herself around that age. I briefly consider asking her about her experience, but decide against it. I don't need to know details; I have a good idea already.

This isn't a tit-for-tat situation, talking about Valerie isn't the same as asking her to relive her trauma. My sister was forced to relive every detail during her testimony and it ultimately broke her spirit. There was nothing I could do.

So, no, I don't want to be responsible for doing damage to Kate's strong and extraordinary essence.

I wrap my arms tighter around her and, for a moment, let myself imagine waking up with her like this every morning. Then I press a kiss on the top of her head.

"I'm going to put on some coffee. Feel free to use the shower, clean towels in the closet in the hallway."

I release her and she rolls over on her back, but when I swing my legs out of bed, I feel her sit up behind me. Her arms snake around my waist and her lips press against my shoulder.

"Are you all right?" she asks.

I twist to cup her face with my hand.

"I am. Surprisingly." I smile at her, brushing the pad of my thumb over her soft cheek. "I haven't talked about her in a long time. It reminded me of something I overheard you tell Melissa yesterday. That what happened to her doesn't have to define her. I only just realized what happened to Valerie shouldn't define her either. I can choose to remember the bright, loving girl she was before."

She nods, her eyes shining as she smiles back.

I drop a featherlight kiss on her lips.

"Better get your ass in the shower or I'm gonna beat you to it."

I get up, pull on a pair of track pants I grab from my dresser, and am on my way out the door when she calls my name.

"One day, when this is over, I may tell you my story."

I smile at her. It doesn't escape me she's implying the possibility of a future, and that pleases me to no end.

"But for now..."

She pauses briefly before she continues.

"My full name is Katherine Faith Jones."

"THAT WAS PEARL. THEY FOUND MY TRUCK."

Judging from the look on her face as she sits back down, this somehow isn't good news.

We stopped at the IHOP by the on-ramp to the I-75 for a quick bite. Fuel for what would surely be another busy day. The plan is to head back to Lanark to share what we learned last night with the team and follow up on some of that information. In particular, the reference Melissa made to law enforcement. That may require some finesse.

We'd barely had a chance to place our order when Kate's phone rang and she stepped out to take the call.

"Where?"

"In the ditch on a back road not too far from the equestrian center off of the Bluegrass Parkway," she replies solemnly.

"The one south of Versailles?"

She confirms with a nod.

"Pretty much totaled, from what I hear."

Her phone pings a few times in rapid succession, announcing incoming messages.

"Pearl, sending pictures."

I glance across the table as she opens the files and swears softly.

"Can I see?"

The vehicle looks like someone took a sledge hammer to it. Someone very pissed. It looks personal.

"At least my gun safe survived," she comments, pointing at an image of the truck's interior.

The safe looks to be bolted into the floor behind the front seat and although dented, the lid still appears firmly closed.

"Did she tell you where the truck was taken?"

"State police towed it."

"They have a small impound lot on the south side of Lexington, not far from the highway. We can swing by on our way through."

She nods and takes a sip of her coffee as she stares off in the distance.

"Did Pearl have anything else, anything new to report? Is she still in Louisville?"

Her eyes snap back to me and she almost looks guilty. I wonder what that is about.

"Yes, sorry. Onyx had a breakthrough with Kaylie last night after sharing with her Melissa is safe. She'd been freaked out when you showed up at the library because she was supposed to meet someone there."

"Who?"

"Paul Krebs."

Another nail in the man's coffin. Too bad he's already dead.

"Maybe he recognized you with Kaylie at the library," I suggest. "Perhaps that's when he contacted Kendrick."

It wouldn't surprise me if it turned out Kate was the target all along, and Krebs was acting on Kendrick's instruction. The man certainly seems to have succeeded in making sure any concrete evidence points squarely at Paul Krebs.

"That's possible," she contemplates. "Although I wasn't wearing my wig. But that might explain how Kendrick figured out it was me."

"Makes sense. Then he had Krebs pick him up behind the strip club and one or both of them broke into your motel room and stole your truck," I surmise.

"That was Kendrick," she states firmly. "You saw the truck, rage did that. It was personal."

I figured as much, which fills me with concern. Kate is a moving target.

"And one more thing," she continues. "Kaylie confirmed Krebs hadn't been the name Melissa gave her or she wouldn't have agreed to meet up with him at the library to interview for a job."

A job, *right*.

"So what name *did* Melissa give her?"

"Doug."

Congressman Melnyk.

Fuck.

So far, we've been focused on Krebs because we haven't come across anything incriminating on any of the other people we've been able to identify.

The shit is definitely going to hit the fan on this one.

"We need to tread lightly."

Matt is preaching to the choir.

I think we all realize the minefield we're about to walk into. Melnyk has deep roots and vast connections in this district.

"This needs to be kept off the books for now."

Jacob Branch's voice is tinny over the speakerphone with a low hum of peripheral noise. He sounds like he's in a vehicle.

"That's what I just said," Matt responds with a bite.

The already tense atmosphere in the room just ramped up a bit. Whenever an investigation involves someone who has a lot of pull—like an elected official in an influential position—it puts everyone on edge.

"Not exactly the same," Jacob counters. *"Being careful isn't going to be enough. This information can't go any further than your team or mine."*

"We're gonna need more manpower than that. Heck, we're not going to get very far running on a skeleton crew," Matt points out.

"This hits the wrong ears; we won't be running at all. We'll get shut down before we have a chance to dig up anything."

"You want us to work with our hands tied behind our backs," Joe Lampert pipes up, clearly annoyed.

The other members of my team nod in agreement. They're frustrated. Hell, we're all frustrated, all we have to show for weeks of work are two dead bodies, two terrified teenagers, and a suspect on the run. Not exactly a successful investigation so far.

"And what about the danger it would put Melissa Romero in? Or any of the others still missing?" Kate suggests in support of her boss's point.

It echoes what Remington used as an excuse to keep his cards close to his chest last night. It also makes me wonder what else the GEM crew may have kept quiet on to avoid consequences for the victims.

I'm reminded of our conversation over breakfast. She'd seemed uncomfortable—guilty even—when I asked if there was news from Pearl. I realize she never really answered that question.

"She's right. We need to concentrate on finding something—anything—irrefutably tying him to this case before we can risk calling in the troops."

Kate's comment seems to have put things in perspective for the guys, and Branch hammered it home.

As much as I hate this might put the team—but especially Matt—in the awkward position of basically having to go dark, Branch and Kate are right, it's the only way.

Let's just hope the end justifies the means.

"Where do we start?" Joe asks.

"By doing inventory of what we collectively know about Melnyk so far," I suggest before asking a question. "Branch, is Pearl still in Louisville?"

I keep my eyes focused on Kate and the apology is on her face before Jacob has a chance to answer.

"No. She's back in Lanark, at the Airbnb. She's working on some things."

I'm curious why Kate wouldn't have mentioned that, but I don't want to call her out in front of everyone.

Instead, I ask Chance, "Did she learn anything from Kendrick's computer?"

There's a hefty pause before he answers.

"That's what she's still working on."

It's Matt who reacts first.

"Should I ask how that is possible when the computer is behind lock and key in the FBI tech lab?"

"It wouldn't be wise. Trust me when I say it's better you don't know."

"I don't need to tell you that any evidence obtained by illegal means is evidence we can't fucking use," Matt reminds him tersely.

"That's the part where you have to trust me."

Matt lets loose with a few choice swear words.

Holy shit.

Pearl must've found a way to bypass the lab's security measures. How else would she be working on information contained on that computer?

Now I get why Kate seemed torn.

"Twice now you've mentioned trust," Matt grinds out. "Forgive me if I find that ironic. Trust you when you don't trust us? It's a two-way street, Branch."

"I'm well aware. So consider this, I could've lied to you," Jacob responds. *"Believe me, it would've been prefer-*

able, but I've been as honest with you as I can be, without forcing you into a situation where you'd have to take some kind of action that would effectively make any information Pearl can pull in unusable."

He's making his point clear, and everyone in the room knows it.

TWENTY

*O*PAL

"Who the fuck is Lee Remington?"

I hold up my finger to Mitch and Sally Kendall, and back out into the hallway outside the offices.

"Janey? What's going on?"

Janey and Raj left a few minutes ago to head back to the rental place after spending most of the morning with us, talking to what kids we were able to catch after breakfast. Sadly, we're not much wiser.

The center is still open and operating as normal, despite its director's glaring absence. The only person who seems affected is Sally, who is trying to function as his interim replacement. She looks a little the worse for wear.

Mitch and I stayed behind to question any available staff members again. With their director missing, we're hoping someone with information about him will come forward. Unfortunately, only Brian and Sally were available, and Brian didn't really have much to add, so we'd moved on to Sally.

At this point, we're desperate for any hint as to where Kendrick may be holed up.

"Janey?" I prompt again, hearing her cursing under her breath.

My friend has an explosive temper and it appears something—or maybe I should say, someone—has triggered it.

"A fucking reporter who says his name is Lee Remington cornered us in the parking lot. He looked aggressive so I took him down. Now he's threatening to sue me and claims to know you."

I sent my report in last night and I'm sure I mentioned something to her this morning when she called to tell me about the truck, but apparently it didn't register.

Janey can have tunnel vision to the exclusion of everything else when she's in the zone.

Visions of my friend—a hundred pounds wet, if that—taking down the tall, solid man I talked to just yesterday has me rushing toward the front doors.

"I do know him," I pant, out of breath as I scan the parking lot. "And if you'd read my emails or even just listened to me when we talk, you'd know who he is too."

"Shit."

I notice Raj leaning against the back of her SUV, arms crossed over her chest, and an amused look on her face. It isn't until I get closer and can see between the parked vehicles, I notice Janey.

She's standing over Lee Remington, who is slumped on the ground with his back against the front fender. He's holding a hand over his face and blood seeps through his fingers.

Jesus.

"Couldn't stop her," Raj says with a shrug of her shoulders. "But in her defense, he was holding on to her door."

I know right away what happened. If there was a tug-of-war over the door, Janey wouldn't have had the strength to match, but I'd be willing to bet she used the reporter's own strength against him by abruptly letting go. A fundamental principal of many martial arts. The sudden lack of resistance would've had the door slam into him with the power of his own strength.

This is why—despite her small stature—my friend is a master in martial arts and a force to be reckoned with.

I tuck my phone in my pocket, glaring at Janey, before I crouch down beside Lee. I peel his hand away from his nose, which is flowing like a faucet.

"Friend of yours?" he asks in a grumble.

"Yeah." I pinch his nose and force his head back. "She doesn't like people in her space uninvited."

"No shit."

"Make yourself useful and get me the first aid kit?" I ask Janey.

To Lee I say, "Lee, meet Pearl, and the one laughing over there is Onyx. These are the other members of the GEM team."

"Wonderful."

He darts a glare at Janey when she crouches on his other side and pulls some gauze and scissors out of the kit.

"You broke my nose."

Janey barely appears to register his words as she continues to carefully roll gauze packs for his nostrils without sparing him a glance.

"Technically, you broke your own nose," she says calmly.

"What are you doing here?" I ask Lee, feeling the need to diffuse the situation before it has a chance to escalate.

"Same thing you are," he says defensively. "Looking for answers." Then he turns to Janey, narrowing his eyes. "For a moment I thought you were Melissa's friend, Bobby-Jean."

My friend scoffs.

"Why? Because I'm Asian?"

"No. Because you're tiny, have short black hair, and look like a fucking kid. Although," he adds, "up close I can see you've got a couple of decades on her."

Ouch.

I feel the air crackle with Janey's indignation. Aging is a sensitive reality for her. I swear she was almost in tears the first gray hair she discovered, and Janey hates to show any emotion other than anger. To an outsider, she can come across as hard, but the truth is her curt manner and occasionally fiery temper are her tools of self-protection. It makes her feel strong and in charge, but aging is the one thing she cannot control.

I know his remark hit her true when she lifts her chin

high and looks down her tiny nose at the man, before addressing him in an icy tone.

"That's all right. I initially felt you might pose a threat." She gives him a good once-over before adding with a cool little smile, "I see now my concern was entirely unfounded."

Then she hands me the rolls of makeshift nose packing, gracefully rises to her full length—such as it is—and climbs into the passenger seat.

"Are you dizzy at all?" I ask Lee, who is glaring up at Janey through the window. "Hit your head? Need an ambulance"

"What?" He swings his head around. "No. I'm fine."

"Good. Then let's put these in and get you to your feet. Otherwise, I can't promise she won't make Onyx drive over you."

Mitch is looking for me just as Remington drives away from the center. He insisted on driving himself when I prompted him to get to a clinic to make sure his nose wasn't broken. In all honesty, I think his ego sustained more damage than any other part of him. Our Janey doesn't take prisoners. Her words can be as lethal as her martial arts skills.

"Was that?"

"Lee Remington. Yes. He just met the rest of my team and now he needs medical care."

I don't blame Mitch for looking confused so I quickly explain what happened.

"How did things go with Sally?"

"She's hanging in, but is worried they'll likely have to

shut the doors next week. Bills will need to be paid, suppliers will start cutting them off, and she has no idea how the finances were run."

"Isn't there a board of directors she can contact?"

"There should be, but Sally can't find any information in the office."

"Maybe Russel Germain can help?" I suggest.

We've been so focused on Kendrick, Krebs, and now Melnyk, I'd almost forgotten about the lawyer.

Mitch

"We found Jamie Lyons."

I almost run the car off the road at Phil Dresden's statement and I feel Kate virtually jump beside me.

"Say what?"

"Jamie Lyons. He was arrested last night by the Paducah City Police Department for car theft. Matt is on his way to talk to him. His name was flagged when they entered it into the system."

"Was he alone?"

Kate is leaning over the center console, her eyes big on mine.

"As far as I know he was alone," Phil confirms, adding, "Although, according to the officer the kid wasn't very cooperative."

"He's probably terrified," she mumbles before asking. "How long ago did Matt leave, Phil?"

In my peripheral vision, I catch her pulling out her phone.

"Couple of minutes ago, why?" Dresden wants to know, but Kate is already dialing.

"Probably so she can ask him to pick up Onyx," I guess, earning me a nod and a smile.

It's not like we haven't had some training and plenty of experience interviewing children, but it's possible the kid will respond better to a woman than a man. This way we'd have all our bases covered.

I thank Phil for the heads-up and end the call just as Kate connects with Matt.

By the time I pull up to Germain's law offices—a swanky building in downtown Lexington—Kate has everyone organized.

"Do you think he's been there the whole time? In Paducah?" she asks when I turn off the engine.

I internally smile at her excitement.

"We won't know for a while. The drive to Paducah is around four hours and it's already coming up on two o'clock," I point out, turning toward her.

"I know," she concedes, pressing a hand to her chest. "God, I hope he knows something about the others."

The bleached blonde behind the glass desk makes no effort to hide her disinterest when we walk into the pretentious reception area. It's cold and impersonal, much like the receptionist who seems engrossed in whatever she's doing on her cell phone. She only briefly glances up before dismissing us as not worth her attention.

On the other side of the lobby, two well-dressed men with briefcases at their feet are sitting in a waiting area on an uncomfortable-looking couch.

I ignore them and we make our way over to the desk.

"Excuse me."

"What can I do for you?" she asks without averting her eyes from some kind of TikTok reel playing on her phone.

Fuck, I hate social media, or what passes for it these days. Not a single damn thing social about it.

"Is Russel Germain in?"

This time she puts her phone down and checks something on her computer.

"Do you have an appointment?"

"No."

Then she finally glances up and looks from me to Kate and back.

"In that case, no."

Having had my fill of her attitude, I pull my badge from my pocket and show her.

"Let's try this again." I purposely raise my voice. "Agents Kenny and Berry, FBI. We need to speak to Russel Germain about the murder of—"

"One moment, please," she stops me, shooting to her feet as she grabs for the phone on her desk.

Then she turns her back to us and whispers urgently into the receiver.

A few moments later, we're being led down a long

hallway to a pair of tall black doors at the end. Next to the doors an older woman sits at a workstation, observing us as we approach. She nods curtly and addresses the receptionist.

"I've got it from here, Kimberly," she says, standing up to walk out from behind her desk.

She knocks discreetly on the door before opening it and turns to face us.

"Mr. Germain will see you now."

Just then my phone starts buzzing in my pocket but I ignore it. Whatever it is will have to wait.

It's clear what Russel Germain lacks in stature is made up for with the size of his office. I almost missed him sitting behind the massive oak table in front of the large windows.

He doesn't bother getting up but motions for us to sit down across from him.

"So...what can I do for you, Officers?"

"Agents," I correct him before I continue. "We'd like to ask you some questions about your involvement with The Youth Center."

The pompous little man leans back in his chair, folding his hands over his stomach.

"My involvement?"

I can already tell he's not going to make this easy.

Once again, I ignore it when my phone buzzes in my pocket.

"Are you saying you have no involvement with the center?"

"Not directly, no. That is, not recently. I believe I may

have done some work for them a while back, but I'd have to check with my assistant."

He's lying through his fucking teeth. I can feel Kate bristling beside me, but I hope she keeps herself in check. As shifty as he's being with me, I have a feeling this douchebag won't respond well to a woman with a brain and a set of balls bigger than his.

"That's odd," I say quickly. "I'm pretty sure you were seen having breakfast there just a couple of weeks ago."

He pretends to think before responding.

"Ah, yes. I vaguely recall—"

I've had enough of these games. While he dicks us around, we're not getting any closer to answers.

"Let's stop beating around the bush, shall we?" I suggest, leaning back, mimicking his pose. "I'm sure even you wouldn't likely forget sharing a meal with Congressman Melnyk and former NFL star, Paul Krebs."

Apparently, Germain is tired of the game as well, because his arrogant smile is replaced with a stern look as he sits forward and leans his arms on the table.

"Yes, what of it? It was a business meeting. Mason Kramer was looking for additional funding for the center and asked me to attend."

No sooner has the buzzing of my phone stopped and it starts up again.

"And now Kramer is missing and Krebs is dead," I volunteer as I pull my phone from my pocket.

Dammit. It's Becky.

"Wait. What?"

I glance across the table and see Germain is genuinely

shocked at what I said. He turns so pale there's no way he is acting.

"Excuse me." I push back my seat and get up. "I have to take this."

I walk across the office for some privacy before I answer.

"Becky? What's so damn urgent. I'm in a—"

"Where is Sawyer?"

I freeze on the spot, icy fingers crawling up my spine.

"I assume at school. Why?"

"The school secretary called a while ago. Sawyer didn't show up for classes today."

I force myself to follow logic.

"Did you try her phone?"

"Of course I did. There's no answer. I've been trying for the past hour."

Okay. It's possible her phone is out of juice. Wouldn't be the first time.

"Did she say anything to you this morning? Plans with a friend? Have you tried Tawna?"

"This morning? How would I have seen her this morning; she stayed the night with you?"

Those icy fingers find their way into my chest, wrapping firmly around my heart and squeezing hard.

"Mitch?"

I barely hear Kate's concerned voice over the sudden ringing in my ears.

TWENTY-ONE

*O*PAL

It was clear something was wrong as soon as Mitch answered his phone.

By the end of the call, he was already on the move and I had to hustle to keep up with him as he stalked out of the lawyer's office without a word.

"It's Sawyer. She's missing."

That's all he bit off when I prompted him.

I did manage to convince him to hand over his car keys and let me drive so he could make some calls.

We're on our way back to Richmond, to his ex-wife's place. Mitch already notified the rest of his team and they are on their way as well. Now he's talking to Matt, while barking occasional directions at me.

I wish I could talk to my team but I'm focused on driving. Knowing Raj is in the car with Matt, I trust she'll take care of making sure my team is informed as well.

Sawyer missing.

God, I hope this is just an act of teenage rebellion and Mitch's daughter stayed at some friend's house, deciding to skip school today. However, I have a really bad feeling this is not some random coincidence.

"Left here. Third house on the right."

I follow Mitch's instructions and pull up to the two-story house in, what is clearly, an affluent neighborhood.

I'm a little hesitant to follow Mitch to the house, but I remind myself I'm here in an official capacity and not as the woman who is sleeping with him. That would be all kinds of awkward.

The door opens as we step up on the porch, revealing a gorgeous, statuesque brunette I have no trouble identifying as Sawyer's mother. I thought the girl was a clone of her father, but seeing her mother, I realize she's probably the perfect mix of both parents.

"Oh, Mitch," the woman cries, throwing herself in his arms.

"Where's Chad?" I hear Mitch ask as he appears to untangle himself from her long limbs.

"Who's that?" the woman answers with a question of her own as she spots me for the first time.

Mitch turns his head, following her eyes on me.

"Opal Berry, she's a colleague."

"Opal, this is Becky Miller, Sawyer's mom."

I opt to nod with a slight smile, keeping my presence on the back burner for now. Good call, since his ex already seems to have dismissed me, aiming her attention back on Mitch.

"Chad is out of town at a conference."

"Have you spoken to him?"

"Briefly," she answers, but her eyes slide to the side.

Uh oh. I'm assuming Chad is a new husband, and her reaction suggests things are not copacetic between them.

"Is he on his way back?" Mitch presses.

"He was supposed to be home last night but got delayed." She follows it up with, "Let's go inside, it's cold."

A distraction tactic for sure, but it works as Mitch follows her in the door with me trailing behind. I don't miss the tight clench of his jaw.

Money is definitely not an issue, judging from the Porsche Cayenne in the driveway and the lavish decor in here. I'm guessing the little red car Sawyer was driving last night did not belong to her mom as I assumed.

The girl is sixteen and has her own wheels? Shit, my feet were my only mode of transportation until I enlisted at eighteen.

"What did she tell you last night?" Mitch asks his ex, who busies herself in the kitchen with a complicated looking espresso machine.

"She said she was heading over to your place and would go to school from there in the morning." There's an accusatory tone to her answer. "Didn't you see her last night?"

"I did. Briefly. She never talked about spending the night," Mitch says as he glances my way. "She walked in on something, we had some words, worked it out, and then she left."

"Words? You fought?"

The pitch of Becky's voice rises and I know this situation is going to disintegrate within seconds if I don't jump in.

"I understand you tried calling her friends," I say, drawing her attention. "Did any of them have any ideas where Sawyer may have gone? Any boyfriends she may have gone to see?"

I ignore the growl coming from Mitch.

"No boyfriends. None that I know of anyway, and none of her friends mentioned anyone."

"Family members close by?"

Becky shakes her head, tears welling in her eyes.

"No," she sobs.

"You wouldn't happen to have her license plate, would you?" I quickly press on, hoping to avert a meltdown.

She recites the number and I type it in a text to Pearl to do a quick search.

"And she drives a red Mazda3?"

Becky starts nodding and then suddenly narrows her eyes on me.

"Wait. How do you know what car she drives?"

Fuck.

"Because I told her," Mitch intercedes, saving my bacon. "Look, we need to talk to Chad, see if maybe he has any idea where she is. Maybe she mentioned something to him."

"She wouldn't have," Becky responds, turning back toward the espresso machine hissing behind her. "She and Chad aren't exactly on speaking terms."

"Since when?"

"They haven't gotten along in a while," she admits, keeping her face averted.

I have a feeling there may be some general domestic discourse in this house, but I keep my mouth shut. I'll let Mitch prod while I keep my ears open. As unlikely as it may seem, it's still a possibility finding me at Mitch's house on top of some kind of domestic dispute may have caused Sawyer to bolt under her own steam.

It's a preferable option to the one where she's being forcibly kept from home. It's even entered my mind perhaps Kendrick or his so-called friends have somehow gotten hold of her. Although I can't imagine how they would've zoomed in on her.

Unless, they've had eyes on Mitch—or even on me—and want to send a message.

Or more likely, cause a distraction.

It would've been a logical assumption our focus would shift if a daughter of one of our own went missing.

And that might give Kendrick and his buddies time to tie up any loose ends.

That would also mean we are getting close enough to make them uncomfortable.

We can't let up now.

"I'll just be a moment," I mumble, heading toward the door.

"Where are you going?" Mitch calls after me.

"I have to make a few phone calls."

I just step out on the porch when a familiar vehicle pulls up to the curb and Joe Lampert and Adam Byron step out.

"They're inside," I tell Mitch's teammates as they walk up.

While they go in, I move away from the front door and dial Jacob.

"What've we got?" he asks right away, and I know Raj has already notified him.

"Sawyer Kenny, sixteen years old, drives a red Mazda3."

I rattle off the license plate number I already forwarded to Janey.

"Mother, Becky Miller, stepfather, Chad Miller. Well-to-do but I don't know their professions. Looks like there may have been some domestic issues."

"You think she ran?"

"It's possible," I admit. "But I was also thinking the timing of this could be very convenient for Kendrick, since half of the CARD team is now here at the Miller house."

"And Matt and Raj are on their way back to town," Jacob mentions.

Dropping what could be a direct lead to the missing kids.

Jesus. The hair on my neck stands on end.

"Jamie Lyons. If I'm right, he might be in danger."

"He's in police custody," Jacob reminds me.

"That may well be, but from what we learned from Melissa and Remington there's reason to think there may be some police involvement. And even if there isn't, most police departments maintain a public blotter online. All it would take is a simple Google search to have the news of his arrest pop up."

Much like the search I did for Lee Remington the other day, except with a simple software you could loop the search to run continuously, sending an alert when there's a hit.

"You need to call Matt."

"Already on it. Gimme a sec."

I take in my surroundings as I wait for Jacob to get back on the line, and notice a tiny security camera tucked in a corner where the porch soffit meets one of the columns. It looks to be aimed at the front door. Walking toward the corner where the garage is set back a bit, I spot another one.

Good. In a neighborhood like this, I would bet every house has some kind of security. We may be able to get some information from a feed.

I make a mental note to ask Mitch about any security he or his neighbors might have.

"Driver has a buddy in the Paducah FBI satellite office he trusts. He'll ask him to take the Lyons boy into protective custody immediately and transport him back to Lexington so he can be questioned here."

I blow out a breath of relief. I had visions of that poor kid in a holding cell, getting shanked by someone who fakes a drunk and disorderly charge to get close to him.

However, there are still four other kids who might be

considered loose ends. As much as I want to find Sawyer and stand by Mitch, I can't give up on them.

"We can't lose sight of the big picture, Jacob."

"I know."

Another thought suddenly occurs to me, turning my blood cold in an instant.

"I'm going to need some wheels of my own to get around."

"I'll get a rental dropped off for you," he offers immediately.

"Thank you."

I rattle off the address and promise to call as soon as I hit the road.

Then I hang up and quickly dial another number.

"Remington."

"Lee, it's Opal. Are you home yet?"

"No I'm just leaving the ER. They had to set my fucking nose. Why?"

"Have you been in touch with Melissa?"

"Yeah, I called her earlier, why? What's going on?"

Shit.

If Kendrick in fact has eyes on either Mitch or me, we may have been followed to Remington's address.

"Her location may have been compromised," I share, my heart beating in my throat.

"How the fuck did that happen?" he snaps, understandably upset.

"Long story, I'll tell you as soon as I can get there. Call her now, tell her to lock herself in a bathroom until you get home."

"I'm right around the corner."

"Are you armed?" I ask, wishing my own guns weren't stuck in my truck at the impound lot.

It takes a minute for Lee to respond.

"I'm covered," he finally answers.

"Good. Stay inside, lock everything, and don't move until I can get there. I'll see if I can get someone to keep an eye on the house in the meantime."

Next, I call Pearl, explaining why I need to ask her to head over to Remington's place to keep an eye on it until I can get there.

By the time I get back inside, Adam is sitting at the kitchen table, a laptop open in front of him, while Joe and Mitch hover over his shoulder. Becky is nowhere in sight.

Mitch lifts his gaze when I walk up.

"What are you working on?" I ask.

"Seeing if we can trace her phone."

"Good. I've got Pearl looking into the car. Have the police been contacted?"

"We put out a BOLO on Sawyer and the car," Joe answers.

A BOLO is a be-on-the-lookout order that can range from a missing person to a hardened criminal. All it means is that officers are going to keep an eye out for anything or anyone that matches the description given.

"What about you? Anything?" Mitch wants to know.

I pause. If the possibility Kendrick somehow took his daughter hasn't occurred to him, I really don't want to be the one to put that image in his head. Especially since I'm running on instinct alone. But I may not have a choice. There's too much at stake.

"Where is Becky?" I counter instead.

"She's upstairs, trying to get a hold of her husband."

The way Mitch says it, I'm guessing there's no love lost between the two men.

Now is my chance, since I don't want to ramp animosity if Becky were to hear how Sawyer's disappearance may have been the result of the case we're working.

"Matt and Raj are on their way back, but Matt is having someone he trusts put Jamie in protective custody. I just spoke to Remington, who is on his way home to make sure Melissa is safe."

I let that hang for a moment, giving the guys a chance to put one and one together.

"Kendrick," Adam is the first to guess.

"It's possible."

"I didn't want to think it," Mitch says, sounding defeated.

"We have to account for that possibility," I tell him gently, putting a hand on his arm.

The expression on his face is raw and I resist the urge to put my arms around him. Given these are his colleagues watching on, and his ex-wife's house we are in, he may not welcome that kind of public display. So instead, I give his arm a little squeeze.

"*She's my world,*" he whispers, breaking my heart.

"We'll find—"

"I've got a location," Adam interrupts, leaning closer to the screen.

We all gather around him.

A red dot is blinking on the screen. It looks like a park, but I can't quite make out where it might be.

"Where is that?" Joe gives voice to that question.

Adam zooms out and I feel Mitch freeze beside me.

It takes me a second but then I recognize it too. It's a small neighborhood park.

Two blocks from Mitch's house.

TWENTY-TWO

MITCH

"Who the hell was that?"

Kate turns around, a set of keys in her hand as the guy she was talking to takes off down the driveway where he hops into a waiting car.

"He dropped off my rental car," she says, bumping the door closed behind her.

"Why do you need a car?"

I can tell from the apologetic expression on her face I'm not going to like her answer.

"I need to be mobile, Mitch. I'm more use out there doing my job than I am here. I can't afford to take my eyes off the ball. There is too much at stake, too many lives in the balance."

With emotions already close to the surface, that comment hurts. Sawyer is all I can think about right now, and my anger flares up when Kate reminds me there are others.

"You want to leave? Then go. Everyone else has."

My tone is sharp, but I don't care. I reach around her and pull the front door back open.

Everyone else being Joe and Adam, who left to find my daughter's phone in a park near my house. I was ready to dart out the door but it was Kate who suggested it was better to let my colleagues go. It killed me, but I had to concede when she reminded me emotions as a parent would diminish my effectiveness as an agent.

It's an argument I've used myself on parents of missing or abducted children. Leave the investigating to those who know what they're doing. Right now, all I know is fear, panic, and you can add anger.

Becky is a mess. I could hear her arguing on the phone earlier with that asshole husband of hers. Apparently, Chad is too busy lobbying on behalf of a large pharmaceutical giant to crooked politicians in Washington to come home when his stepdaughter is missing. Piece of shit.

Yeah, I'm angry. But if I'm honest with myself it's mostly from guilt. Why didn't I put my foot down last night and drive her home? Instead, I let her drive home by herself, eager to get back inside to the woman who has slowly but surely started filling a void in my life I hadn't realized existed.

I feel like I'm adrift in the middle of a storm, and the only one I can hold on to, to keep my head above water, is leaving me to drown.

"I'll be in touch," Kate says softly, lifting a hand to touch my face.

I turn my head at the last minute, afraid if I let her touch me, I'll be begging her to stay.

Jesus. How did I get so weak? So lost?

The distinct sound of my phone ringing has me running for the kitchen where I left it on the table. Just as I reach for it, I hear the door close with a soft snick and guilt overwhelms me. I shake it off and answer Joe's call.

"We've got her car. The phone was lying on the ground beside the driver's side door, which was unlocked. Her purse is sitting on the passenger seat, and the keys are still in the ignition."

The urge to puke is so overwhelming I have to bend over. Whatever little hope I was holding on to she might just walk in the door at some point evaporates instantly. I focus on breathing for a few moments.

When I regain some control over my faculties, I ask, "Anything else?"

"Nothing else. No sign of any struggle, my friend," he says carefully, instinctively knowing what I'm getting at.

She would've passed the small parking lot to the park on her way out of my neighborhood.

"Call—" I start.

"Adam is on the phone with SAC Walker to get a team out here. Hang tight, Mitch. I'm heading back now and Adam is staying here to wait for a CSI unit to get here. Walker will take care of logistics."

I sink down on a kitchen chair after ending the call, and rest my head in my hands.

"Mitch? I heard you on the phone. Who was it? Is there news?"

Becky's face still shows signs of her earlier meltdown. Kate had calmly handled her, suggesting she lie down while we wait for news, but Kate isn't here now.

"Sit down, Becky."

Her face pales, but she doesn't argue and takes a seat, resting her clasped hands on the table in front of her. I reach over and cover them with one of mine.

"We still don't know where Sawyer is, but we found her car."

While I'm talking, Becky opens her hands and grabs on to mine.

"No sign of her?" she asks in a quavering voice.

I shake my head.

"None," I tell her, giving her fingers a squeeze. "The guys found her phone and her purse was still in the car."

"That's not good, right?"

Shit. This is too fucking hard.

"No, Becks, it's not."

The name I used to call her slips out in a moment when joint parenthood trumps any acrimony that remains between us.

"There was no evidence of a struggle though. No sign of any force."

I squeeze her fingers again to get her attention before I add, "No sign she was hurt in any way."

She nods a few times.

"Okay. Okay. That's good. So what do we do now?"

I'm about to answer when a knock sounds at the door.

Becky is about to jump up, but I hold her back.

"Let me get the door," I tell her.

It may be Matt, or Joe made serious time getting back here, but I'm not taking any chances and unholster my gun. Then I peek out the bay window.

It's Matt, alone. I put my gun away and open the door.

"Hey, pal."

He shakes my hand and claps me on the shoulder. Then he looks beyond me.

"Hey, Becky."

I've worked with Driver long enough he knows my ex, who is currently being folded in his arms.

"Just talked to Joe, he should be here shortly," he tells me over Becky's head.

I'm sure Joe filled him in, but I'd still like to talk to him without my ex listening in.

Becky offers to make Matt a coffee and heads for the counter where she starts messing about with that massive machine again. The damn noise the thing makes annoys me to no end but I guess it keeps her busy.

"Where is Opal?" Matt asks suddenly.

"She took off."

I hope my tone conveys I don't want to talk about it, but that's never stopped Matt before.

It doesn't now.

"Where'd she go?"

"Don't know. Don't care."

That last comment is a lie, I fucking care, although it would be easier not to. It took hearing the door close behind her to bring on regret about my parting words for her.

The truth is, she was right, she does have a job to do and would be more useful out there than she is here, holding my hand. But dammit, I already have one person I care about out there exposed to a danger I have no control over. The thought of Kate vulnerable out there as well was too much to take on.

Still, like the idiot I am, I showed her the door anyway.

"Bullshit," is Matt's response, calling my bluff. "You forget, I've seen you with her. You care a great fucking deal."

I look over at Becky, who still has her back turned. Then I return my focus to Matt.

"Fine, I care, but right now my focus has to be on finding my daughter and I don't have a fucking clue where to even start."

"We start with the CCTV feed from the gas station across the street from the park."

Shit, I'd forgotten about the Mobil right when you turn into my neighborhood. Goes to show my mind is not running on all cylinders.

"Joe got hold of the manager, who was cooperative. He's getting a copy ready for Joe to pick up."

Becky walks up and hands Matt a mug before turning to me.

"Do you want another one?"

I've had several of the high-octane coffees by now

which, combined with adrenaline flowing through my system, already has me crawling out of my skin.

"I'm good, thanks."

"Can I get you something to eat?"

I guess we missed dinner somewhere but food is the last thing on my mind right now. This preoccupation with food and drink is starting to annoy me, and I'm about to blow her off when Matt speaks up.

"You know what? That's a good idea. We all need some fuel. I'm sure Joe and Adam would appreciate something as well when they get back." He smiles at her. "Maybe soup and sandwiches? Keep it easy."

I watch her head back to the kitchen, probably glad to have a purpose, and squeeze the bridge of my nose with my fingers.

Fuck. I almost snapped at the woman.

"Where's the husband?" Matt asks under his breath, making sure Becky can't hear him.

"DC, where apparently he has more important things to tend to."

"What a piece of work."

We're interrupted by the beam of headlights coming in through the front window as Joe's vehicle pulls into the driveway. I have the door open before he makes it to the porch.

"Any luck?"

He holds up a thumb drive.

I'd forgotten her propensity to bake or cook when she's stressed, but Becky appears to be making soup for an army when I ask if we can use Chad's office. It's right off the hallway by the front door. She hesitates only for a moment before shrugging her shoulders.

"Go right ahead. It's not like he's around enough to use it himself."

She sounds so deflated and I feel a sudden wave of empathy for her. Her child is missing, her asshole husband chooses not to be here to support her, and she's in the kitchen cooking for her ex and his teammates who are taking over her house.

Chad's office is spotless, more for show than an actual functional space. There are no files out in the open, not even a computer or phone on the desk, just a blotter and a wooden penholder. On the credenza behind the leather executive office chair I spot a few framed pictures, including a family portrait showing Sawyer framed by her mother and that douche. They're all smiling, but it looks far from genuine.

I close the door behind us as Joe sets up at the small conference table, opening his laptop and inserting the USB key.

"I asked the guy to include everything from the night prior to last," Joe says as a black-and-white image of the gas pumps pops up.

Behind it the road is visible, including the entrance to the park's small parking lot across the street. There's a date stamp in the corner, a clock counting underneath.

"Do you remember about what time you got home last night?" Matt asks me.

I can't believe it was only last night. Feels like days have passed.

"Probably seven thirty or thereabouts."

Joe rewinds the clip to seven fifteen, yesterday evening, and lets it play while we crowd around. In the next ten minutes only six vehicles drive into the neighborhood as they pass the gas station. One I recognize as one of my neighbor's, one is a UPS van that reappears three minutes later on its way out, just like a small SUV we see pass twice, both coming and going. Could be a pizza delivery or something like that.

At seven twenty-eight my car comes into view. I point at the screen.

"There."

We all bend closer, waiting to see if we might've been followed. Thirty-two seconds later a dark-colored, four-door sedan rolls by.

"Is that an unmarked police car?" I wonder out loud.

"Looks like," Joe agrees. "Not really close enough to be following you."

Unfortunately, from this angle it's impossible to see a license plate.

"Can't rule it out. We came from Irvine so I would've made a left at the traffic light to drive into the subdivision. They might've caught a red light and been forced to wait."

Matt taps Joe on the shoulder.

"We'll know soon enough. Keep going."

Watching that little red car drive by is harder than I thought.

If not for that damn car, Sawyer would've been safely at home.

Chad bought it for her when she turned sixteen. Of course, my daughter was over the moon and Becky didn't see a problem with it, so by the time I found out it was a done deal, I'd been set up to be the bad guy once again. That didn't mean I dropped the issue, and that car was the cause of many an argument since they've allowed her to drive it by herself when, by law, she's supposed have a fully licensed driver beside her until she's fucking eighteen. It's been an ongoing dispute, and the reason I no longer even attempt to be civil when I bump into Chad.

"There it is again," Joe says, pointing at the screen where I can just make out the front of the car.

"Slow it down frame by frame," Matt instructs him.

Under the beam from the streetlamp, you can clearly see a single person outlined in the car as it slowly comes into view.

Sawyer.

Then suddenly the Mazda is lit up from behind by flashing lights and we watch her abruptly turn into the small parking lot.

The unmarked police car pulls in right behind her, only briefly showing an individual behind the wheel.

"*Sonofabitch*," Matt mutters under his breath.

My blood chills as I watch both cars pull almost out of view of the security camera. The only thing visible is the trunk of the police car, its brake lights bright.

Damn, no license plate.

Then, suddenly, they go dark and the flashing lights are turned off. I know whoever is in that car is getting out and walking up to my daughter's window. All the hair on my body stands on end as my eyes stay glued to the screen for what seems like an eternity, but is likely only a few minutes.

There's no visible movement until the taillights come on, and the car starts backing up.

One more flash of a single individual behind the wheel before he speeds away and out of sight.

Taking my daughter with him.

Twenty-four hours ago.

I drop my head when blood rushes in my ears and my knees feel weak. Twenty-four hours is a long fucking time.

"Back it up a bit."

Matt must've seen something and my head snaps up as I watch Joe play it in reverse, frame by frame. I'm focused on the inside of the car, trying to catch a glimpse of either my daughter or the bastard who took her.

"There. Freeze it."

On the screen, the vehicle is just about to turn onto the street. All I can distinguish is a decent set of shoulders and part of his head. The face stays in the shadows so I can't make out any features.

"What are you seeing?"

Matt taps on the screen where the light beam from the lamppost across the road just reaches the car's grill.

"It's a Crown Vic," I point out. "Not an active department vehicle. Those were all replaced by the Ford Police Interceptor as the standard police issue vehicle by 2020."

"Exactly," Matt concurs. "Zoom in?"

When Joe does as he asks, I notice the license plate on the bumper.

Unfortunately, it's virtually illegible.

"I'm gonna send this to my contact at the crime lab, he might be able to clean it up some," Matt says.

I don't hold out much hope, but there may be another way to try and track down whose car that is.

"When the old cruisers were decommissioned, they were auctioned off. I bet you those records are still around somewhere."

Matt turns to me with a smile.

"Looks like we've got some work to do."

Despite the dire situation, I find myself grinning back.

It's a start.

TWENTY-THREE

OPAL

I can see the lights on at Remington's house from a distance.

I'd called Lee when I left Richmond to let him know there would be an SUV parked in front of his house belonging to GEM. I didn't want him to get spooked while I'm trying to get there.

I reach beside me, comforted when I encounter the cold steel of my personal arsenal, which I moved from the trunk to the passenger seat a block from the Miller residence. Jacob sent a message as I was leaving the house, telling me he'd left something in the rental's trunk for me. I don't know how he managed to get the contents of my gun safe from the impound lot, or how it got from there into the car, but that's Jacob for you. His connections are as much of a mystery as the man himself.

I'm not about to question it, not when having my

weapons within reach makes me feel better prepared for any situation.

Janey's vehicle is parked a few doors down across the street. When I back into the driveway—easier for a quick getaway if needed—I see her get out and start crossing the street toward me.

"All quiet," she says, looking past me at the house through narrowed eyes.

"Good."

"How's Mitch?"

"Angry, frustrated, scared out of his mind," I inform her, trying not to feel hurt by his reaction earlier.

I've dealt with enough parents to know their reactions can be unpredictable and emotion driven. They often feel useless, frustrated, and can lash out—even at each other—with little provocation.

I could handle his angry words, but when he turned away from me, avoiding my touch, it hit harder. I remind myself it wasn't personal.

At least I hope it wasn't.

Not that it would make any difference, I wouldn't do anything different.

The best chance we have of finding Sawyer, or any of the other kids, is if we can do our work without the restrictions law enforcement is limited with.

"Understandable."

"Any luck with Kendrick's hard drive?"

I know Janey didn't walk out of that FBI office without the information contained on that computer. Exactly how she manages to do that without anyone noticing requires an impressive level of expertise, quick hands, and nerves of steel, none of which I possess.

Now, ask me to hit a grape on a tree trunk at a distance of seventy-five feet and I'm your woman.

That's why we are stronger as a team. We each have our talents to bring to the table.

"A few possibilities. A couple of pieces of information I was able to hand off to Jacob, who is working on confirming their validity."

Because we're a small team, Jacob likes to follow a lead as far as he can take it himself, before handing it to one of us to pursue on the ground.

"Can you give me a hint?"

I'm hungry for information. Anything to set this investigation on the fast track because I have this sinking feeling our time is running out.

"Our congressman has his fingers deep in the pie Kendrick has been serving."

"We already knew that," I point out.

"Right, but it looks like he doesn't just partake, he's part of the operation."

"How do you figure that?"

"The direction of the money flow," she explains. "I found financial files for the center masked as a listing of donations from a slew of big players, including, but not limited to, Krebs and Germain. Some of the names would make your hair stand on end. Nominal amounts, mostly. A couple of thousand each, a cluster of them paid on or around the same dates." She cocks a hip and gets comfortable leaning against the car's fender. "I figured that wasn't the whole story so I dug a little deeper and found an encrypted file named *Pure*. I was able to get in to find a matching spreadsheet of names but with amounts almost ten times higher. It looks like only ten percent of the actual donated amount ended up with the center, while the other ninety percent was funneled to the Cayman Islands. The account there belongs to a company by the name of Pure Caribbean. Jacob is trying to find out who it belongs to."

"And Melnyk?" I prompt her.

"Oh, yes. Our congressman. Here's the kicker; Melnyk is listed as a minor donor to the center, but his name is not on the other list. I had a peek at Melnyk's financials and found the small donations to the center, but no other withdrawals. Curiously, every time a donation was made from Melnyk's personal account to the center, a large sum of money was deposited into his campaign account on the very same day. Fifty thousand buckaroos each time a cluster of those donations are listed. Guess where that money came from?"

Holy Jesus.

While Kendrick was grooming kids for exploitation, Melnyk was out there recruiting customers.

Sick fuckers. All of them.

This kind of information would've stayed hidden, perhaps forever, if we had to work within legal limitations. At the very least we would've lost time we already don't have enough of.

I'm about to prompt Janey on the source of the deposits when I'm distracted by a dark sedan coming down the street. Something about the vehicle's cautious approach puts me on edge. My alarm is only heightened when I spot the lights mounted on the car's grill.

"I thought Crown Vics were phased out years ago?" Janey mumbles behind me as I automatically start reaching for the door handle.

"They were."

As I respond, I open the driver's side door, keeping a close eye on the approaching car. All I can see is a single person inside. Judging by the way he fits behind the wheel, it's a large man.

I sidestep so the bulk of my body is covered by the open door. Janey does the same behind me.

When the car is level with the neighbor's driveway, I see the passenger side window sliding down.

"Cover!" I yell when I see the light reflect off a barrel in the open window.

I dive into the rental, grabbing for the first gun I encounter, when I hear the first muted pops of a fully automatic weapon.

Fuck.

My Glock 19 fits smoothly in my hand, it almost feels like a physical extension. As I back out of the car and duck low, Janey is already returning fire from the far side of the door. Thank God she was carrying.

"Vehicle stopped at eleven o'clock from our position," she yells over the ongoing gunfire. "He's firing at the house."

Shit. I hope Lee and Melissa are safe in there.

"Cover me," I tell Janey, who immediately starts

firing rapid shots at the vehicle while I slip the barrel of my Glock in the opening between the door and the rental.

The angle is sharp and the shooter is ducking low behind the wheel, but I think I have a shot through the windshield. I wish I'd grabbed my rifle instead, it's more accurate, but the Glock will have to do.

I smoothly rack the slide to load a bullet in the chamber and take aim, slowly but steadily depressing the trigger.

Unfortunately, just as I fire off my shot the shadow in the vehicle shifts. The windshield shatters, but the sedan is already taking off with tires squealing. I get off one more shot which catches the vehicle's rear fender.

Janey darts out from behind the door and hustles down the driveway, firing a few more shots at the disappearing vehicle.

"Janey! House!"

Tucking my gun in the back of my jeans, I run toward the house.

Every single front window is shattered and the door has been destroyed under the barrage of bullets.

"Lee! Melissa!"

I climb in through the front window, avoiding the shards of glass as best I can, while yelling their names. I can feel Janey right behind me.

"We're okay. We're down here."

Lee comes up the basement stairs and looks around at the devastation of his living room.

"Fucking hell."

"Anyone hurt?" I ask, looking beyond him to see Melissa peeking out. "Watch out for the glass."

"We're not," Lee answers, his eyes slide over my shoulder. "But she was hit."

I swing around to find my friend with blood dripping down the side of her face.

"By a piece of glass," Janey returns crisply. "It's a scratch. Now let's get the hell out of here before they come back, or worse; the cops show up."

She's right. We need to get out of here ASAP.

What felt like hours probably just lasted minutes, but the gunfire would not have gone unnoticed. Someone is bound to have called 911. If we're still here when the cops show up, we'll only lose more valuable time.

Besides, at this point I'm not sure who we can trust.

"I need a few files, my laptop," Lee says, moving toward the bedrooms.

"No time," Janey barks, just as we hear sirens in the distance. "Now!"

Her urgent tone doesn't stop the man from darting into one of the doors off the narrow hallway.

Leaving Janey to deal with the reporter, I grab Melissa by the hand and help her over the worst of the debris and outside. There I notice one of the tires is flat on the rental, which has not gone unscathed. It appears to have caught a couple of stray bullets.

Shit. We'll have to pile into the SUV.

I can't risk leaving behind my weapons, so I dive into the passenger side to retrieve my guns.

Poor Melissa looks scared as she takes in what I'm

cradling in my arms, but I don't have time for explanations. Those sirens are coming closer.

"The SUV across the street, Melissa."

She doesn't argue and follows me to the other side of the road.

Luckily, Janey left the vehicle unlocked so I urge the girl to climb in the back. I join her after tossing my guns in the cargo space. By then Janey is running toward us, the much smaller woman dragging Lee across the street.

"Airbnb," I say when she gets behind the wheel.

She nods and starts the engine.

I look behind me when she peels away from the curb, and just as she turns a corner to get to the highway, I catch sight of flashing lights pulling into the street behind us.

That was too close.

I keep an eye out the rear window while pulling my phone from my pocket, dialing Raj, who answers after only one ring.

"Heads-up. There was an incident at the reporter's house. We're coming in hot with Remington and the girl. Doesn't look like we have a tail, but you never know. We're getting on to the 4 South. I need you to wait for us at the bottom of the airport exit and check for tails. We'll use backroads to backtrack to the Airbnb."

"On my way." I can hear she's already on the move. "Want me to get on the horn with Jacob?"

"No. I'd better call him myself." I wince, not looking forward to the prospect. "Keep your fingers crossed he took out full insurance on my rental."

"Ouch," Raj says softly.

Ouch, indeed.

"Yeah. Oh, and Ra-Onyx?"

I only barely catch myself using her real name and immediately am concerned someone heard me call out for Janey earlier. Dammit. I know better.

"Yeah?"

"Keep an eye out for an unmarked police vehicle."

I hear her muffled curse before she comes back with, "Will do."

By the time Janey pulls the SUV into the garage of the rental house, I've already warned Jacob about the shooting. He'd been about to call Janey, having heard a call about a disturbance come in over the scanner.

Figures. Any time I try to get a visual image of our boss, I envision someone in some kind of command center in a bunker, surrounded by telephones, computers, and an array of electronics, monitoring the world. The man seems to have eyes and ears everywhere, yet manages to stay invisible himself.

The garage door rumbles closed behind us, and I rush to get out and make sure we get Lee and the girl safely inside.

Raj comes in the front door, and I hand the impromptu guests over to her care while I head back to the garage to collect my weapons. I pass by the open door of the powder room, showing Janey in front of the mirror, lifting one side of her hair to examine a nasty-looking gash on the side of her head.

That's no cut from flying glass.

"Glass, huh?"

Her eyes snap to mine in the reflection of the mirror.

"It's just a graze."

I shake my head.

"Raj is in the kitchen. Get her to put some clotting powder on there. You're bleeding all over the place."

It's a fairly shallow groove, but head wounds are notorious for bleeding, and there's no way this one can be closed up any other way. She'll have a nice scar, good thing it'll be covered by her hair.

"Oh." I remember as she squeezes by me. "I still don't know where those deposits came from."

She swivels around, a grin on her bloodied face making her look almost maniacal.

"GlanTox."

"Never heard of it," I tell her, wondering why she's wearing such a smug expression.

"It's a new, up-and-coming biotech company, and one of Melnyk's biggest campaign sponsors."

None of what she says means anything, but it clearly means something to her.

"GlanTox is a subsidiary of Glan Industries."

Glan.

The penny drops.

GlanTox, Glan Industries, and I'm willing to bet Glan Development is yet another branch.

Glan Development, the company that chartered the yacht in the Caribbean.

The company putting on the personal development seminar Krebs, Germain, and Melnyk all took part in.

That cannot be a coincidence.

TWENTY-FOUR

MITCH

"Jacob, you're on speaker."

Matt places his cell phone in the middle of the table.

"It's just Joe, Mitch, and myself here."

"Good. We've had a bit of a situation at the Remington house."

I surge to my feet and grab the edge of the table. The energy in the room immediately pitches higher, and renewed fear claws at my throat.

I meet Matt's eyes over the table.

"What kind of situation?" he asks, holding my gaze.

"Drive-by shooting. Pearl and Opal were in the driveway when the car drove up. Bastard destroyed the house, but Remington and the girl are unharmed."

What the fuck does that mean? Is Opal hurt?

I want to ask but my fucking chest hurts so bad I can barely get my breath.

"The women? Are they okay?" Matt asks for me.

"They're fine. They returned fire and the guy took off, but we moved..."

I'm no longer listening as I lean forward over the table, willing my heart to stop hammering and trying to force air into my lungs.

A heavy hand lands on my shoulder, pushing down, as Joe's voice sounds right by my ear.

"Sit down before you fall down, and breathe, motherfucker."

I unlock my knees and make a hard landing on the chair. The white dots dancing in front of my eyes dissipate as the tight band around my chest slowly releases.

I just catch Jacob saying, *"...says it looked like an older model police cruiser."*

"We have video of my daughter being taken in an unmarked Crown Vic," I tell him, my voice hoarse.

"Security feed?"

"From a gas station across the street," Matt fills in.

Branch is quiet for a moment.

Then he says, *"I'm guessing you didn't get much?"*

"Other than the make, and the fact it's still rigged up with lights, no. I have a buddy at the lab trying to clean up a still shot we have of the license plate."

"Chances are, it's a stolen plate anyway."

"Probably, but we're about to go over departmental vehicle auction records."

"Ah, smart. Let me know if something pops up."

"Will do. And if you have something..." Matt returns.

"Actually, I might have something interesting.

Nothing substantiated, mind you," Jacob is quick to disclaim. Probably code for: not obtained by legal means. *"And I'm not sure it's helpful at this point, but we have reason to believe Congressman Melnyk is a bigger player in this sex ring than we thought."*

He doesn't elaborate much before he ends the call, only to say that they discovered information suggesting Melnyk may be recruiting like-minded perverts with fat pocketbooks.

Interesting, but it doesn't really help me get any closer to finding my daughter, who is in the hands of someone who apparently thinks nothing of shooting up a peaceful family neighborhood in his attempt to tie off loose ends.

That's pretty fucking brazen and quite frankly, terrifying.

I'm feeling more powerless by the minute.

The urge to call Kate to hear with my own ears she's unharmed is hard to resist, but I opt to shoot off a message to her instead.

Are you okay?

I STARE STUPIDLY AT MY PHONE, WAITING FOR AN instant reply, but none seems forthcoming.

"Okay, guys." Matt separates the stack of papers he was printing off before Jacob called into three equal piles, handing one to each of us. "Let's focus."

In the past half hour Dresden and Punani have joined Adam Byron, across from the Mobil station, helping local cops who were called in to knock on doors of neighboring houses to look for possible witnesses to Sawyer's kidnapping. They'll be paying particular attention to houses with security systems, hoping for cameras that may have caught the actual abduction. Even just a glimpse of whoever took her would be helpful.

Until those guys come back with something, these records are all we have.

As Matt had pointed out earlier, to assume it was Kendrick might seem logical, but we have to keep an open mind to the possibility there are others involved.

Still, Kendrick's alias is the first name I scan for when I flip through the stack of papers in front of me. I suspect Mason Kramer may not have been the only alternate identity he used, but Walker's team hasn't found evidence of any other names they've been able to connect.

To the world, Josh Kendrick no longer exists. Official records state the man perished in the fire at Transition House and what were supposed to be his remains—there wasn't a lot left—were buried at the county cemetery when they were still unclaimed after three months. The man even has a simple stone marker listing his name.

Unfortunately, the county coroner who would've been responsible for identifying those remains as Kendrick died seven years ago, and no autopsy records could be found. I'm sure SAC Walker will eventually have those remains excavated and tested, but that doesn't help us much now.

Four hundred and seventy-three police-issue Crown Vics from law enforcement departments in Lexington as well as the surrounding counties were auctioned off between 2012 and 2020. Each of the listings in the file showed manufacturing year, model, mileage, the overall condition, its former use, the date of the auction, and the winning bid and bidder.

My initial focus is on the names beside each entry, going carefully down the page, but nothing jumps out at me. No Kramer or Kendrick listed. I move on to the next one, hearing the rustle of paper as the others slip through their own stack.

"Can I get you guys anything else?"

Becky pokes her head in the door, looking more ragged than I've ever seen her before.

"We're fine, Becks. Why don't you try to lie down for a bit? Try to get some rest?"

I repeat what I told her half an hour ago after we had some of her soup and a sandwich. She didn't listen then either, has been in the kitchen doing God knows what to keep busy.

Earlier I asked if there was a friend she could call who could come to be with her, but she didn't want that. My guess is because she's embarrassed her husband isn't home to support her. Becky and Chad are very much about outward appearances, and I suspect any friends she has are equally skin deep. Image is everything.

Fucking Chad Miller.

"Okay," Becky says, surprising me. "Let me know if..."

She doesn't finish the sentence and looks so sad and

lost standing there. I get up and go to her, noticing her eyes swimming with emotions.

"You'll be the first to know," I promise her, folding my arms around her.

There's no one else here to give her comfort.

At first, she seems immobile, but then a sob breaks free and the full weight of her body sags against me.

All of a sudden, the front door swings open and her husband walks in the door. He takes one look at us standing in the doorway to his office and turns beet red.

"What the fuck do you think you're doing?"

Becky abruptly jerks from my arms and swings around on her husband.

"How dare you!"

Opal

"That's him."

I look up to find Melissa in the doorway.

She'd dozed off on the couch in the family room off the kitchen, watching TV, while Lee and I were in here downloading.

Janey disappeared to her room almost immediately when we got here, claiming to need peace and quiet to work. Raj has been on the phone in hers, talking to Jacob and trying to pull strings to allow her to interview Jamie Lyons once he arrives at the FBI office.

Apparently, getting his house shot up, and the shared news Mitch's daughter was now also missing, prompted Lee to share a little more of what he was able to uncover in the years of research he's put in. Some of this stuff—especially what he has on the congressman—is pretty interesting.

It turns out the Caribbean is a frequent travel destination for him. Not for family vacations though. Every one of the five trips he's made there in the past two and a half years, his family stayed home. It confirms our suspicions he's involved in the organization.

Lee has a picture he took of Melnyk sitting in an airport lounge with Kendrick up on his screen.

"That man?"

I point at the congressman, already knowing from what Kaylie told Raj, Doug was the one she was set up with at Krebs's cabin.

"He said his name was Doug," she says in a soft voice, lowering her eyes to the floor as a shiver appears to roll through her. "I'd seen his picture before. I knew he was some kind of politician. I was scared."

"I don't blame you," I tell her gently. "And I know it's not easy to talk about, but is there anything else you may have remembered since the last time we talked?"

I could swear she's about to mention something when she seems to change her mind and shakes her head. I don't want to push the girl when I know she doesn't really trust anyone at the moment. I might risk her shutting down completely, but we need something to go on. Anything.

"Melissa, another girl was taken last night. She's only sixteen years old." Her eyes snap up so I press on. "Do you remember Agent Kenny, who was with me the other day? It's his daughter. Her name is Sawyer."

She pushes away from the doorpost and walks toward us, taking a seat across the table. She glances furtively at Lee.

"Is it easier if I go?" he asks immediately with genuine concern.

Despite my poor first impression of the man, he is fast winning me over.

"No. That's all right."

"Okay. I'm just going to make some tea though. I'll just be over there," he says, pointing to the stove.

Smart move. It gives the girl a sense of privacy without losing the security of having him close by.

He's definitely rising in my esteem.

"I'll have some too, if you don't mind," I tell him as he passes, before turning to Melissa. "You want some too?"

When she nods, he says, "I'll make a pot."

He grabs the kettle off the stove and holds it under the faucet. As soon as the water runs, the girl starts talking.

"There was someone else."

"At the cabin?"

She nods.

"Okay, so Ke-Kramer was there because he drove you there. And you already mentioned Krebs, so who else?"

"I don't know his name. It was when..." She pauses for a moment. "When we were upstairs, in a bedroom."

Then she falls silent again, undoubtedly reliving the ordeal.

I reach over and cover her hand.

"Where this man took you," I prompt her gently.

"I heard an engine. Thought maybe I could get their attention and call for help. I was able to get away from... him. Saw a man on one of those four-wheelers coming out of the trees."

"An ATV?"

"Yeah. He pulled up to the house so I started banging on the window. He looked up, but..."

"He didn't help," I fill in for her.

"No. When I heard footsteps coming up the stairs and saw the door open, I thought maybe..." She swallows hard and gives her chin a little jerk. "But he sat down on a chair in the corner to watch as..."

She gives her head a hard shake as if she's trying to clear the mental image.

A loud bang from the sink has both our heads snap around to see Lee bent over, his arms braced against the counter, and his head hanging down.

"Hey," I draw Melissa's attention. "If I showed you some pictures, do you think you would recognize him?"

She shrugs, and I pull out my phone, ready to pull up a few photos I've been collecting, when Raj walks into the kitchen.

"I've gotta run," she announces.

I glance at the clock on my screen and note it's well past midnight.

"It's the middle of the night."

She grins. "I know, Matt's agent friend arrived from Paducah. I'm meeting them downtown."

As gentle and soft-spoken as Raj may appear, there is steel underneath. She's a force to be reckoned with when she sets her mind to something, and what she wanted was an interview with Jamie Lyons.

Looks like she's about to get it.

By the time she's gone, Lee is back behind his laptop, a teapot, three mugs, a carton of milk, and a bag of sugar in the middle of the table.

"Can I show you the pictures?" I check with Melissa.

"Sure."

I slide out of my seat and sit down beside her, locating the photos the CARD team took at the sex club, showing a few people going into the private room. But first I want her to look at a picture I took at breakfast at the center.

"I know you know these two." I point at Krebs and Melnyk. "But how about this man? Do you recognize him?"

I indicate Russel Germain.

She nods, and I feel excitement surge.

"I've seen him before at The Youth Center," she says. "But he wasn't the one at the cabin."

Dammit. I would have loved to nail that slick bastard.

"Okay. How about one of these guys?"

I hold my phone up so Melissa can see and start flipping through the surveillance pictures from the night at the club.

"Wait. Go back one?"

In the picture she asks me to return to is the man who was a few years ahead of me in school.

Fuck, I was supposed to have looked into him, but I never got around to it.

"He was wearing a beanie though," she explains. "I didn't know he was bald. I've never seen him at the center."

"Who is it?" Lee asks and I turn the screen toward him.

"Marshall Browning. He's the son of the former—"

But Lee doesn't let me finish as he slams a fist on the table.

"Son of a fucking bitch. I knew it!"

TWENTY-FIVE

OPAL

I shoot off a quick message to Mitch, letting him know
I'm fine.

It warmed me to notice a text had come in from him,
asking if I was okay. He must've heard from Jacob what
happened at Lee's house. I would've loved to have given
him a quick call just so I could hear his voice, but we may
be on to something and my gut tells me my time is better
spent seeing where it leads us.

I look over Lee's shoulder as he zooms in on the satellite image of Krebs's mountain property.

On the screen, I recognize the clearing and part of the
cabin's roof, as well as the barn where we found the
Yukon I saw barreling at me outside the library.

"Here, you can see the trail leading to the cliff where
Krebs was found," I point out on the image.

I'm able to follow the trail farther up the mountain

until it abruptly makes a sharp left, veering back in the direction of the main road. About halfway down you can clearly see another structure. Much smaller than the Krebs cabin.

"Looks like a hunting cabin to me," Lee suggests.

"She's asleep," Janey announces as she walks in from the family room and pulls the French doors closed behind her.

She'd come down at Lee's outburst and was about to rip him a new one when she noticed Melissa huddled on the chair next to me.

With a gentleness she doesn't usually put on display, she took the girl's arm and guided her into the next room.

It didn't escape me the reporter observed my friend's uncharacteristic behavior with great interest.

Janey sat down on the couch with Melissa and appeared to talk to her softly before changing the channel on the TV to an episode of *The Big Bang Theory*.

"I'm glad. Come have a look, we may have something here."

I wave her over.

"It's got to be a hunting cabin," she echoes Lee when she takes in the image on the screen.

"The girl said she saw an ATV coming from the direction of that trail," I explain.

"The same trail we think Kendrick disappeared down?"

"Same one," I confirm.

She nods. "Give me a minute to grab my laptop."

It takes her all of ten minutes to find a title for the

cabin and apparently a total of sixty-five acres surrounding it. Unfortunately, there's a name on the title I don't recognize.

Elizabeth Allen.

"Gotcha," Lee mutters, opening up a new window on his screen. "There it is."

I peer at the file's small font, a reminder it's time to get myself some reading glasses. The Excel file lists a bunch of names in the first column and I spot George Browning. The name Elizabeth Allen right beside it in the second column.

"George Browning's late wife," Lee clarifies. "Marshall Browning's mother. She died in 2003."

In the third column, beside Browning, I see an address which doesn't match the hunting cabin we were looking at.

"Where is that?" I want to know.

"Cave Run Lake. It's where Browning bought a property when he retired."

Janey looks over her computer at Lee.

"Any reason you've been collecting information on Lanark's former chief of police?" she asks with a healthy dose of suspicion.

"Yeah. The man is as dirty as the day is long, and I've spent years trying to prove it."

His calmly delivered honesty has one of Janey's eyebrows lift almost imperceptibly.

"Is that a fact?"

Lee shifts in his seat and angles his body toward her. I step out of the way, curious to see how this plays out.

"Damn right it is. His fingerprints were all over what happened at the Transition House."

"How do you figure?"

"My mother worked there."

"I heard," Janey answers, glancing at me.

So she took the time to read my earlier report. Finally.

"Then you probably also heard she took concerns she had about some of the stuff she'd seen at the house to the cops. She ended up talking to the chief himself. A few days later she was dead, and it was written off as an accident when it clearly wasn't. Same thing with the fire that burned the damned place down, there was never a proper investigation into a possible cause. Did you know no autopsy was ever done on the remains they found? All of it stinks to high heaven," he concludes passionately.

Janey huffs but doesn't challenge him further, which is probably as much of a concession as he's going to get. Then she turns back to her laptop and with a few keystrokes she brings up another satellite image.

I notice this one is of a lake.

"What's the address? The home address?" she asks.

Lee rattles it off as I walk over to her.

"That's pretty remote," I point out when I catch sight of a red flag marking a spot covered by trees, much the same way most of the land for miles around it is. The only recognizable proof of civilization is a glimpse of a roof almost obscured by the tree cover and a dock jutting out in the lake.

"Yup. I think we should go have a look," Janey announces.

"Why there and not at the hunting cabin?" Lee wants to know.

"Because the FBI was crawling all over that place after finding Krebs dead and would've found the cabin and cleared it. Besides, that place doesn't look to be much bigger than a room or two, and the only way to it is through town which is too close anyway," she explains. "The property on Cave Run Lake is about fifteen miles from Salt Lick, which is the closest town, and five miles from the nearest neighbor. It's also far from any law enforcement activity, and that water access makes it easy to get out of there in a hurry should the need arise. That's the place I'd pick if I wanted to hide someone."

She shoves back from the table and stands up, looking at me.

"Wanna take a drive?"

"Now? It's the middle of the night," Lee points out, getting up as well.

Janey shrugs. "No one'll see us coming."

"Fine," Lee snaps, like he has a say in the matter. "But I'm coming."

My friend barks out a rare laugh.

"Like hell you are. Two-fingered typing skills and a decent grasp of the English language hardly qualify you. Leave it to the professionals. Besides," she adds when he is about to object. "Someone has to stay here with the girl."

If looks could kill, Janey would be a pile of ashes on the kitchen floor, but she doesn't spare him another glance as she heads toward the stairs.

"You may wanna grab your gear," she tells me over her shoulder.

I'm about to follow her when I hear Lee mumble.

"*Fucking ballbuster.*"

I clap him on the shoulder in passing.

"You have no idea, my friend."

Mitch

Jesus, what a shit show.

In the past few minutes, I've learned more about my ex-wife's current marriage than I ever cared to.

She and Chad have taken the verbal battle to the kitchen after Matt, quite unsuccessfully, tried to intervene. When emotions are this charged and the parties this intent on confrontation, it's sometimes easier to let them simply battle it out instead of trying to soothe the waters.

Hard to focus when we can hear the two yelling.

"Anyone else wondering how he managed to get home from DC so quickly?" Joe observes.

"If he was in DC at all," I point out.

The fight next door has been peppered with accusations of infidelity from both parties, and I can't help wonder if Sawyer ever had to listen to arguments like this. It makes me feel even more guilty about my reaction when she showed up at my place, and explains her uncharacteristically rude reaction to Kate.

"True," Joe concedes. "Shouldn't be too hard to verify though."

Matt isn't paying us much attention, he seems glued to the papers in front of him, and I force myself to go back to the auction list as well.

The loud arguing has been ongoing in the background but when the asshole mentions my daughter's name, it draws my attention.

"...a drama queen. The little bitch is probably just off—"

I'm no longer listening, but up on my feet and on the move.

"That's enough!" I bark, startling them both when I storm into the kitchen. "We have a daughter missing," I direct at Becky. "And you're fucking fighting about your miserable goddamn marriage? You two are un-*fucking*-believable!"

Then I jab a finger at Chad, who jerks back.

"And if I hear you talk like that about Sawyer ever again, this'll be my fist coming at your face. I'll fucking wipe the floor with you, you miserable piece of shit!"

"You can't threaten me in my own house," the jerk postures, puffing out his chest.

So I lean in, my nose inches from his.

"No? Try me, Chad."

"Kenny!" Matt yells from the office. "Get your ass in here!"

I shoot the man a final scathing glare before I rush back to the office.

Matt is standing behind Joe's chair, both are looking at something on the screen of his laptop.

"Five years ago, George Browning bought a retired 2009 Crown Vic at auction," Matt informs me. "Recognize that name?"

"Former Lanark chief of police," I recall. "He'd be well in his seventies now, but his son was one of the guys Kate identified from the surveillance pictures at the sex club."

"Kate?" Joe echoes.

Fuck, I slipped up.

"Opal Berry."

Matt looks at me hard. "Not her real name," he concludes.

I meet his eyes straight on. I don't want to betray her trust, but there's no way I can lie to my teammates.

"No."

"I figured the names Opal, Pearl, and Onyx were a little too cutesy to be a coincidence," he comments. "What about Jacob Branch? That his real name?"

I shake my head. "Don't know."

I'm convinced this won't be the last of it when Matt returns his attention back to the screen, but for now it looks like I'm off the hook.

"Marshall Browning?" Joe asks.

"Yeah, that's the son," I clarify. "A couple of years ahead of Opal..." I make sure to use the right name, "...in high school, so probably mid-forties."

Joe pulls up the surveillance picture of the man. Tall, built, with a bald head and goatee.

"What've we got on him?" Matt snaps.

"Marshall Browning, forty-five, address; 2785 Polo Club Blvd, Lexington, apartment three twenty-seven," Joe rattles off while pulling up another screen. "Oh, and this is interesting; the guy is a physical training instructor at the Lexington Police Training Academy."

Interesting indeed. Between the father and the son, the family has deep roots in law enforcement.

"Maybe we should pay Marshall Browning a visit," Joe suggests.

Sounds reasonable enough—there's no way Browning isn't somehow involved in this—but I don't think wasting time rushing out to his apartment is going to get us anywhere.

"Assuming he's the one we're looking for and he has Sawyer, he's not keeping her in an apartment. First of all, it'd be hard to get her inside without someone seeing or hearing something. Too risky, especially since he would've had to leave her there to shoot up Remington's place," I argue, trying not to think about the possibility Browning had no reason to worry about Sawyer making any noise. "Also, where would he have kept the Crown Vic? In the apartment building's parking lot? He might as well have marked himself with a big red X on the map."

"He's right," Matt agrees. "Plus, we already know he's not working alone. Where does the old man live?"

During the few minutes it takes Joe to pull up the information, I notice the rest of the house has gone quiet.

Chad and Becky must've put their argument to rest. For now, at least.

Good thing too, or I might've put a bullet in the guy.

Still, the silence is as welcome as it is a little unnerving and I decide to poke my head out of the room to spot Becky sitting on the couch, obviously crying, and there's no sign of her husband. I would've noticed if he'd left so I'm sure he's somewhere in the house. Who knows, maybe he's on the phone with his lawyer complaining about FBI brutality. Like I fucking care.

I leave Becky to her own devices and turn back to the guys.

"He's got a place on Cave Run Lake."

I'm surprised when Joe mentions the place where Sawyer and I went camping what now seems like ages ago.

"I know the area," I volunteer. "It's pretty remote."

"It's also an hour and a half from here. Not exactly next door," Joe points out.

"That would only work in their favor," is Matt's response. "It's also about the same distance from either West Virginia or Ohio, giving them a way out of state fast. Plus, there'd be virtually no neighbors to speak of and little to no local traffic, making it easy to monitor anyone approaching."

I'm already shrugging into my jacket when he adds, "It would be the perfect hideout."

"Let's go," I announce.

"Hold on one second," Matt stops me. "Let me see where Byron and the others are. They can go—"

I shake my head abruptly.

"Any chance my daughter's there, I'm going. I know the area," I repeat my earlier comment.

Matt glares at me, but I won't back down. I'll quit if I have to. Either way, I'm going.

"Goddammit, Mitch," Matt barks, but he's already grabbing for his coat as well. "Joe, you stay. I'll send Byron here to join you. Punani and Dresden should stick around so you have wheels on the ground if something should move here. Oh, and keep your eye on the husband," he adds.

"You're going in without backup?" Joe questions him.

"No. I'm calling Walker from the road."

We rush out the door, leaving it to Joe to pass on to Becky what is going on. He can handle it. We don't have time for explanations.

"I'm driving," Matt orders when I'm heading for my car.

I've barely gotten into the passenger seat when my phone starts to ring.

"It's Jacob," I tell Matt.

The timing is curious to say the least. It's after one in the morning and it looks like no one is sleeping.

"Jacob," I answer. "I'm putting you on speaker."

"*I won't keep you long. Wanted to give you a heads-up. My team may have found a possible lead to a place the kids may be held. Possibly your daughter as well. They left about fifteen minutes ago. I'll call you as soon as I get any more information.*"

"Where?" Matt snaps, but is met with silence. "Fucking hell, Branch. Where?"

"I'm sorry, I seem to have a poor connection. What was that?"

The phone goes dead after that.

"That son of a bitch cut us off."

"Before you could tell him to stand his team down," I observe. "What do you want to bet they're heading for Cave Run Lake."

"Fucking amateurs will only get in our way," Matt grumbles.

I think amateurs is a bit of a misnomer—so far these women have more than proven their intelligence and their mettle—but that doesn't mean I want them facing off with the kind of power I'm afraid these men can pull together.

Especially when my daughter's life is in the balance.

Or Kate's, for that matter, because there's no doubt in my mind, she'll probably end up leading the charge.

I glance over at Matt.

"Floor it."

TWENTY-SIX

Opal

"It's Mitch again," I tell Janey.

It's the third time he's called and just like the other times, I silence the call. We'd contacted Jacob on our way out of town, and he said he'd give us a head start before contacting the CARD team. His faith in us to get the job done a confidence boost I welcome. Doubt had been creeping in since we left, wondering if I didn't owe it to Mitch to let him know right away. After all, his daughter's life could be on the line if we fail.

This time when the ringing stops it is shortly followed by the ping of an incoming message.

"Mitch as well, I presume?" she suggests.

It is.

"He says they're about fifteen minutes behind us and to pull over and wait for them."

"Ha! Not a chance in hell, buddy," Janey comments.

As much as I know ignoring his wishes and forging ahead is a risk, every minute of delay could be the difference between life and death for those kids, and that includes his daughter.

I can apologize later when we hand over his girl.

Provided she's alive and breathing.

"We can do this," my friend reassures me gently, clearly not oblivious to my internal struggles. "We gather intel, evaluate the information and strategize, then we mobilize and execute. Like we've done before."

She quotes GEM's mission statement almost verbatim, one Jacob drilled into us from the beginning.

I nod in response before focusing on the satellite app open on my phone, showing all the different routes of approach open to us. Unfortunately, all of them will require a fair bit of trudging through the woods to sneak up unseen.

The last thing we want is to alert the men I've become convinced are hiding out there—Kendrick, Browning, and likely his son—and cause them to panic.

The route I instruct Janey to follow is one that avoids populated areas as much as possible once we get off Highway 64. It also stays away from what would be a more direct route to the property. I found a trailhead where we can leave the SUV about a two-mile hike from the residence. Rough terrain too, but nothing we can't handle, even carrying our gear.

The thirty-or-so-minute drive, once we get off the highway, passes quickly as I actively navigate every turn, and by the time we pull onto the dirt road leading to the trailhead, I'm fully focused and ready.

Janey pulls the SUV under the cover of a large tree, out of sight from above, and from anyone driving past the small parking loop. When we get out, we make sure to close the doors quietly. Noise carries, especially close to water and in the quiet of night.

Getting our gear, we strap on the Kevlar vests Jacob insists we wear going into potentially dangerous situations, and adjust the two-way radio earpieces, making sure we're on the same channel. Then Janey fits her night-vision goggles over her head, while I change the scope on my M24 sniper rifle for a nighttime one. Daylight is still a few hours away.

Checking my cell phone before tucking it back in my pocket, I see there's no reception, which doesn't worry me, I know Janey carries a sat phone.

The rest of my gear and extra ammo is tucked in the small backpack I have strapped on. My Glock is in my pocket, a stun gun hooked to my belt, and I'm holding a satellite GPS in my hand. My classic-looking M24 is slung over my shoulder.

When I look over at Janey, I see she's ready as well, and nod to let her know to go ahead.

She's much faster than I am and limber on her feet, which is helpful in the dense brush with fallen trees and limbs littering the way. However, leading the way she hits any obstacles first so all I have to do is follow close behind her and manage to stay upright.

Still, I'm breathing heavy by the time she motions for me to stop.

"Two o'clock," she whispers.

My eyes pan to the right and catch sight of a faint glow of light through the trees. I check the GPS in my hand.

"Could be the house."

"Maybe."

The next moment the light abruptly disappears. Perhaps someone turning off an outside lamp before turning in late. We're going to need to proceed with extra caution.

Janey starts moving and I fall into step, pulling my Glock from my pocket as we get closer. With the reflection of the moon off the water as a lighter backdrop, we can see the dark outlines of the house appear.

Ahead of me, Janey appears to stumble and starts falling forward. I reach out and barely manage to grab hold of the back of her vest, narrowly keeping her from falling face-first into a tree trunk.

Suddenly we're bathed in a flood of bright light, coming from directly above us. Janey curses loudly, ripping the goggles off her head as she's instantly blinded. I need to blink my eyes a few times to adjust, still hanging on to her vest as I jerk her back into the shadows.

"Motion sensor light," I tell her, just as a shot rings out.

It strikes the tree I just pulled us behind, sending pieces of bark flying, and has us ducking down. I keep my eyes peeled on the house which is still dark. No lights are on.

A second shot immediately follows, barely missing us, but it gives me an idea where the shots are coming from. I caught the flash.

"Rifle. Second floor, to the left of the front door," I inform Janey, no longer worrying about my volume.

She's already firing off a couple of shots as I lift my rifle from my shoulder and try to sight in on the window. With the night-vision scope, I can't see a thing because of the damn floodlight. Any movement we make gets picked up by the sensors, so unless we move out of range, I can't accurately fire off a shot.

"We need to move for me to get a clear shot."

"I know," she answers, already darting to the left, while staying crouched low.

She ducks behind another tree and fires off a few more shots, giving me the cover I need to hustle up behind her. Unfortunately, we're looking up an incline and I don't have a good vantage point.

"I want to get over there."

I point out a tree about twenty feet up ahead on slightly higher ground.

"I'll cover you," Janey says and I immediately brace to run. "*Three, two...*"

When she starts firing on *one*, I'm already hoofing it, pumping my legs as I run a zigzag pattern, praying I don't fall over a root or fallen branch. I hit the trunk of the tree and brace my back against it, sliding down until my butt hits the ground. Then I roll over on my stomach, pulling my M24 in front of me. Staying low to the ground, it'll be hard to spot me since our shooter no longer has the advantage of elevation.

Now when I line up my sight, I can see movement in the window and catch the light reflect off a barrel. I don't hesitate and take a shot.

Whoever was holding the rifle drops it instantly and I can hear the clatter when it hits the ground below. I'm not sure if I hit my target, but getting the weapon from his hand is good enough for now.

Janey heard it too and is already crouching down beside me.

"We can't afford to wait," she points out.

She's right. We have to capitalize now, when whoever is in the house is hopefully momentarily distracted.

"We need to split up."

It's the only way we can have at least both obvious exits blocked. Going in different directions can also throw off whoever is watching.

"I'll go around the back," I add. "You see if there's an alternate way to the front door to get in."

She gives me a thumbs-up and, staying as close to the ground as I can, I start moving. I'm able to use the woods for cover until I'm almost at the house, when I hear a shriek.

"*No!*"

The voice is female, comes from the rear of the house, and sounds scared as hell. I'm pretty sure it's Sawyer's, but there's no way to know for sure until I get a glimpse. It makes my blood pump a little faster.

Without thinking too hard, I dart out of the trees toward the side of the house and with my back pressed against the siding and my Glock leading the way, I ease my way toward the rear. I move carefully and every so often I look behind me. The last thing I want is someone sneaking up on me from behind.

Another screech pierces the night, this one seems to come from farther, closer to the water.

Shit. The dock.

"*I heard that,*" Janey's voice crackles in my ear.

I press my finger to my earpiece.

"*I'm investigating.*"

When I step away from the wall, I can see all the way to the water. I think it's Kendrick, the tall man teetering on the floating dock. He seems to have a hard time keeping his footing as he struggles to lift the smaller figure of a girl into the motorboat moored alongside it.

"*Have visual. Kendrick is trying to escape with a hostage,*" I whisper.

"*Need assistance?*"

"*Negative. Cover the house.*"

"*About to make entry,*" Janey confirms.

They're a couple of hundred yards from me, and I have a clear line of sight. Lifting my rifle, I brace it tightly against my shoulder, line my right eye up with the scope, and find the pair on the dock.

I'm pretty sure it's Mitch's daughter and it's definitely Kendrick. If the situation wasn't so dire, I'd be smiling at the girl's grit. Even with her hands apparently tied behind her back, she's giving him a hard time, kicking her legs as he lifts her from behind.

As it is, I need to focus on making sure that boat doesn't leave the dock.

Unfortunately, they're moving too much for me to get a clear shot and I can't risk hitting Sawyer.

A volley of shots coming from behind me breaks my concentration, and for a moment I turn away from my target. By the time I realize the sound was coming from inside the house and focus back on the dock, Kendrick and the girl are inside the boat. The sound of an engine starting has my heart dropping.

My chance to stop him gone, I start running straight toward the water's edge, hoping I can get a clear shot as he takes off.

I watch the boat veer away from the dock and kick it into high gear, cursing the extra pounds I'm carrying for slowing me down. I used to run like the wind, but my condition isn't the same as it was even ten years ago.

There's an outcropping of land jutting out into the lake I'm pretty sure Kendrick is aiming for. If he can make it around the tip he'll be out of sight and out of reach.

The moment my feet hit the dock, the damn thing starts bobbing up and down, almost throwing me off-kilter. Despite that I manage to make it to the end, widening my stance against the movement of the water. Panting like a racehorse, I lift my rifle and relax my neck, letting my cheek fall against the stock as I squeeze my left eye shut.

The first thing I notice through my scope is Sawyer,

sitting upright in the bow of the boat, facing me. She appears to be looking right at me.

Kendrick has his back to me and is ducked down, making himself as small a target as possible.

Despite the boat speeding toward that strip of land, I need to take in a few deep breaths, letting the air deflate from my lungs. Everything seems to slow down as I wait for my opportunity, which comes sooner than expected when the girl shifts over to the side of the boat. Almost half of Kendrick's torso is now a clear target.

That's enough for me.

I line up my shot and curl my index finger into the trigger guard.

I breathe in, but hold this one.

"Don't shoot!" I hear a man yell, but it's too late; my finger is already pressing down on the trigger.

The shot echoes loud over the water.

TWENTY-SEVEN

Mitch

"Is that what I think it is?"

I follow the direction Matt is pointing in and it takes me a second to spot the sparse light bouncing off a section of a headlight.

We left Matt's truck at the side of the road at the base of the long unpaved driveway up to the house and decided to walk in.

I never heard back from Kate, but I have to assume she's already here and hopefully proceeding with caution as well. I doubt the message I left her to cease and desist did much to slow her down, so we broke every speed limit to get here.

Agents from the Lexington office can't be far behind us. Matt called SAC Walker from the road. He promised to dispatch backup right away, but we can't afford to wait for them to catch up.

The Crown Vic is covered with fallen branches in an attempt to hide it. Matt starts walking toward it but I whistle softly between my teeth and motion for him to come back. The more urgent objective is to get to the house where my gut says we'll find Sawyer, we can check the vehicle later.

He shrugs and turns back when a shot rings out in the distance. Both of us snap our heads in the direction of the sound. Then a second one.

"*Rifle,*" Matt mouths.

It's followed by a salvo which sounds like return fire, this time from a smaller caliber. Maybe a handgun.

Fuck, this is not good.

We start moving at the same time, breaking into a run up the left side of the long driveway, no longer bothering to hide under the tree cover. More shots ring out, making my legs pump harder. My heart too. Running with the extra weight of equipment doesn't make it any easier.

I struggle to keep up with Matt, who's ahead of me, and vow once this is over, I'm going to add running to my exercise regime.

The sharp report of a rifle seems to sound closer—or maybe that's just wishful thinking—but after that, silence appears to return to the night. I hope to God it doesn't mean Kate and her partner are hurt, or worse.

The only sound is from our feet pounding the packed dirt.

Up ahead, Matt comes to a stop and holds up his hand to alert me. I ease up alongside him and notice the house up ahead. Visibility is better here, closer to the water the night is not quite so dark.

My legs burn and my lungs are straining for air, as I take stock of the place.

The house is large, but nothing special to look at. A two-story construction covered in beige siding, with a centered front door. One of the upstairs windows appears to be open and off to the right of the house is a separate double garage. A sliver of the lake is visible directly ahead.

It looks almost deserted; no vehicles out front and no lights on inside. If not for the sound of gunfire, we might've been tricked into believing if someone was in there in the first place, they'd be sleeping.

A scream pierces the silence and all the hair on my body stands on end.

"Fuck, Mitch, wait," Matt hisses, but my feet are already moving.

Nothing short of a bullet is going to stop me, and even that might not be enough.

Logically that scream could have been from anyone, but somehow, I know down to my bones I just heard my daughter.

It's amazing what the body can do when fueled by fear and adrenaline. I can't even feel my legs as I race toward the house.

I catch a glimpse of movement on the right side of the house. A small shadow slipping between the house and the garage and out of sight. I could swear the scream came from the other side, where I can see the glimmer coming off the water.

The dock.

I'm about to dart across the path between the trees and the house when gunfire erupts again. Swiveling around, I just catch Matt sprinting along the front of the house, ducking into the alleyway separating it from the garage.

As more shots ring out, I'm torn whether to follow him or rush toward the water where I heard Sawyer's scream. Backup or rescue? My mind is still struggling when my body already makes the decision.

The right one: I'm running toward the back of the house when I hear the sound of an engine starting up.

My eyes quickly take in the scene before me as I round the corner. The moonlight illuminates the end of the dock where I just catch sight of a boat moving away. Two people inside, one of whom I have no trouble identifying as my baby girl.

An invisible fist punches all the air from my chest.

Then I notice the figure running onto the dock. The hair gives her away.

Kate.

I take off after her, registering a moment too late she's lifting a rifle, lining up the boat in her sights.

Does she not see my daughter in the boat?

I open my mouth to yell, but nothing comes out. I stop and try again, cupping my hands around my mouth.

"Don't shoot!"

Too late: the rifle's crack reverberates across the lake.

My eyes seek out the retreating boat, and I just catch sight of something big hitting the water with a big splash. Was it Sawyer or her captor?

Jesus, I can't see anyone else in the watercraft, which appears to aim straight for a piece of land extending into the lake.

I hear yelling behind me and the sound of running footsteps as I stand by, helplessly watching as the boat slams into the shore.

A fraction of a second later, the sound of an explosion reaches my ears.

Then I turn my head back to the dock, seeing only a rifle and what looks like a Kevlar vest left on its planks.

There's no sign of Kate.

Opal

She jumped.

Even as I pulled the trigger, I saw her leap over the side.

The next instant my bullet hit true, toppling Kendrick off the other side of the boat, which seems to veer slightly off course, straight for land.

She jumped.

Unless she managed to get out of her bindings, she is virtually helpless in the water.

The moment my brain processes the information, I drop my rifle from my hands, strip off my vest, and without a second thought, dive into the lake's frigid waters.

I gasp at the cold when my head breaks the surface, but force my limbs to move anyway. I'm not a great swimmer by any means, but I'm no slouch and fueled by determination, although I regret not kicking off my shoes first.

Keeping my eyes on the tip of land the boat had been aiming for I don't see the impact, but I hear the sound of an explosion and feel the vibrations in the water around me.

My focus is on Sawyer, and while making sure I stay on course, I also keep an eye out for any sign of her in the water.

I hope to God she is able to at least tread water and keep her head elevated, because no matter how hard I swim, that piece of land doesn't seem to get any closer. My arms and legs burn with the effort, and my strokes get sloppier as my water-soaked clothes pull me down.

Under any other circumstance I might've given up, but this is Mitch's daughter. If anything happens to her, he'll never forgive me.

Hell, I'll never forgive myself.

There.

Up ahead, maybe a hundred yards from me, I see movement in the water. Just a slight splashing.

"Sawyer!"

A head pops up and I can see her pale face against the dark water.

Clever girl. She'd been floating on her back, the splashing I saw probably the kicking of her legs.

Ignoring the cold creeping into my bones, I attack the water with renewed energy. It still takes me a couple of minutes to get close.

A quick glance at the shore shows we've still got a ways to go.

"Sawyer, I need you to roll on your back again. Use your lungs for buoyancy," I tell her.

I'm having a hard enough time keeping myself afloat, the last thing I need is the girl desperately grabbing on to me, potentially drowning us both in the process.

When I see her do what I asked, I approach and tread water beside her. Even in the moonlight I can see her skin is pale and she's having a hard time focusing her eyes. I can't expect her to be too much help in her own rescue.

Underwater, my numb hands are fumbling with the buckle on my belt.

"Hey, Sawyer? I'm going to need you to hook your arm through my belt so I can pull you to shore."

Dammit, hypothermia is getting to me as well. I'm starting to slur my words.

"Opal?"

I smile at her despite my chattering teeth.

"You've got it."

Finally I'm able to pull my belt free and quickly help her stick her arm through the loop I created by slipping the end through the buckle.

"All you have to do is breathe, do you hear me?" I ask the girl.

Her faint, "Yeah," will have to do.

Grabbing on to the end of the belt, I aim for shore. Long strokes with one arm and a kick of my legs, while I hold on to Mitch's daughter for dear life, dragging her behind me.

Somewhere along the way my mind goes blank and my body functions on instinct alone, the drag in the water behind me like dead weight. I have no idea how long I've been in the water when I feel hands hook under my arms, dragging me ashore, but I don't let go of the belt.

"Oh fuck, Sawyer..."

The agonized voice is the last thing I hear before I lose my battle with consciousness.

Mitch

"Air Evac chopper will meet us just outside of town. ETA is five minutes."

I glance up at the EMT, who is hooking another bag of warm fluids on the IV pole.

Sawyer's skin is almost translucent and her lips are blue against the mylar blankets she's covered with.

If not for her slow heart rate showing on the portable monitor, I'd think she was already gone.

Kate's condition had been only fractionally better as she was loaded onto the second ambulance.

It had been second nature to jump in the back of the ambulance with my daughter, but my heart ached not being able to be two places at once.

That had been the longest forty minutes of my life, waiting for the ambulances Matt had called to arrive.

We'd done what we could, stripping both of them down to their underwear and wrapping them in layers of our clothing. Two SUVs with Lexington agents had arrived, and we were able to get the women into the back of one of the vehicles, blasting the heat as high as it would go.

"Where is the other ambulance going?" I ask as I glance out the small window in the back.

The second rig is transporting Kate, with Pearl by her side. It's been behind us all the way to Salt Lick and just turned right where we went left.

"Morehead. The other patient is more stable and she'll be at the urgent care center in fifteen minutes or so," the young man clarifies. "Your daughter's flight to Lexington should take about the same time."

But it'll take me a fuckofalot longer, since I've already been told there's no room for me on the chopper. One of the Lexington agents should be behind us to drive me to town since Matt has to stay and manage the scene.

I haven't even asked who was shooting or what was found inside the house. The only thing important to me right now are the two people I care about most in this world.

The ambulance stops at the edge of a sports field, and I can already hear the sound of the helicopter rotors.

When the stretcher is pulled from the ambulance, I barely have a chance to kiss her cold forehead and tell her I love her, before she's rushed toward the waiting chopper.

I watch it take off with a heavy heart, hoping like fuck I didn't just kiss my girl for the last time. When I turn around the Bureau's Ford Expedition is already waiting.

After a mumbled thanks and a nod for the agent, whose name I already can't remember, I aim my eyes out the window as I replay the longest hour or so of my life.

When Matt caught up with me, I'd just tracked down Kate in the water. She was swimming away from the dock and I started running in that direction when his hand grabbed my shoulder.

"Easier to keep up with her running along the shore," he'd pointed out.

A better idea than jumping in the water after her, which is what I'd been about to do. Chances would've been all three of us ending up hypothermic and in need of assistance, and not enough people to do the rescuing.

One look at Sawyer and I knew she was in trouble.

Kate was a powerhouse, having been in the water about as long as my daughter, she'd still found the strength to drag her almost all the way to shore before passing out.

My emotions are all over the fucking place. Anger still

rushes through my veins when I think about the risk Kate took when she shot at that sick bastard—the bullet might've hit Sawyer—but at the same time I'm overwhelmed with gratitude she saved my daughter's life.

Then there's the guilt. *Christ*, so much guilt.

The weight of responsibility sits heavy on my chest.

It doesn't help when we arrive at the hospital Becky is the first person I encounter. Tears are streaming down her face but her mouth is an angry line.

She plants the heels of both hands in my chest and shoves me with all her weight.

"You bastard! This is all your fault," she spits at me. "If not for that precious, goddamn job of yours, none of this would've happened."

Chad stands behind her—suddenly the picture of a loving and supportive husband—and folds his arms around her waist, bending low to whisper something in her ear as he pulls her out of my path.

Her outburst is like a kick to the nuts, but I manage to walk right past them without a word.

At the desk, I ask immediately about my daughter's condition.

"She was flown in by helicopter sometime in the past half hour. I'm her father," I explain.

The young nurse seems surprised as her eyes glance beyond me.

"I'm sorry," she starts a little awkwardly. "Maybe there's been a misunderstanding. That gentleman told me he's her father."

I don't even have to look behind me to know she's

talking about fucking Chad. Instead of turning what is already a testy situation into a full-on brawl, I pull my badge from my pocket.

"My name is Mitchell Kenny and I'm Sawyer Kenny's father. If you'd like I can pull up the court order indicating shared custody."

The girl turns beet red and shakes her head.

"That won't be necessary. I'm sorry about the confusion."

"Not your fault. Now, can you please give me an update on my daughter?"

TWENTY-EIGHT

Opal

"So what happened?"

I'm shivering under the warm blankets piled on top of me, and my mind is still a bit groggy.

"You shot Kendrick. They were able to pull his body from the lake. Nice head shot," Janey says.

I'd been down in the emergency room when I woke up and was told my friend was in the waiting room, but the treatment rooms were so overrun, no visitors were allowed.

Once the attending physician decided my vitals were stable, they moved me up here for monitoring. I'll be here for at least twenty-four hours I was told.

I was relieved to see Janey walk into the room.

"Good, but I meant what happened with the girl? Is she okay?"

"Sawyer? She was airlifted to LMC in Lexington. Last I heard, she hadn't regained consciousness but was deemed stable. Mind you, this is at least third-hand information Jacob passed on. He sends you his best, by the way."

I blow out a relieved breath. Stable is good.

The girl already had a traumatic day and a half before she ended up in the water. I hope she simply needs a little more time before she's ready to face the world again. She just learned firsthand how ugly it can be.

"Did you find the other kids?" I ask hopefully.

"Bobby-Jean," Janey says, a tense expression on her face.

"Please, tell me she was alive."

"Yes. For what it's worth," she grinds out. "The old man kept her in a dog kennel in the basement, which had been turned into some kind of playroom."

Bile crawls up my throat. That poor girl.

"I had to crawl into that crate, she wouldn't come out."

That can't have been easy for my friend, who has a severe case of claustrophobia, with good reason.

Janey goes on to tell me how she encountered George Browning trying to get to the garage. Presumably to get away in one of the trucks parked there. He fired a few shots at Janey first, who only had a few of the thirteen rounds in the magazine of her Smith & Wesson left to return fire. She wasn't able to take him down before he ducked into the garage for cover.

She'd been about to follow him inside when Matt stormed past her out of nowhere, and took the former police chief to the ground.

He's in custody, along with the younger Browning, who was found in a bedroom upstairs, alive but bleeding from a shot through the shoulder.

"No sign of Jesper or the two girls?" I want to know.

Bryonne and Chantel are also still missing.

Janey shakes her head.

"Not yet, but that house is crammed full of junk. I'm sure the feds will be going over every inch of it. Let's hope they find something useful."

My eyes feel heavy so I close them and lie back. Three kids still out there.

Shit. We're not quite done yet.

"Do you need to sleep?"

"No. Just resting. What else? Any word from Raj? What about the other players, has Melnyk been picked up?"

My eyes snap open as the questions suddenly flood my mind.

"What about Russel Germain? We can't let those guys slip through our fingers. We can't let them get away with this."

Janey snickers.

"Slow your roll, Kate. You're not going anywhere anytime soon. You know Jacob is all over it, and so is Driver and his CARD team. No one is going to get away with anything."

She sits on the edge of my bed and pats my hand before she checks her phone.

"Nothing from Raj yet, but I'm sure either she or Jacob will let us know."

I only have one question left, and I'm not sure I want the answer, but I ask anyway.

"How is Mitch?"

Janey's face softens.

"Distraught, terrified, angry, anything you can imagine, he's probably feeling."

I nod. I'm sure the anger is for me.

"He yelled at me not to shoot," I whisper.

"He did?"

"It was too late. I was already pulling the trigger." I shake my head. "She saw me, trusted me, and jumped right off that boat."

"That girl would've been dead if not for you," my friend defends me.

"She might still die…"

The words taste bitter on my tongue as I think how many lives it would impact. Including my own.

"She will pull through," Janey says confidently.

"Maybe if I—"

"What?" she interrupts. "Did what? Let Kendrick take her? Would that have been preferable? Or she could've stayed on that boat and would've been blown to bits. You gave her a chance."

Rationally, I know she has a point, but I doubt Mitch would see it that way.

I smile at her even as tears burn my eyes.

"Yeah, you're right."

It's clear from the weary expression on her face she doesn't buy my capitulation. She knows me too well.

"You should get some rest," she says when I close my eyes.

Sleep sounds good right now, not like I've had much of it in the past days, but I'm not sure I'll be able to.

"Okay," I respond nonetheless.

"I should give that reporter a call, give him an update. He's been blowing up my damn phone," she grumbles as I feel her get up off the bed.

"I don't even know where my phone is," I share.

"Probably at the bottom of the lake, but leave it to me. I'll pick up a new one when I'm out. I have to find a way back to the lake to pick up my ride anyway. I'll leave my number at the nurses' desk, in case. Shouldn't be too long."

Her footsteps retreat and I hear the swoosh of the door closing.

The first tear escapes and rolls down my cheek.

Mitch

"No."

Chad startles when I block his way.

He tries to look into the room behind me but I shift and cut off his view of my daughter. I don't want him even looking at her.

"I have a right to—" he starts, but I cut him off.

"You have no rights and you know it. Take a walk, Miller."

Becky must've let him know Sawyer was awake because he's been MIA since shortly after I got here this morning.

"Mr. Miller," Matt says behind me. "Your wife is down the hall in the waiting room, feel free to join her, we shouldn't be too long."

He hesitates briefly, making one more attempt to catch a glimpse of my daughter, before he presses his lips together and stalks off.

"Punani will keep an eye on him," Matt reminds me in a low voice.

I close the door, lean my back against it, and smile reassuringly at my daughter, who's sitting up in bed, the color back on her cheeks.

Thank fuck.

"Go on, Pumpkin," I encourage her.

Becky and I had sat at her bedside for what felt like forever when she'd finally started waking up a few hours ago. A little groggy at first, but that didn't last long. She'd quickly perked up after a nurse brought her something to drink and some soup to eat.

Then she surprised me when she said she needed to talk to me alone. Becky didn't much like that, but Sawyer insisted, reminding her mom she was a witness and had information for the FBI.

I made her wait until Matt could get here, mainly because I was afraid of what she might tell me. I had no idea what happened to her in the roughly thirty-two hours she was in the hands of these perverts.

To my immense relief, she'd been lucky. She'd been shoved around a bit but hadn't been touched sexually.

"Dad, don't leave him alone with Mom," she says, her eyes on the door.

"Who, Chad? They won't be, John Punani is keeping your mom company."

That seems to appease her as she settles back against her pillows.

"Good. Because, Dad? He was behind it."

It's like the air is sucked out of the room and every muscle in my body tenses up.

"Your stepfather?" Matt asks.

She nods.

"Like I said, the guy who claimed to be a cop wouldn't talk to me after he arrested me, and locked me in the back of his car. When we finally got to the house, he handed me off to the other guy, not the old man, but the guy on the boat. That one tied me up in the small bathroom and told me if I behaved, they wouldn't have to hurt my mom. Then he said I could thank my stepdad for that."

She closes her eyes briefly, looking pale again. I push away from the door, taking a seat on the edge of her bed and brushing the hair off her forehead. My anger momentarily pushed aside with concern for my girl.

"You need to take a break?"

She shakes her head and grabs on to my hand.

"I didn't understand what he meant at first," she continues. "But I could overhear them talk in the living room. They planned to sell me. Said I'd probably fetch them a good price, that I was worth more than the girl Chad traded me in for. They thought it was funny."

She sniffles and turns her eyes on me.

"The worst part is, I had no trouble believing he'd do something like that. He gave me the creeps, Dad. The way he'd look at me, or sometimes touch me, I knew it wasn't right. Last week he walked into the bathroom when I was in the shower. I know I locked the door. I'm sorry I didn't tell you."

I shoot off the bed with murder on my mind when Sawyer starts crying.

"Dad, please..."

Matt, his phone to his ear, is already rushing out the door.

I tamp down my rage and turn back to the bed. Then I climb in beside her, rest my back against the headboard, and collect my little girl in my arms.

She's had enough trauma for a lifetime, the last thing she needs is to have her father charged with murder.

"Nothing for you to apologize for, Pumpkin. Not a damn thing."

I trust my team; they can take Miller down.

My daughter needs me.

"I DID NOTHIN' WRONG."

The girl jerks her chin up defiantly.

"No one said you did," Matt returns.

It had been getting dark when he poked his head into Sawyer's hospital room and asked me to step outside.

Becky had come in at some point, her eyes red-rimmed from crying. Sawyer had fallen asleep and I'd moved to sit in a chair beside her, still holding on to her hand.

I was already moving out of the way when Becky mouthed, "Sorry," and climbed into bed with our daughter, gathering her in her arms. I slipped out to get a coffee from the hospital cafeteria and put a call in to Jacob for an update on Kate. He was able to tell me she was doing well and would likely be released in the morning.

As much as I wanted to go see her, it would've taken me at least two and a half hours just to get to Morehead and back. I did try her number but it went straight to voicemail, and when I called the hospital, I was told she was sleeping. I didn't bother leaving a message.

What I have to say to her has to be done in person.

"I turned eighteen last month," the girl says defensively. "I'm legal. I can do whatever I want."

"But you weren't eighteen when you met Chad, were you?" Matt probes. "Did he force himself on you that first time?"

She tries to keep her face impassive, but only partially succeeds.

"It weren't like that. Not like them lowlifes on the

street who take what they want without anything in return. Look at this place."

Chantel Staffman gestures around the cozy apartment that lowlife Miller had set her up in.

Joe found out about a lease for the place in Covington, just south of the Ohio River, when he interviewed the man's secretary. According to her, Miller hadn't been scheduled to go to DC until this coming week.

The bastard was probably hanging out here.

"I ain't on the streets, I got food in my fridge, and he's gettin' me a car."

That's not likely to happen now and I can't help feeling sorry for the kid. She's been gaslighted.

"When's the last time you saw him?"

"Couple'a days ago. Stayed for a few days."

"Did he do that often?"

She shrugs. "A few times for the night, but mostly he'd just show up for a couple of hours."

"Did he say why he was staying longer this time?" Matt asks.

"He didn't say, he was kinda busy on the phone most of the time."

"Do you know who he was talking to?"

"Some guy about a girl."

"Did you get a name?"

"Nah, I just heard him say they could pick the girl up at her dad's place." Suddenly, she turns to me. "What'd you say your name was?"

I'm surprised, I've been keeping a low profile, letting

Matt run the interview, but I did introduce myself when we came in.

"Agent Mitch Kenny. Why?"

She nods.

"Cuz I'm pretty sure I heard him mention your name."

Matt and I share a look.

Chantel Staffman has given us the final nail in Chad Miller's coffin.

That son of a bitch is going down.

"He lawyered up, by the way," Matt shares when we get in his vehicle.

"Miller?"

He hums in confirmation.

"Let me guess; Russel Germain?"

"Got it in one."

"Would be nice to find something concrete we can use on that dirtbag," I suggest.

"And Melnyk," Matt adds. "So far, we have the word of a high-school-dropout daughter of a meth head against that of a well-respected member of Congress. Doesn't require a degree to see how that would play out."

He's not lying.

It's no wonder these kids never bothered to seek out help from law enforcement or any other grown-up for that matter.

All they've learned in their young lives is that they're not worth listening to.

That's where I'm hoping the FBI's Violent Crimes Against Children Section, our CARD unit, and organizations like GEM can make a difference. Give kids a voice, be advocates.

Which reminds me...

"What's happening to the Lyons kid? Anything from him yet?"

There are still two kids out there, and the hope remains Jamie Lyons may be able to tell us where to look.

"Onyx was still working to soften him up. The kid is tough. Let me give her a quick call."

"Agent Driver," the woman answers in that elegant voice. "I was just about to call you."

"Tell me you got somewhere with him."

"He was warming up once I informed him both Melissa and Bobby-Jean were found. Quite chatty, ultimately."

"How would he know those girls were missing? He was already gone for months by then," I point out.

Unless, of course, he stayed in touch with someone. Maybe one of the kids?

"Ah, yes, I was wondering the same thing. It turns out Jamie kept himself abreast of what happened at the center by way of monthly phone calls to a friend."

"Who's the friend?" Matt wants to know.

"Apparently, the cook. Brian Tapper."

Wow.

That's one twist I didn't see coming. I remember Kate mentioning the man seemed rather fond of the kid and suggested perhaps talking to him again, but we never really had the chance.

"He knew?"

"Jamie swears he never told Brian where he was and begged him not to tell anyone. He'd been afraid the information might fall into the wrong hands."

"Whose?" I ask, making a mental note to finally pay this Brian a visit.

"It would appear our rather shady attorney has a penchant for boys. Unwanted interest in young Jamie, who felt he had no choice but to run. However, he did not go alone," she adds.

"Jesper Olson."

Those two were friends, it seemed a logical conclusion.

But the response I get from Onyx is a surprise.

"Actually, no. It was Bryonne Taylor. I'm on my way to pick her up in Paducah now."

"Are you kidding me?" Matt exclaims. "Paducah?"

"Hiding under the Clark Memorial Bridge across the Tennessee River," she confirms.

"Fuck me. She was right under our nose. I'll call my friend to go pick her up," he offers.

"I'd rather you didn't. The girl is bound to take off. As a woman, I'll present less of a threat."

Onyx makes a good point, one that has become more obvious these past weeks.

I never really thought about the fact we don't have women in our unit, but I'm starting to wonder if that should not be amended.

"Fair enough," Matt concedes. "But at the very least let him provide some backup."

"I won't say no to that."

All the kids accounted for except for one.

"What about Jesper Olson?" I prompt. "Did he say anything about him?"

"Yes, he did."

A lengthy pause follows before she clarifies the statement.

"Jesper Olson was the one who lured them in."

TWENTY-NINE

*O*PAL

"Okay, hold on one second..."

I glance over at Janey who—as expected—is glowering at Lee Remington. The man is virtually leaning across the conference table, an expression of disbelief on his face.

"Are you saying one of the kids was in it with Kendrick?"

"We have reason to believe Jesper Olson was, yes," Jacob's tinny voice confirms from the speaker in the center of the table. *"The boy was well-liked by the other kids, a bit of a heartthrob, and generally looked up to by his peers. He made for the perfect decoy."*

It had been Jacob's idea to invite Remington to our office for a 'briefing,' after the journalist hounded us relentlessly for information since we found Sawyer and Bobby-Jean. Our boss is hoping to satisfy Lee with a few salient tidbits only pertaining to the missing kids, but referring him to the FBI for the rest. Personally, I'm not so sure the man will be that easily put off.

"Has he been located?"

"Not yet," I answer. "We're still working on it."

It's been two weeks since Janey and Raj drove me home from the hospital. *Home*, home, as in, my place a couple of miles outside Dry Ridge. Jacob had insisted on one week's rest before he'd allow me back to work. It had been one of the longest weeks of my life. Luckily, Janey took pity on me and delivered a new laptop, in addition to the new phone she'd already provided me with.

Still, I watched more TV than I ever had. Mostly Hallmark Christmas movies that were incredibly lame, but very addictive and inevitably made me cry.

I did a lot of that too. Went through a six-pack of Kleenex boxes in seven days, although I can't say it was just because of the sappy movies.

Mitch never called. He contacted Janey a few times and apparently inquired about me, but I never got a call myself, or even a text.

It's the risk I took when I walked out of the house when Sawyer was missing, but I'm not going to lie, it still hurt. Mitch was the first guy I let down my guard with. Could envision something long term with.

So yeah, I felt the loss. Still do.

It was a relief when the week was over and Jacob allowed me back into the office.

Since then, I've spent most of my time trying to find out what happened to Jesper Olson. Yesterday, I got a lead that pointed us in the direction of the Cayman Islands.

In her interview with Jamie Lyons, he'd informed Raj that Jesper offered him, Chantel, and Bryonne, a chance to make a few extra bucks by serving drinks and food at some private Christmas party. It was supposed to take place at the Bluegrass Scenic Railroad and Museum in Versailles. By his account—which was later confirmed by Chantel—Kendrick drove them to the location in a van but it had been Jesper who handed out hot chocolates. Those had apparently been laced with something. Rohypnol, most likely.

Jamie says the only thing he remembers is finding himself half-naked in a railway car with Russel Germain. He freaked out, knocked the lawyer on his bare ass, and took off. He found Bryonne puking in the walkway of the next car and dragged her along.

They managed to get away and kept running.

I found a charge on Mason Kramer's credit card account around the same time for two business class tickets to the Cayman Islands over Christmas. One in his name and the other traveler listed was Oliver Cade. Kendrick flew back to the U.S. two days after Christmas, but the return portion on the second ticket was never claimed.

Yesterday, a Delta flight attendant was able to identify both Jesper Olson and Josh Kendrick as seated in her section on the flight to Grand Cayman.

So yeah, we're still working this case.

It could be months yet before we can see the full

scope of this operation. Nailing Kendrick was a victory for GEM for sure, but who's to say it ended with him? Sure, we succeeded in finding those kids, but none of them came away unscathed and they will all need extensive therapy. Besides, who knows how many of them are still out there we don't know about?

The truth is, we may never get all the answers we want but it certainly won't be for lack of trying.

I'm exhausted. A common aftereffect of hypothermia, I'm told. It's been a full day of planning, even after Remington finally left. I'm convinced we haven't seen the last of him, but there's little more we can do about it. Like every member on our team, he won't rest until the last T is crossed and I is dotted.

The man is like a dog with a bone.

"Go home. Get some rest," Raj orders.

Home.

It used to be my sanctuary. I'd walk in and leave everything on the doorstep. These past few weeks it has become a bitter reminder of what feels like a surprisingly lonely existence.

I don't even own a pet, for crying out loud.

Stopping at Kroger on my way through town, I pick up a few odds and ends to make a hearty stew. Something filling and wholesome that will last me at least a couple of days.

It's been getting colder and, apparently, we're expecting snow tomorrow afternoon. We don't generally get a whole lot of the white stuff here, and I'm not exactly looking forward to it.

I wish I could trade places with Janey. She is flying to Grand Cayman the day after tomorrow for a bit of recon.

Maybe a trip to the islands would get my mind off Mitch Kenny.

It's dark when I pull up to my small, two-bedroom farmhouse, so I'm glad for the outdoor lights I have on a timer. Most of the three acres of property that came with it are treed, the original farmland surrounding those long sold off to neighboring farmers by a previous owner. The lights make it look a little more welcoming.

I turn off the engine of the small SUV I've been driving. Another rental while I shop around for a new truck. It looks a little out of place in the country, but it'll have to do until I can find something better.

Grabbing the two bags of groceries, I get out, lock my doors, and head for the ramshackle front porch. The front door sticks, so I have to use both hands to open it.

The moment I step over the threshold, a bright beam of light hits me from behind.

Mitch

Jesus, she lives in the boonies.

Don't get me wrong, it's pretty country, but a little remote for a woman alone.

I shake my head and chuckle. What the hell am I thinking? This is Kate we're talking about.

A one-woman army.

But also the softest, kindest, and most passionate woman I've ever had the pleasure to get close to.

Although that may have changed, after letting two weeks pass without getting in touch. Granted, I was pretty messed up those first few days with Sawyer in the hospital and then had my hands full with the aftermath, but that's not really an excuse.

The longer you let time pass, the harder it becomes.

It was actually my daughter who got on my case and, more or less, shoved me out of the door this afternoon. A bit ironic, given the way she reacted to Kate the first time they met, but since the rescue at the lake, Sawyer has become Opal Berry's biggest fan.

The headlights hit the mailbox with the number Janey messaged me, in bold black letters.

My palms are damp as I turn my car up the driveway. Could be I'm a little nervous about the reception I'll get.

The answer is obvious when I catch sight of her, framed in the doorway as she swings around, the rifle in her hands pointing straight at me.

Maybe a call would've been a good idea.

I slam my foot on the brake just as she tilts her head to the side.

Then she slowly lowers the barrel and I blow out the breath I've been holding. I ease my foot from the brake and continue to the house, pulling my car next to the silver SUV.

"I guess I deserved that reception."

She already has the rifle tucked out of sight when I climb up her steps.

"What are you doing here, Mitch?"

I stop in front of her and notice the dark circles under her eyes. She looks tired. Dropping in unannounced may not have been a great idea, but I'm here now.

"I wanted to talk to you."

"A phone call would've been easier."

She's quick with her response and perhaps a little touchy.

"You're right, it would've, but then I wouldn't have been able to look at you when I tell you the ways I've fucked up."

She opens her mouth and immediately snaps it shut again. Then she drops her head and, for a moment, I think she's going to tell me it's too little too late, but instead she steps to the side.

"You may as well come in then."

Not exactly a warm invitation but an improvement on the promise of a bullet between the eyes.

She takes off her coat and reaches for a couple of grocery bags just inside the door. I quickly take them from her before following her down the hall to a surprisingly modern kitchen. It's clear that at some point someone did some renovations, knocking out a wall between the kitchen and the living area, creating an open L-shaped space, and adding sliding glass doors in the back.

"Just put them on the counter."

I do as she asks and she immediately starts putting

groceries away. She avoids looking at me as she moves around the kitchen, going on about refreshments.

"I don't have much to drink, but I can make a pot of tea. Unless you prefer coffee? I may be able to find a dusty bottle of wine left somewhere, but I'm afraid milk and water are the only other things I can offer. I'm gone a lot of the time..."

She's nervous.

"Kate."

"...and even when I'm home I rarely have people—"

"*Kate*," I repeat, a bit more firmly as I step in her path and put a hand on her shoulder.

Her pretty gray eyes finally look at me.

"Tea is fine."

She nods briskly and goes about filling a kettle at the sink.

"How is Sawyer?" she asks, with her back to me.

"She's recovering well. She's been on my case about getting in touch with you."

Darting me a glance, she turns, sets the kettle on the stove, and lights a burner.

"You needed encouragement?"

She leans with her hip against the counter and her arms crossed in front of her.

"Not really, but I thought I needed time to get my head and my heart and my gut back in sync before facing you."

Time for honesty.

"I was torn, Kate. And pissed and scared witless, and frankly, confused. Mostly about the force of my emotions.

In this line of work, you develop an on and off switch, you know that. A simple mechanism that allows us to shut out everything but the case we're working."

"I get that," she says, slowly unfolding her arms.

"That switch never worked on you," I continue, wanting to get it all on the table. "You were everywhere and there was no shutting it off even if I'd wanted to, which I didn't. Then when Sawyer went missing..."

Suddenly she pushes away from the counter and crosses the space I'd been struggling to keep between us.

"I turned off emotion in favor of the investigation," she finishes for me, placing a hand in the middle of my chest. "It hurt you."

I take her hand and press my lips to the pulse on the inside of her wrist.

"And I lashed out," I admit. "I'm sor—"

"No," she says firmly, pressing her fingers against my lips. "We both did what we needed to do. No apologies."

Slipping my arms around her waist, I pull her flush against me and lower my head, looking into her eyes.

"I'm in awe of you," I confess right before I close my mouth over hers.

As seems to happen any time I touch Kate, the initial spark turns into an inferno in seconds. She moans against my lips and her fingers curl around my neck, pulling me even closer.

My focus is complete as I map her body with my hands, memorizing every soft curve and enticing dip. The need to touch her bare skin has me tugging up the hem of her sweater, when a shrill whistle has both of us jump.

"Water's boiling."

She breaks away with an apologetic smile and lifts the kettle from the burner, turning off the gas. Then she reaches into a cupboard beside the stove.

"I have Earl Grey or Orange Pekoe. Do you have a preference?"

Fuck, yeah, I have a preference, and it's got nothing to do with tea.

Moving in behind her, I put my hands on her hips and press my hard cock against her round ass. Then lean down and brush my lips against her ear.

"I do. Show me your bedroom."

She turns slowly, purposely brushing my dick with her ass, a seductive smirk on her lips. Then she grabs my hand and pulls me toward a narrow staircase leading upstairs.

"Watch," she warns when we reach a small landing.

I narrowly avoid hitting my head on the low doorway into her bedroom.

Letting go of my hand when we reach the bed, she turns to face me and whips her sweater off, dropping it to the floor. Helpless to stop myself, my gaze locks in on the swell of her breasts. Beautiful creamy skin, almost matching the color of her nondescript bra barely containing them.

I love how she doesn't try to hide any part of her as she strips in record time. I'm still frozen on the spot when she starts tugging on my clothes.

"Kate..." slips from my lips right before my jacket lands at my feet.

Her fingers work feverishly on the buttons of my shirt next, but I'm right out of patience. Brushing her hands out of the way, I make short work of my shirt, simply pulling it over my head.

Moments later I'm as naked as she is and eager to feel her skin against mine. I reach for her, but she's faster, planting her hands in the middle of my chest and shoving me toward the bed where I land flat on my back.

"God, I missed your body," she mutters when she climbs on top of me, straddling my hips.

Her spread palms slide from my stomach up to my chest as she leans forward. When the tip of her tongue plays with my nipple, her hair brushes over my skin and sends shivers down my spine.

Then she starts sliding down my body.

"Kate, baby..."

I hadn't planned for this. Hoped, maybe, but at most I'd wished for a chance to talk to her.

As I should've expected by now, Kate is a surprise as she slowly licks the thick, throbbing vein running the length of my cock from root to tip.

The warm, wet drag of her tongue breaks the last of my control.

"Knees," I grunt as I roll her off me.

She doesn't argue and rewards me with the sight of her ass in the air.

Fuck, yeah.

I'm already close when I enter her pussy, feeling those slick muscles close around me like a fist. Determined not to go off without her, I slip a hand between her legs and work her clit.

My mouth drops open as I piston my hips, unable to control the pace until that tingle at the base of my spine starts to build. Quickly wetting it in my mouth, I slip the tip of my thumb past the tight ring of her asshole.

Right away her whimpers turn to grunts as she grinds herself against me. The next moment she yells and as I feel her body clench around me, I can finally let go.

"MITCH?"

She's sprawled over me, her fingertips drawing figure eights through the hair on my chest.

I'm still willing my heart rate to come down after round two, as I press my nose in her hair, breathing her scent.

"Hmmm."

"Do you think we've got enough to put Melnyk away?"

Seriously?

Groaning, I roll both of us so she ends up under me and push up on my elbows to look down into her flushed face.

"Let's make a rule," I suggest. "No discussing him or any other sick pervert when we're naked after mind-blowing sex. Or better yet, how about a ban on discussing work in bed altogether?"

A smug smile spreads over her lips.

"Mind-blowing?"

I groan again and plant my face in the crook of her neck.

"Babe, sex with you is the toughest cardiac workout I've ever had."

Her small hand pats my ass.

"We'll just have to practice more."

I chuckle against her skin.

"Only you could make me excited about working out."

Her limbs wrap around me, holding me in place, and we stay like that for a few minutes until she asks another question.

"So can we talk about us?"

I lift myself off her again.

"Always."

She hesitates for a moment, smiling almost shyly.

"Where do we go from here? You and me."

"Forward, hopefully."

I lift my eyebrows in question, which she answers with a nod. Leaning down, I brush her lips with mine.

"We'll figure it out as we go," I promise. "We both have demanding jobs, we live in different cities, I'm sure it'll be a challenge at times to match up our schedules. But where there's a will, there's a way, and I'm willing. I want this," I emphasize, looking deep into her eyes.

"So do I," she admits, making me feel like a million bucks.

"One thing though," I continue. "We'll have to start with a do-over on meeting my daughter to start with. She's eager to redeem herself. In fact, I had to deter her from coming with me tonight."

She chuckles softly before turning serious again.

"I'd love that. As long as you're sure Sawyer's not going to hate me."

Now it's my turn to laugh.

"My sweet Kate...she's gonna love you, I promise."

I kiss the tip of her nose and add in a whisper, "It's impossible not to."

THIRTY

*O*PAL

"Hey, what are you doing here?"

I'm surprised to see Mitch walking into the GEM office, he's never been here before.

Not that we haven't seen each other these past two months whenever we had a chance, but there's never really been a reason for him to stop by my work.

A pleasant surprise, as I lift my face so he can drop a kiss on my lips.

"I wasn't expecting you until Wednesday. I hope you didn't make plans, I'm about to go into a meeting with the team."

Janey is supposed to call in from the Caymans to give us an update in twenty minutes and we're supposed to strategize a plan of attack. It's not a meeting I can afford to miss.

Mitch grins down at me, his eyes sparkling.

"Who says I'm here for you?"

I glance around the open office space and catch Raj's smiling eyes. She gets up from her desk, picks up a file folder, and walks toward us. Then she reaches to shake Mitch's hand.

"Good to see you again, Mitch."

"Same to you."

"These are for you," Raj says, handing him the folder and a pen.

I'm more confused by the minute.

"Can someone please explain to me what's going on?"

Mitch holds up a finger.

"Gimme just a minute." He points at the empty desk across from mine. "Can I?"

Nobody sits at that desk, I suspect it's just there for balance, to match Raj and Janey's desks which face each other as well.

"Sure," Raj answers. "It's all yours."

Mitch shrugs off his coat and hangs it over the back of the chair before sitting down. I'm surprised to see him wearing casual clothes. He never mentioned being off today.

"Okay, really, guys," I complain, when he opens the folder and starts signing documents.

Neither of them says a thing and I'm starting to get annoyed when Mitch slaps the folder shut and walks over, sliding it in front of me.

"What is this?"

"I need you to know something first," he finally says, handing the pen to me. "The decision is yours. If anything about this makes you uncomfortable, there'll be no hard feelings."

I flip open the folder and immediately notice four signatures at the bottom.

"It was Mitch's idea we should all sign for it to be legally binding," Raj explains, "Even one missing signature would make it null and void."

I realize I'm looking at the last page of a contract. I flip it over to find the first page, and it all becomes clear.

"Are you serious?"

My voice rises in pitch.

"As a heartbeat," he returns without hesitation. "You know I've been frustrated these past few months."

He did mention that a few times, but never once had he suggested anything like this.

"You know, you're the only man who can make me cry," I sniffle, adding my signature beside my name.

"It's true," Raj says helpfully. "I don't think I've ever seen her cry as much as she has since meeting you."

I huff unhappily and hold up two fingers.

"Twice." That she's seen anyway.

Then I get up and wind my arms around Mitch's neck.

"I can't believe you quit the team."

He shrugs and puts his hands on my hips.

"They know things changed for me after Sawyer was taken," Mitch explains as I notice Raj slipping into the adjoining conference room, closing the door behind her.

"I never had a problem handing over any case to the Criminal Investigations Division once our part was done, but you know I've been having a hard time letting this one go."

I nod at him.

It's frustrating even for us, knowing we haven't answered every question and tied up every loose end, but at least we're able to actively plug away at it. That's not possible for Mitch within the parameters of his job.

"So you called Jacob?"

"Actually, he first called me. I think it was a little over a month ago. He said if ever I was interested in a career change that would allow me a bit more flexibility to let him know. Dangled the carrot so to speak. It's almost like he knew."

"Uncanny, isn't it? He seems to know exactly what to say to put a bug in your ear."

"Yeah. I couldn't stop thinking about it, ended up talking to Matt about it."

"Yet you didn't talk to me," I observe, giving him a little shake. "In fact, looks like I may have been the last to know."

"You were, and for good reason," he hurries to add. "It was important to me your team was on board with it before you even knew. They might've felt obligated to say yes, thinking that's what you'd want."

"You took quite a risk, what if I'd said no?" I'm curious to know.

"I'd have probably done some investigating on my own, I've got some money saved up to tide me over. But Jacob was quite certain you'd say yes."

I lean back a little and raise one eyebrow.

"He was, was he?"

Not sure whether to be insulted or grateful I'm apparently an open book to my boss.

"Hmm," Mitch hums. "He was more concerned about how serious I was about you."

Did I say boss? Apparently, now he thinks he's my father.

"And? What did you tell him."

A slow grin emerges on his face until lines fan out from the corners of his eyes. He tucks me a little closer.

"I told him I was dead-serious."

"Yeah?"

I smile back at him, more than a little pleased. It's not like I don't know he loves me—I'm pretty sure he knows I love him—we just haven't really put it into so many words.

To me this is as good as.

"Don't plan on letting you go, Kate. Ever."

Even better.

I lift a hand to his face and run my fingers over his stubble.

"I'm okay with that."

Mitch

"A few discreet candles might've been better, Dad."

Glancing over at Sawyer, I notice she has the cake box open, staring inside.

"Why? What's wrong with those?"

We just picked up the cake I ordered the day after GEM officially became my new employer. During Pearl's Cayman briefing, which Jacob asked me to sit in on—he wanted me up to speed before I officially start on Monday—she'd let it slip it was Kate's birthday Wednesday.

When I asked Kate later if she wanted to do something special for her birthday; she brushed it off, saying she doesn't really put much stock into birthdays. It didn't quite ring true, so I came up with the idea to do something special for her. Just the two of us.

It was my mistake to mention anything to Sawyer, who turned the idea for a private party for two into a celebration for three. Complete with the balloons and wrapped gifts stuffed in the back seat, and the hot pan of lasagna wrapped in towels in the trunk, all courtesy of my daughter, who invited herself along.

I didn't have the heart to say no to her. The couple of times my daughter was there when Kate visited, the two had really hit it off. With Becky a royal mess since Chad was arrested, it's not that shocking. Sawyer craves a strong, stable female influence and Kate fits that bill perfectly.

So my girl made this surprise her mission, and I'm keeping my fingers crossed Kate won't shut the door in our faces.

The damn cake is the only contribution I was allowed

to make, and now it sounds like I may have fallen down on the job.

Sawyer glances up, a doubtful look on her face.

"Really? Forty-one candles? What were you thinking? You'll be lucky if she doesn't put them out on your face. No woman wants a visual reminder of her age."

I'm not sure what it says about me that I need to be schooled on women by my sixteen-year-old daughter.

"Can you pull them out?" I ask, leaning over to check the cake which has forty-one tiny white candles perfectly spaced over the iced top of the triple-layer Black Forrest cake I picked.

"No," is the immediate response. "It'll ruin the icing."

I practice apologies in my head the rest of the drive to Kate's place while Sawyer messes with her phone. She doesn't look up until I pull into the driveway.

"Oh my God, that's so pretty!"

I smile at the Christmas lights wrapped around the porch and following the roofline of Kate's farmhouse.

Sawyer's right, it does look pretty. Homey.

Welcoming.

I hope that's still true when she opens the door and finds both of us on her doorstep.

Sawyer grabs the presents and the balloons, leaving me to carry the cake. The door opens shortly after I knock. The expression on Kate's face is one of shock.

"Happy birthday!" my daughter squeals.

Then a smile breaks through. A genuine one, thank God.

"Oh wow, what a lovely surprise."

She shoots a grateful look my way but I cock my thumb at my girl.

"It was all her."

It's the last word I get for a while as Kate hustles a chatting Sawyer through to the kitchen. I close the front door and head after them.

"Your house is so cute," I hear my daughter gush.

I wince when I look around and see two settings on the table and candles lit all over the house. Clearly the plan was an evening for two.

When I glance at her she's smiling, giving her head a slight shake when she catches on I notice. I watch as she surreptitiously turns off the oven before grabbing an extra plate from the cupboard, while Sawyer explores the main floor, providing nonstop commentary.

"Oh, I almost forgot, Dad? Is the car unlocked?"

"It is."

"Awesome, I'll go grab dinner."

She dumps the gifts on the table and lets the balloons drift to the ceiling.

"You brought dinner?" Kate asks, looking at my daughter.

"Hope you like lasagna. I made it myself."

No lack of confidence for my girl. Guess that's not a bad thing.

"My favorite comfort food."

"Good," Sawyer says, pointing at the box in my hands. "Dad brought dessert."

Then she adds in a stage-whisper, "Forgive him. He

knows not what he's doing," before sashaying down the hall.

"What was that all about?" Kate wants to know.

Instead of answering, I open the box and turn it toward her. She may as well see for herself.

"Oh my," she says softly as her eyes fill with tears.

"Shit." I slide the cake box on the counter and cup her face in my hands. "Sawyer warned me I missed the boat. All I can say is it was well-intended. I asked them to put on those candles, one for each birthday I missed, plus today's."

She shakes her head, smiling through the tears on her face.

"The last time I had a cake for my birthday was when I turned eight. I helped my mom bake it and my brother put the candles on. I'd almost forgotten it. Thank you for reminding me."

"So these are good tears?" I want to assure myself.

But before she can answer, Sawyer walks in, carrying the large lasagna pan that could probably feed a family of ten.

"It's still hot, we should eat it now," she announces, sliding the pan on the stove before turning around.

One look at Kate's face and my daughter immediately aims a glare at me as she points an accusing finger.

"See? I knew those candles were a bad idea. You made her cry."

Kate starts laughing and turns to me, wrapping her arms around my neck.

"I love all forty-one of them. I love you."

EPILOGUE

*O*PAL

"It's Matt."

I groan as he rolls off me and swings his leg over the edge of the bed to take the call.

I'm blissfully tender everywhere.

I was never a morning person, but in the last few weeks—since Mitch started with GEM and ends up spending a lot of nights at my place—they've become my favorite time of day.

"Yeah, she's here. I'll put you on speaker."

I automatically scoot up in bed and pull the sheet up to my chin. Not that he can see I'm naked, but it seems wrong.

"I wanted to tell you both myself. Douglas Melnyk and Russel Germain were taken into FBI custody this morning on a slew of charges. The ones that will interest you most are federal charges of sexual exploitation of children, rape, and sexual abuse of a minor. SAC Walker personally slapped the cuffs on the congressman."

I'm sure the smile on my face matches the massive one Mitch is wearing as he looks at me.

"*Fuck*, that's great news," he says.

"Yes, it is," Matt agrees. "But there's still a long road ahead and these two are well connected and have substantial resources. I don't think they'll go down without a fight. Walker is not letting up either though. He says this will remain an ongoing investigation until a conviction is in."

As we drive to the office, the news is all over the media already.

Raj is waiting, waving us into the conference room as soon as we walk in.

"Jacob is on the line and we're waiting for Janey to call in."

Now that Mitch is part of the team and signed that non-disclosure agreement as part of his employment contract, he knows everyone's real names.

I don't even have a chance to ask if Raj heard the news when Janey's disembodied voice chirps from the speaker in the middle of the table.

"I'm here!"

My eyes shoot to Raj who looks as puzzled as I feel.

Janey doesn't chirp. Ever.

"*Everything all right, Pearl?*" Jacob—sticking to code names—inquires.

"I'm great," is the response.

Something's definitely up with her.

"All right. First things first."

Jacob shares the news of Melnyk and Germain, which apparently is news only to Janey, who is back in the Caymans.

"Do you have anything new for us, Pearl?"

"Do I ever," she answers. "I found him."

"Please tell me you're talking about Jesper Olson," Mitch pleads.

"That would be him."

"Can you give us a little more?"

"Goes by the name Martin Duyvenvoorde now."

"Where did you find him?" Raj wants to know.

"At the Battleground Gym in West Bay."

"And you are positive?"

"Not a single doubt," Janey confirms.

I'm waiting with bated breath.

It's cold here and I wouldn't be averse to a surprise trip to the tropics.

Jacob wasn't about to send the whole team unless we had a solid lead.

Looks like we might have one now.

"Very well then, people." Jacob finally comes back on. *"You all know what to do."*

I can't contain my excitement.

"We're going?"

"Be ready in six hours. We're heading to Grand Cayman."

The smile on my face is even bigger when I swing around to Mitch.

"We're going to the Cayman Islands."

He shakes his head and grins indulgently.

"I heard," he comments dryly.

Mr. Cool and Collected.

"I'm packing a bikini," I tease.

CONTINUE READING FOR A PREVIEW OF PEARL,
BOOK 2 IN THE GEM SERIES.

"HI, JANEY. MY NAME IS SANDRA. I'M A SOCIAL worker with child protective services."

I hear her voice but I don't want to turn around. I'm too embarrassed.

Stupid Billy Crocker and his big mouth. He's the reason the teacher brought me to see the school nurse and now I'm in a heap of trouble. Even the principal got called in.

I should've worn my black sweatshirt but it's been hot out for days and I was afraid I'd get laughed at. Hoping my back had scabbed over, I ended up putting on a T-shirt and kept my long hair loose.

That was a mistake.

Billy, who sits behind me in class, noticed blood on the back of my chair.

"Janey?" The nurse bends down in front of the bed I'm curled up on. "I'm going to show Sandra your back, okay?"

I squeeze my eyes closed when she reaches over me and pulls the sheet down. I'm mortified when I hear the other woman hiss between her teeth.

I've never looked at my back, but I've felt the ridges and scars my mother's switch left behind.

"Who did this to you, Janey?"

I PEEK OUT FROM UNDER THE SCRATCHY BLANKET AND look around the dark room.

It looks spooky, with only a little bit of moonlight coming in through the windows.

I share a bunk bed with Kate, another new girl here. She already picked the bottom bunk, so I took the top. I would've picked that one anyway, I feel safer up here.

We share the room with five other girls but they're all older and mostly ignore us. Except maybe Rajani, who seems nice enough, even though I haven't said much to her. Or anyone else, really.

The boys have a dorm room on the other side of the building and we're kept mostly separated except at meal times.

It's only been four days since the social worker brought me here, but I already know I don't like it. Every day I have to meet with this woman for therapy. She's supposed to be a doctor, but she asks strange questions and makes me feel really uncomfortable.

There's also a guy—his name is Josh—and he runs education and activity programs. Some of the kids seem afraid of him.

He gives me the creeps.

I'm pretty sure something weird is going on here.

Pearl

"You..."

Asshole. How the hell did he find me?

"Pearl, fancy meeting you here."

I'd like to wipe that arrogant smirk off his handsome face. What a waste of good looks.

"You're trespassing," I snap, pointing at the small sign indicating 'Private Beach.'

The beach house I'm staying at sits on a few acres of land with about two-hundred yards of ocean frontage. GEM—the organization I work for—rented the place when the rest of my team joined me here on Grand Cayman a few weeks ago. The rental I had before only had one bedroom and was in town, near the airport. Nothing much to look at, unlike this house.

Sadly, I've spent most of my time here holed up inside, working. Raj, Kate, and Mitch—the rest of my team—headed back home yesterday and I'm supposed to fly out in two days.

I stayed behind to follow up with the captain of luxury yacht scheduled to be back sometime tomorrow from a two-week-long chartered trip around the Caribbean. The man has eluded me for the two months I've been here—doing little more than dropping off a load of passengers and picking up the next before taking off again—but I plan to be at the dock when he shows up tomorrow. I'm not going to let him slip through my fingers again, but for today I'd promised myself a leisurely day on the beach.

Well, so much for that. There is no way I'll be relaxing with Lee Remington hovering over me.

The first time I met him was in a parking lot and I gave him a bloody nose when my car door slammed in his face. That's by far my favorite memory of all the interactions we've had since then. The man just rubs me the wrong way.

Maybe it's because I suspect he's one of those guys who wouldn't hesitate to use the fact he's tall, dark, and good-looking to open doors for him. Or, perhaps, it's his job as freelance journalist that doesn't sit well with me.

Another reporter had left a sour taste in my mouth when he caught me in the parking lot of the club I worked at in Cincinnati many moons ago. He claimed he was doing a story on an assault that had taken place behind the club a couple of days prior. I guess I'd still been a little naïve at the time and shared way too much with the guy. Next thing I know, a covert picture taken inside the club of me dancing was featured next to his article titled "Sex Trade in the City" in a local newspaper a few days later.

The bastard used my name as he blasted the industry. It cost me my fiancé, my job, and quite a few friends I'd made.

So yeah, I'm not a fan and I have a really long memory.

I huff when Lee wordlessly plops down in the sand beside me, looping his arms around his knees. I'm trying hard not to notice how he looks even better in cargo shorts and a well-washed Pink Floyd shirt than he does in jeans.

"I don't recall inviting you."

He turns his head and grins at me. His eyes are hidden behind the shades he's wearing, but I swear I can feel him scrutinizing me.

"I bumped into Mitch and your friends at the airport when I was getting in yesterday. They told me to check in on you."

"Bullshit," I grumble, wrapping my towel around me.

Although...I wouldn't exactly put it past either Kate or Raj to send him by to needle me. They know how I feel about the man.

"What are you doing in the Caymans anyway?"

"I'm not allowed to have a vacation?"

I roll my eyes at him. He's as likely to take a vacation as I am. There's a reason he's here.

He stretches his long legs, crossing them at the ankles, getting comfortable. His dark skin gleams in the sun, mocking my almost pasty complexion. I've barely caught any rays while here, having spent most of my time inside behind the computer.

"Sorry, not buying it."

I get up, tying my towel tightly around me as I gather up my things. The man makes me uncomfortable and I've got better things to do than hang out on the beach with him.

"Where are you going?"

"Some of us have work to do."

I know I'm being snippy, but Remington brings it out in me. It doesn't deter him from jumping to his feet and following me back to the house.

"You're meeting with Robert Justice tomorrow," he says casually, stopping me in my tracks.

"How would you know that?" I ask suspiciously.

I'd be shocked if my teammates shared my hopes of intercepting the captain at the dock.

He shrugs, turning his eyes to the endless blue ocean.

"I'm here to talk to him and assume since you're not on the flight with the rest of your team, you're hanging around for the same reason."

It shouldn't surprise me Remington is chasing down the same leads I am. The big difference is he's chasing a story for a byline, while we're chasing down criminals to make sure they receive justice. Not exactly the same objective. Although, I grudgingly admit his knowledge came in handy earlier this year when we managed to shut down a youth center in Lanark, Kentucky.

Several teenagers had gone missing and we uncovered what can only be described as a ring of sexual predators. What had been a shock was finding Josh Kendrick at the helm. A man who supposed to have died twenty years ago.

Oh, he was using an alias and his appearance had changed dramatically over the years, but Kate who'd been at the center posing as Opal Berry—her cover name— recognized his voice immediately.

You'd think, after two decades, the sound of a voice would be hard to remember, but I don't think any of us would ever forget Kendrick's voice.

The man is dead now, his center shut down, and the sick perverts using his services are in jail and awaiting trial, but we have reason to believe this case was only the tip of the iceberg.

It's why I ended up in the Caymans, following a lead by the name of Jesper Olson. He'd gone missing from the center as well, however, we discovered later he was not a victim but rather part of the plot, acting as a decoy to lure the other kids.

Jesper ended up on the islands and I tracked him down working on the Distant Promise, the yacht captained by Robert Justice, but sometime in the past few weeks the boy disappeared again.

I suspect he may have been dropped off during the yacht's previous cruise, which is why I need to talk to the captain.

Alone.

Lee

I watch her stomp off.

Although, with her small feet sinking into the fine beach sand, it doesn't really have the required effect.

As small as the woman is, I know better than to underestimate her. The one and only time I did, I ended up on my ass. That tiny package packs a big punch in more ways than one.

You'd think someone who weighs significantly less

than what I bench press wouldn't be able to take down a man twice her size, but you'd be wrong. Pearl looks deceivingly young and innocent with those delicate features and funky, angled, bob haircut.

I don't bother following her, knowing I'd undoubtedly get the door to the beach house slammed in my face. She's prickly, to put it mildly, which is why I opt not to share how I ended up here. Given that it was Jacob, her boss, who asked me to come and, apparently, he didn't share that with her, I can only assume she won't be happy.

He's touched base with me from time to time these past months, looking for the same answers I am. Recognizing the mutual benefit to sharing information, I've been keeping him abreast of any progress I've made and vice versa.

Even though I'm not sure what his motivations are, our objectives seem to run parallel: to bring down the three individuals responsible for atrocities that took place two decades ago. Including the murder of my mother, who'd been a housekeeper at Transition House—a youth home at the center of the depravities—and was killed for what she knew.

Transition House burned down, its management supposedly having perished in the fire, but I've always had my suspicions around that. With good reason, as it turned out. Josh Kendrick—once program manager for Transition House—appeared back in Lanark as director of the new youth center.

The sick bastard wasn't back for long though. If he hadn't made the mistake of kidnapping the daughter of an

FBI agent, he might've gotten away and started up shop elsewhere, but Opal—another GEM operator—took him out.

One down, two more to go.

I get to my feet and wipe the sand off my ass. I'm hungry and could go for some conch fritters. For a second, I wonder if I should ask Pearl along to try and break the ice, but I'm pretty sure that would be wasted energy.

I'll catch up with her tomorrow morning at the dock.

I CAN'T HEAR WHAT SHE MUMBLES UNDER HER breath when I saunter onto the dock, but I have no doubt it's far from complimentary.

Pearl's almost-black eyes regard me with disdain.

"You're going to be in the way."

I shrug. "Who knows? I could be useful. I understand you haven't had much luck so far."

Her scowl makes it clear she's not happy with the reminder.

"You think you can do better because you're a man?"

"Yes, I do," I tell her honestly.

It just so happens, in this case, being a man—a Black one at that—he is more likely to talk to me than he would to an Asian woman. Not because I think I'm superior, but Robert Justice might.

It's on my tongue to tell her Jacob Chance called me for that exact reason, but with the yacht coming around the end of the pier, this might not be the best time to get into that.

Pearl caught sight of it as well and spreads her stance, folding her arms over her chest as we wait for the ship to dock. I catch the older man eyeing her suspiciously as he orders his crew to fasten the lines.

The moment he steps foot on the dock, Pearl marches up to him, determined not to let him pass her by.

"Excuse me, Robert Justice?"

"*Wah gwaan,*" I interrupt, asking the man how he's doing as I brush by her and hold out my hand.

With his narrowed eyes still on Pearl, he accepts the shake.

"*Wah duh yuh want?*"

"*Lee Remington, mi ah journalist,*" I introduce myself. "*Mi a luk fah information, cyaah wi talk?*"

I can feel the steam coming off Pearl, but I ignore her as I follow Justice, who starts walking toward the small office building at the end of the dock.

"*Mi know nutten,*" he mutters, trying to cut me off.

"*Eh bout Martin Duyvenvoorde he wuk fi yuh.*"

At the mention of his employee—the name Jesper Olson used here in the Caymans—he glares at me with guarded eyes.

"*Nah nuh muh,*" he responds.

Maybe not anymore, but we know he went out on the previous cruise as part of the crew.

It takes a bit to get him to admit the kid debarked in Florida three weeks ago, but that's about as much as I can get out of him.

Last year, his yacht was chartered by a company by the name of Glan Development, but the moment I mention that name he blanches, shutting me down.

"Deh ask tuh bai questions a dangerous," he warns me before he shuts the door in my face.

He's obviously scared and I don't blame him.

Glan Development is a subsidiary of Glan Industries, which is part of an almost impenetrable network of shell companies. I've tried.

Pure Caribbean is another one we found when following the flow of illegal funds. This company has a physical address here on Grand Cayman, but there's nothing but a run-down, empty warehouse. The moneys paid by rich fuckers paying for the sexual exploitation of minors landed in Pure Caribbean's local bank account, shielding it.

These people are sick and ruthless. They have money, connections, and will do anything to protect those interests and their own asses. They wouldn't flinch at killing Robert Justice or anyone else for that matter.

"Of course you speak Patois," Pearl snarls when I turn to her.

"Jamaican born," I explain.

Portmore, Jamaica, to be more specific, although I did most of my growing up in Kentucky. My mother moved us there when I was only three but continued to speak Patois at home.

"What did he say?"

"The kid was dropped off on Key West. That's all he was willing to tell me."

"He's back in the U.S.?"

"So it seems."

She mutters a string of unladylike expletives before she turns on her heel and heads for the parking lot.

"Hey!" I call, jogging after her. "Wanna grab some lunch? I know a place—"

"I have to pack," she says, already getting into her rental vehicle.

Of course she has an excuse ready.

Don't know why I even bother trying to be friendly, she obviously hates my guts.

———

ALSO BY FREYA BARKER

GEM Series

OPAL

PEARL

ONYX

High Mountain Trackers Series:

HIGH MEADOW

HIGH STAKES

HIGH GROUND

HIGH IMPACT

Arrow's Edge MC Series:

EDGE OF REASON

EDGE OF DARKNESS

EDGE OF TOMORROW

EDGE OF FEAR

EDGE OF REALITY

EDGE OF TRUST

PASS Series:

HIT & RUN

LIFE & LIMB

LOCK & LOAD

LOST & FOUND

On Call Series:

BURNING FOR AUTUMN

COVERING OLLIE

TRACKING TAHLULA

ABSOLVING BLUE

REVEALING ANNIE

DISSECTING MEREDITH

WATCHING TRIN

IGNITING VIC

Rock Point Series:

KEEPING 6

CABIN 12

HWY 550

10-CODE

Northern Lights Collection:

A CHANGE OF TIDE

A CHANGE OF VIEW

A CHANGE OF PACE

SnapShot Series:

SHUTTER SPEED

FREEZE FRAME

IDEAL IMAGE

Portland, ME, Series:

FROM DUST

CRUEL WATER

THROUGH FIRE

STILL AIR

LuLLaY (a Christmas novella)

Cedar Tree Series:

SLIM TO NONE

HUNDRED TO ONE

AGAINST ME

CLEAN LINES

UPPER HAND

LIKE ARROWS

HEAD START

Standalones:

WHEN HOPE ENDS

VICTIM OF CIRCUMSTANCE

BONUS KISSES

SECONDS

ABOUT THE AUTHOR

USA Today bestselling author Freya Barker loves writing about ordinary people with extraordinary stories.

Driven to make her books about 'real' people; she creates characters who are perhaps less than perfect, each struggling to find their own slice of happy, but just as deserving of romance, thrills and chills in their lives.

Recipient of the ReadFREE.ly 2019 Best Book We've Read All Year Award for "Covering Ollie, the 2015 RomCon "Reader's Choice" Award for Best First Book, "Slim To None", Finalist for the 2017 Kindle Book Award with "From Dust", and Finalist for the 2020 Kindle Book Award with "When Hope Ends", Freya spins story after story with an endless supply of bruised and dented characters, vying for attention!

www.freyabarker.com

Printed in the USA
CPSIA information can be obtained
at www.ICGtesting.com
LVHW021020081124
796073LV00007B/50